PRAISE FOR THE SEASIDE CAFÉ MYSTERIES

"Fun and intriguing, *Live and Let Chai* is filled to the brim with Southern charm."

—Kirsten Weiss, author of A Pie Town Mystery series, for *Live and Let Chai*

"Bree Baker's seaside town of Charm has everything readers could want: an intrepid and lovable heroine who owns an adorable iced tea cafe, a swoon-worthy hero—and murder. Fast-paced, smartly plotted, and full of surprises, it's as refreshing as a day at the beach!"

—Kylie Logan, bestselling author of *French Fried*, for *Live and Let Chai*

"A sun-filled cozy-cum-romance best enjoyed by beach readers."

—*Kirkus Reviews* for *No Good Tea Goes Unpunished*

"This is a food- and tea-filled story, but Baker never loses sight of moving the mystery plot forward and providing ample opportunities for fans to catch up with the engaging series cast."

—*Booklist* for *Tide and Punishment*

"A swarm of bee-centric suspects, a bit of sweet romance, and a surprise sting add up to a honey of a tale."

—*Kirkus Reviews* for *A Call for Kelp*

ALSO BY BREE BAKER

Seaside Café Mysteries

Live and Let Chai

No Good Tea Goes Unpunished

Tide and Punishment

A Call for Kelp

CLOSELY
Harbored
SECRETS

Seaside Café Mysteries, Book 5

BREE BAKER

Poisoned Pen
PRESS

Published by Poisoned Pen Press, an imprint of Sourcebooks
P.O. Box 4410, Naperville, Illinois 60567-4410
(630) 961-3900
sourcebooks.com

Library of Congress Cataloging-in-Publication Data

Names: Baker, Bree, author.
Title: Closely harbored secrets / Bree Baker.
Description: Naperville, Illinois : Poisoned Pen Press, an imprint of
   Sourcebooks, [2020] | Series: Seaside Café mysteries ; book 5
Identifiers: LCCN 2020018066 (paperback)
Subjects: GSAFD: Mystery fiction.
Classification: LCC PS3602.A5847 C56
2020 (print) | DDC 813/.6--dc23
LC record available at https://lccn.loc.gov/2020018066

Printed and bound in Canada.
MBP 10 9 8 7 6 5 4 3 2 1

To my mama,
my best friend

CHAPTER

ONE

I waved goodbye to my last customer of the evening, then set the CLOSED sign in the window at Sun, Sand, and Tea, my seaside café and iced tea shop. Normally, I stayed open until seven, serving snacks and sweets to the after-dinner crowd when they made their way back to the beach, but tonight was a special occasion. The annual island ghost walk began at seven, and I needed to be at the Wharf Museum by six. According to the time on my fitness bracelet, it was officially after five, and I was running late.

I zipped across the foyer of my historic Victorian home and into the first-floor café, where my little logoed wagon awaited. I'd repainted and repurposed the Radio Flyer from my childhood to match my shop's beachy theme, then I'd put her to work. Wagon was now a pretty pale-blue with curly, white letters and peppy, pink flowers. She was adorable and a welcomed assistant on deliveries all over town.

I loaded several jugs of tea in my most popular

flavors onto Wagon beside a stack of boxed finger foods, then took a minute to admire the view. The café stretched through a good chunk of my home's first floor, filling the space from front foyer to rear deck with warm scents of buttery shrimp, spun sugar, and sweet tea. The previous owner had knocked out a few non-load-bearing walls, so the newly renovated kitchen spilled seamlessly into the former dining room and a gathering area with floor-to-ceiling windows. I'd fallen in love with the layout at first sight, then added the final touches after moving in. A little shiplap and wainscoting, fresh paint, and café seating had turned the open floor plan into the perfect seaside escape. I'd chosen soft shades of creams and tans, greens, and blues to reflect the jaw-dropping views beyond the glass. Sand and shells. The sky and sea. With punches of orange and yellow as homage to the unequivocally beautiful sunrises I observed every morning from my deck, usually with the company of a local seagull I called Lou.

I flipped off the light with a smile, then headed out to enjoy the evening.

The sun had set beyond the bay on the opposite side of the island, leaving gorgeous amber and apricot streaks across my world. I hurried to the boardwalk at the end of my driveway with Wagon in tow, enjoying the rhythmic thump-thump of her little tires on historic, sun-bleached planks. Fall had finally won its battle over summer in Charm, and the evidence was all around. Gone were the long, sunny days of incessant humidity and lingering scents of sunblock. Present were the moon at dinnertime, the crunch of drying leaves underfoot, and a lingering chill in the brisk autumn air.

My little costal town was part of North Carolina's barrier islands, known to most as the Outer Banks. The sun rose over the Atlantic outside my back door and set over the sound, or bay. The lighthouse-like tower that rose from the third floor of my old Victorian made views of both possible and perfect from inside, but the space was consumed by clutter, some as old as the house, and I preferred a firsthand account. I inhaled deeply, savoring the moment, then released the breath with a smile. It was good to be home.

I'd left the island once, something my great-aunts believed Swan women should never do. We were cursed, after all, according to family tales and lore. Leaving the island was supposed to end badly for us. Never one to believe everything I heard, I'd spent eight years away, muddling through culinary school while simultaneously chasing a cowboy around a rodeo circuit. None of that had worked out, and I'd returned a couple of winters back, nursing a broken heart. My great-aunts claimed that was the curse in action, but after nearly two years home, I'd come to the conclusion that curse was the wrong word. I was lucky to have a place like this to call home and blessed to have a community like mine to call family. My deep internal desire to be here, and my apparent inability to thrive anywhere else, only meant that the island spoke to me.

That this place was part of me, woven into my fibers and present in my soul. If that was a curse, Merriam-Webster needed to reconsider the definition.

I picked up my pace as the chilly October wind blew, urging me along. Tonight's ghost walk was a tradition started by my family decades ago as a way to raise money for local charities. My grandma and her sisters, my great-aunts Clara and Fran, had become the go-to resources for spooky island legends, and they'd decided to capitalize on the interest by turning their tales into donations for good causes. Now, all the best local haunting stories were told once a year to anyone who wanted to listen. Actors regularly volunteered to dress as various ghosts from the stories and add a little creepy ambience to the outing. At the end, donations were encouraged but not required, and all proceeds went to a pre-selected charity.

This year, the monies would go to rebuilding barns used by the island's cowboys to track and care for our wild horses. Several structures were severely damaged a few months ago during a summer hurricane, and many of the emergency rescue supplies were lost. It was a cause I could easily get behind. Charm's wild horses were some of the last on the East Coast.

I'd volunteered to make the refreshments for a donations-welcome reception following the walk. I'd delivered the bulk of my offerings this morning, using my golf cart, Blue. Wagon was Blue's little sister, and they made an adorable pair, but Blue was best for big jobs. I had a matching thrift-store bike with basket as well, but she didn't get out as much. Bike's basket was cute, but the capacity limited.

I checked the time as I hurried along, twilight quickly erasing the sunset. The beach and sea stretched out on one side of me. The marsh and Charm's small downtown on the other.

According to my bully of a fitness bracelet, I was moving at an acceptable pace for a change. Upon returning to Charm in a size twelve, I'd bought the little drill sergeant disguised as jewelry. Considering I'd left in a size six and was much closer to my thirtieth birthday than my twentieth these days, it had seemed like a good idea at the time. Hundreds of miles and a slightly fluctuating waistline later, I had a love-hate relationship with the bracelet.

I pulled wild, brown curls away from my eyes and cheeks, tucking them behind my ears, while the hearty ocean breeze did its best to set them free. I'd left my hair down tonight, going heavy on the hair product and lip gloss.

Soon, the Wharf Museum appeared, rising like an apparition in the distance, marking the boardwalk's end. The stout, one-story structure was built in the mid-1900s and patched up as needed over time, but the look never changed. Its gray stucco façade had been bleached and weathered to a pale, earthy perfection, courtesy of relentless island storms and the scorching southern sun.

The museum documented and chronicled all things relating to Charm and the sea. Remnants and contents of sunken ships, stories and legends of lost sailors, the area's largest catches on record, and a full account of our marine life through the ages. I'd always loved visiting the museum and reading about the coast, then sitting for hours on the beach or pier, imagining sunken war ships and all their secrets lying just beneath the sparkling surf.

"There you are!" My great-aunt Fran's voice turned me toward the massive, man-made sand dunes, protecting the museum from the tide. She frowned in concentration as she moved through the soft sand, lifting the length of her black cotton skirt in her hands. She'd tied her long, dark locks into a braid over one shoulder, and the silver streaks glinted in the rising moonlight.

"What are you doing out here?" I asked, checking in every direction for signs of another person.

She waved a long-stemmed lighter at me, clutched in one hand. "Lighting up your night." Behind her, a row of candles flickered inside mason jars along the walkway to the museum's rear patio. "Now, come on. Everything is almost ready. The actors are all geared up and heading out to their spots around town. Clara's in her dressing room, rehearsing lines."

"Perfect." I kissed Aunt Fran's cheek when she reached me, then followed her into the building, towing Wagon in my wake.

The museum's interior lights had been dimmed slightly for effect. A gauzy, white faux webbing stretched across picture frames and display cases, as if they were old and neglected instead of well-loved and maintained. The occasional plastic skull or prop spider accented bookshelves and activity areas. Rubber bats and mice clung to piles of nautical rope and old anchors. A skeleton piloted a rotten dinghy with a glaring hole.

I giggled as I hurried past, recalling ghost stories told around campfires and trick-or-treating with friends.

Music and voices poured from a brightly lit room at the back of the building where a dozen people sipped coffees and chatted, already prepared for the night. Excitement filled the air as we drew near, and I felt my stomach tense in anticipation. Everyone looked fantastic, if a little nervous for their roles. They were dressed in costumes from times gone by and traded stories from ghost walks of the past. I recognized most as local historians and Charm Enthusiasts, a club that had popped up while I was in elementary school. Charm Enthusiasts organized fundraisers and promoted local businesses. Tonight, they were helping with decorations and the reception. The remaining handful of faces belonged to members of a group Aunt Clara had joined two springs back: the Society for the Preservation and Retelling of Unrecorded History. Kitty Hawk chapter.

Kitty Hawk was a town not far from Charm. The communities were similar in size and geography, but Charm was friendlier, artsier, generally more charming. The Kitty Hawk historical group fancied themselves a special breed of historians. Ones Charm didn't have. Ones dedicated to preserving and passing on local history by word of mouth. I saw it as a club for the continuation of ancient gossip, but Clara hated when I said so.

By teaming up with the Society for the Preservation and Retelling of Unrecorded History, Kitty Hawk chapter, Charm Enthusiasts had doubled up on marketing and expected an unprecedented number of attendees from multiple island towns. After splitting the anticipated donations, our wild horses were sure to get everything they needed and more.

The sudden sensation of cool breath against my neck sent a mass of chills cascading down my spine. I jerked around in search of the problem. I wasn't standing under a vent or near a fan. I was at least five feet from the nearest person. Still, I dragged an accusatory gaze over the actors dressed as ghosts in case I'd somehow missed something.

"Don't be ridiculous," a nearby woman growled, drawing my attention to a couple in the corner. She smoothed her brown hair and pink tweed skirt when she saw me looking, then set her hand on the arm of the man beside her and flashed him a warning look.

He yanked free from her grip, glaring down at her as he stormed away.

The woman followed.

No one else in the room seemed to notice. Not even Aunt Fran, who'd gone to help someone with a white wig and eighteenth-century-replica ball gown.

A group of men in matching suit jackets with the museum's logo moved through the space between Aunt Fran and me, temporarily disrupting my view of her. The men were presumably on some sort of security patrol, since the museum was open after-hours and would soon be completely stuffed with people. The team ranged in age from younger than me to something more like my great-aunts' ages, and though the individuals looked nothing alike, they shared a quiet, dorkish enthusiasm I'd come to appreciate in all historians.

One of the younger members of the group turned and caught me watching as they passed. He pushed round-rimmed glasses higher onto the bridge of his nose, and I spun away, embarrassed to be caught staring. He'd been reasonably attractive, appeared close to my age, and wore his sandy hair in a schoolboy haircut that suited his round, scholarly face. Cute, but not for me. I already had a hefty set of man problems. Roughly six feet of them.

"Miss Swan," a familiar voice said, turning me around again. Marie Watson, president of the Charm Enthusiasts, approached with open arms. "We are so glad you're here," she cooed, collecting me in a tight hug. "It was more than generous of you to donate all the food and drink for tonight, especially when the event has grown to such proportions. We normally get fifty or sixty participants. Now we're looking at twice that number. Maybe more. We'll have to hold an encore performance just to accommodate the interest.

It's wonderful!" She hugged me again and beamed before taking Wagon by the handle. "I'm arranging the refreshments on the patio for our reception, right beside a big old jar for donations." She spoke the last part with one hand shielding her mouth, as if it was a secret, then winked and was gone.

Aunt Fran moved back in my direction; head tipped toward the narrow hallway lined in small offices.

I followed her to an open door with a piece of paper taped to it. Aunt Clara's name was typed in giant font across the middle.

Inside, Aunt Clara spoke quietly with a white-haired man. He was dressed like a priest, but the way he was looking at her assured me he was in costume.

Aunt Fran cleared her throat, and the couple jumped apart, cheeks pink.

Aunt Clara clapped her hands silently when she saw us. "Oh! Come in! Fran. Everly. This is Tony Grayson."

"How do you do?" he asked, tipping forward briefly at the waist. He shot Aunt Clara a look before making his way to the door. "I guess I should run across town and get into position near the church. Enjoy the walk, ladies. Break a leg, Clara."

I opened my mouth to ask more about Tony Grayson, but Aunt Clara interrupted.

"What do you think?" She spun in a tiny circle, one arm outstretched for balance. The chiffon and lace clung to her narrow frame, its ivory color emphasizing her naturally light eyes and fair skin. Her fine, blond-and-silver hair was pinned high on her head, and simple nude flats covered her feet. "This dress was handmade in 1901 by Honey Swan," Aunt Clara said. "She was such a talented seamstress."

That was true. Honey was inarguably gifted with a needle and thread. A few of her creations were part of a Women's History display at the state museum in Charlotte. She'd been aptly named by her mother for our family's legacy of bee preservation and the creation of endless holistic products made from the honey and wax in the hives. A tradition Aunt Clara and Aunt Fran continued today. "I love it," I told her. "You look beautiful."

"So do you," she said, coming to kiss my cheek. I gave my vintage swing dress and minicloak a careful look. I'd debated long and hard about the right thing to wear tonight and had really wanted the answer to be jeans and sneakers. Unfortunately, I knew better. Luckily, my stubborn and abundant curves worked well in certain 1950s apparel and looking like a pinup instead of plain old plus-sized helped my ego more than I'd ever admit.

"You look just like your mother," Aunt Clara said dreamily, reaching out to sweep the curls from my shoulders, "and your grandma."

My mother died of a broken heart before I was old enough to remember her, and my grandma had raised me in her stead. That was the other family legend my aunts believed in, and the one I hated the most. Swan women were cursed in love.

I pushed the thought away and refocused on the sweet women before me. I shared Aunt Fran's olive complexion, dark hair, and eyes, but my pushover personality leaned heavily on the Clara side of the scale. My great-aunts were sisters with different fathers, giving the women distinct and near opposite appearances, much like their personal styles and personalities.

They were a yin and yang of sisterhood. Aunt Clara with her ready hugs, and Aunt Fran always prepared for battle.

"Ten minutes!" a voice called from outside the room.

Clara made a little peep of surprise.

"Are you ready?" I asked, knowing she was. My aunts lived to tell stories, the older the better, and this was Aunt Clara's night to shine.

"I think so," she said, setting a palm against her middle and releasing a deep breath. "I've led this walk every year since the beginning, but I still get an attack of the butterflies when it's showtime." Her smile slipped a bit as she considered the words. Then a frown began to form.

I slid my gaze to Aunt Fran. I didn't like it when Aunt Clara wasn't spilling rainbows and sunshine. It wasn't like her, and it gave me pause. "Are you okay?"

"Hmm?" She blinked. "Sorry, I just had the strangest sensation."

Aunt Fran shoved a bottle of water in her sister's direction. "Drink. You're probably dehydrated. Then grab a bag of granola on your way out. You've barely eaten today."

Aunt Clara nodded slowly, accepting the water.

I cleared my throat, thoroughly unsettled. "Have you decided which stories to tell between stops?" I asked. She'd been mulling it over for weeks, and I hoped a case of the nerves was all that was bothering her.

Actors would supply added depth to her main stories, but Aunt Clara had to keep the crowd entertained as they moved from stop to stop. She knew hundreds of town and island legends, but only had time for five or six, and it was an annual dilemma on her part.

"I think so," she said. "It's just so hard to choose. I hate to be a broken record for those who've taken the tour a few times. But I also don't want to disappoint anyone waiting for a particular tale that doesn't come."

"Everyone loves to hear about the 'Sandman's Treasure,'" Aunt Fran said. "That's my favorite. People go goo-goo every year over that one."

I rolled my eyes. "I used to think every piece of sea glass I found on the beach was part of that treasure. I wholeheartedly believed it was real."

"It is real," Aunt Clara said.

I shook my head.

She frowned. "It is."

I relented with a shrug and a smile.

"It's fun," Aunt Fran said. "It gets everyone all wound up."

That was true. But saying things like *buried treasure* on an island was always trouble. Every decade or so someone claimed to stumble upon evidence of something grand hidden in Charm. Sometimes it was pirate doubloons. Sometimes the Queen's gold on a sunken English vessel. Then treasure hunters showed up in droves, clogging our streets and generally filling the town with madness for weeks on end. No one wanted that.

"Five minutes!" the hallway voice bellowed again. This time people scrambled outside the door.

"That's my cue," Aunt Clara said, moving toward the hustle and bustle.

Aunt Fran and I followed as far as the threshold, then jumped back against the wall as a headless woman in a black Victorian ball gown came marching through. The dress was floor-length, long-sleeved, and high-collared, with a two-inch strip of peek-a-boo lace between the satin neck and bodice. The actress turned in every direction, appearing to look for something, presumably her head. "Where is it?" she snapped, flinging things off tables and counters. "Who would take it? This is ridiculous!"

"Who is that?" I whispered, recognizing the Mourning Mable costume, but not the voice coming through it.

Mourning Mable was one of the island's most popular legends. She was allegedly beheaded by a jaded British sailor who'd fallen madly in love with her at first sight. Unfortunately, Mable was already happily married and utterly uninterested in his attention. The sailor couldn't fathom such a slight and quickly determined that her husband was the problem. So, he killed him to change Mable's marital status. Poor Mable was lost to grief and agony, crying every moment she was awake. Legend says her sorrow could be heard throughout the land. Eventually, the sailor cracked. Unable to bear her sobs or rejection any longer, he pulled his sword and shut her up. Permanently.

Clearly, Mable had lived in very dramatic times.

People sometimes referred to the murderous sailor as the Sandman and said he left a treasure with Mable out of regret for what he'd done. It was more likely that another legend had gotten mixed up with Mable's over the years, but that was the problem with unrecorded history. It was like a two-hundred-year-long game of Telephone. Details were bound to get messed up. But Charmers loved a good tale of love and murder, so a large memorial had been erected in Willow Park.

Aunt Clara rushed back to our sides, steering clear of the rampaging Mable. "That's Dixie Wetherill," she whispered. "She's the founder of the Society for the Preservation and Retelling of Unrecorded History. Kitty Hawk chapter."

"And?" I asked, noting something odd in her tone. Something that said there was more to the story.

"Someone has stolen my candelabra," Dixie yelled. "Some petty human has taken my only prop in an attempt to ruin me. How am I supposed to rise from the dead properly and walk through the dark without the light from my candles? For goodness' sake, I'm not an actual ghost!"

The massive black gown swished as she spun and paced.

I knew from experience that a harness worn beneath the garment balanced the equivalent of a ten-inch shoulder pad on each side of the wearer's head and forced the dress's collar above her hairline. A black mesh-and-lace insert in the bodice created an eye-level window so the actor could see where she was going. I'd loved to wear the Mourning Mable costume when I was young, then I'd jump out and scare my grandma.

Aunt Clara watched the ranting headless woman march away before answering. "She's not very pleasant, and I made the mistake of handing off auditions to her for the ghost roles. Everyone wanted to play Mable, but she gave the role to herself. She didn't even hold auditions for that one. Now I have to work with her, and she's been a real pain. Every time we practice, she rises from behind her memorial and tries to steal the show with some kind of half-cocked monologue," Clara continued. "It's ridiculous. She can't talk. She's headless!"

The brunette I'd seen arguing with a man earlier blew back into view, scanning the freshly emptied community area before us. "Dixie!" she called, her tone tight, expression hard. She glared at the items Dixie had tossed aside and overturned.

"Aubrey," Aunt Clara said, stepping away from the threshold where we'd gathered. She pointed in the direction everyone had gone. "Dixie was looking for something, and she went that way."

Aubrey turned in the direction Aunt Clara pointed, then rolled her eyes as she coasted past. "I'd like to knock her head off again," she mumbled.

Aunt Fran made a sour face at her sister. "Is Dixie the one who gives you all that trouble?"

I swung my gaze to Aunt Clara, feeling my feathers ruffle. "Someone's giving you trouble?"

Aunt Clara shrugged. "It's not personal. Dixie doesn't like Swans in general."

I balked. "That's not any better. How can she have a problem with our entire family?" And frankly, the idea that anyone could be mean to Aunt Clara, the embodiment of love and acceptance, peeved me off. "What does she do to you?"

"Oh," Aunt Clara waved a hand. "She's harmless. Just rude. I'm not entirely sure why. Could be that she's one of those people who think we're descended from witches because our ancestors came from Salem during the trials. Though, I've told her the Swans left Salem because it was pure hysteria in those times, and the Swan women have always sought peace, but that didn't diffuse her."

"Wetherill," I said, Dixie's last name suddenly ringing a bell. "You *have* mentioned her. She's the woman obsessed with our family tree." I'd completely forgotten.

Aunt Fran crossed her arms. "One and the same."

I made a disgusted, throaty sound. The Wetherill family had a long lineage on the islands as well, and Dixie had always seemed a little jealous that we could trace the Swan women back to the founding of Charm, and farther. She'd been giving Aunt Clara a hard time since the day she joined Dixie's group.

The rustle of fabric drew our collective attention through the now otherwise silent building. Mourning Mable stood a few feet away, hands on hips. "Why are you still standing there, Clara?" she snapped. "People are waiting."

"Of course." Aunt Clara gathered the length of her skirts and glided away.

The headless grouch followed.

CHAPTER

TWO

I grabbed a lantern from the pile outside the museum's rear doors, then handed one to Aunt Fran. The lanterns were black tinged with bronze and styled after those of another era. They were plastic on plastic, instead of glass and metal, to reduce weight and increase durability. I gave mine an appreciative look. A battery-operated votive flickered inside. From the distance between us and the departing group ahead, it was impossible to tell the bobbing lights weren't as authentic as most of the legends being told.

Aunt Fran and I moved slowly through the thick, dry sand near the museum, heading lower on the dark beach, toward the more tightly packed surf. We trailed behind the group, already fifty yards away, steering clear of the water and in no hurry to catch up. The night was beautiful, and we'd heard all the stories before. Plus, the group would stop soon to hear the tale of Blackbeard's ghost, and we'd join them then.

Before the infamous pirate earned his iconic name,

he was known as Edward Teach. Legend has it that Teach was brought to justice not far from Charm, in an isolated cove he'd been rumored to love. The location is known today as Teach's Hole, and its Outer Banks location made it a prime candidate for the ghost walk. That, plus the fact that some folks still claimed to see him there, wandering the land or swimming in the sea.

My favorite of Aunt Clara's eerie tales was about the *Carroll A. Deering*, a massive, five-masted schooner found wrecked on the shores of Cape Hatteras in 1921. The crew and lifeboats were gone, along with all their personal belongings. The navigation equipment and the anchors as well. But the table was set for dinner, as if the missing crew had been about to sit down for a meal. I loved that story most because it was true and well documented, but no one had ever learned where the crew went or why. I'd dreamed up a dozen Hollywood-worthy possibilities while I was growing up, but it seemed the whole truth would never be told. That part was the worst.

I hated an unsolved mystery.

After the Blackbeard story was told, we followed Aunt Clara and her group back onto the boardwalk, moving north, then across town to Willow Park, where we would listen to her retelling of the Sandman and Mourning Mable legend.

I thought of the way Aunt Clara had seemed a little off when the ten-minute warning was called, and I rubbed away the gooseflesh crawling over my arms.

I wondered again what she'd sensed, and if maybe I sensed it too, because even though I wasn't one for superstitions, something felt off tonight. My intuition was screaming, and I didn't know why.

I scanned the world around me, searching for some cause for concern. The moon was big and bright overhead, the breeze hearty and cool. But there was only peace and stillness. A perfect autumn night.

"You feel it too," Aunt Fran said softly.

"What?" I jerked in her direction, having nearly forgotten she was there.

"I don't know," she said. "Something."

I didn't like the faraway look in her eyes, so I was glad when we reached Willow Park and Aunt Clara halted her tour for another story. I needed a moment to center myself.

The bulbous mass of walkers stopped on the walkway outside Mourning Mable's memorial and flattened into a crescent shape before Aunt Clara, silent and ready for the next haunted-island tale. The memorial was composed of a large marble vault and life-sized statue of Mable affixed to the top. The effigy had a head and wore a cape that appeared to ripple in the breeze.

Aunt Fran fidgeted beside me. She craned her neck, searching in every direction, then turned herself in a full circle. "Something's not right," she said.

I followed her gaze with my own, trying to concentrate as Aunt Clara's voice boomed strong and steady through the night.

"Do you think someone's hurt?" I asked Aunt Fran, sliding my fingers around the cell phone inside my pocket.

A soft scraping sound pricked my ears before she could answer. I lifted a palm to stall her response, then closed my eyes to concentrate on the peculiar noise. The hairs on the back of my neck rose to attention. Fear danced down my spine on a thousand spidery legs.

"Do you hear that?" I asked. I opened my eyes and waited for a response.

Wind ruffled the fabric of her soft black gown, raising the oversized sleeves and billowing the material around her as if she might take flight. She shook her head, then released a heavy breath. "No. What is it?"

I listened again, but the sound was gone. "I don't hear it anymore."

"These days," Aunt Clara said, drawing me back to the moment with her spooky campfire-story voice, "legend has it that if you stand in this very spot when the moon is high and its light dapples the earth, you can still hear her crying among the willows."

The group turned collectively for a look at the giant moon above, then dutifully traced its path across the ground. The gnarled reaching fingers of a nearby willow rustled on the breeze. Its creeping shadows slithered closer to Mable's memorial with each bow of the skeletal limbs.

A long moment passed, and the crowd looked to Aunt Clara.

Aunt Fran nudged me with her elbow. "Dixie missed her cue."

Aunt Clara stared at the silent and motionless marble structure, engraved with Mable's name. She cleared her throat, then attempted to rally. "When the moon is high and the earth is still," she projected, trying once more to prompt Dixie into action, "some say they still hear her crying."

Silence.

Aunt Clara glanced nervously at the crowd, then at Aunt Fran and I, still several yards away. Her brow crumpled, and her expression turned wary. "Fran?"

Aunt Fran was in motion as the word registered to my ears, their incomprehensible bond showing its depth once more.

I hurried after her, stopping at Aunt Clara's side. My stomach churned with a growing sense of foreboding. "Where's Dixie?"

My aunts stared in the direction of Mable's memorial, at the stretching and retreating shadows on the ground.

The crowd began to whisper.

The scratching I'd heard earlier replayed in my mind, and I shuffled forward on instinct. Maybe I'd been meant to follow the sound. It seemed reasonable, since I was the only one who'd heard it, and my intuition had been trying to tell me something all evening.

I raised the lantern in one trembling arm, holding it firm against the wind.

Someone moaned, and a massive black mound appeared before me.

Not a shadow, I realized. The Mourning Mable costume was outstretched on the ground. And Dixie moaned inside it.

"Oh, no!" I called, rushing forward. "Dixie!"

"Everly?" Aunt Fran's voice rose from behind me.

"Call an ambulance!" I yelled, crossing the last few feet to the costume, crumpled onto its side. I fell roughly to my knees before her, remembering belatedly that her face was covered by the dark material. "Can you hear me?" I asked the satin and lace as my mind raced wildly through all the reasons she could lying there.

Had she fallen and hit her head? Collapsed from the lack of free-flowing air inside the dress? Was she dehydrated? Did she faint? Had she suffered a stroke or heart attack? "Dixie," I said. "Are you okay?"

The faux flames of my little lantern licked the curves of something metal behind her. "The candelabra," I said, flashing back to the snow outside my Christmas party. Aunt Fran had found a broken garden gnome and collected it, only to unintentionally place her fingerprints on a murder weapon.

I stifled the urge to touch the discarded prop. Six unobstructed, battery-powered candles, one affixed to each of the candelabra's arms, had to produce more light than the single faux tealight behind my plastic-paneled lantern. But I wasn't willing to accidentally follow in Aunt Fran's mistakes.

I shook my head, erasing the ugly memory and refocusing on the moment at hand.

"Dixie." I flattened myself on the ground before her and used the lantern's light to peer through the narrow line of lace. Her eyes appeared to be closed, and I wasn't sure what to do. I knew better than to move her, but I didn't know what was wrong or how to help. "Ms. Wetherill," I pleaded. "Are you hurt? Did you fall? Are you ill?" The final question was ridiculous I realized as I spoke it. It wasn't as if she'd decided to take a nap.

"I've called an ambulance!" Aunt Clara exclaimed, rushing to my side. "Fran's staying with the group. Is Dixie okay? Dixie?" she asked, resting a hand on the gown as she lowered to my side.

"She moaned when I found her," I said. "But she hasn't spoken to me or made any noise since."

"Don't worry, Dixie," Aunt Clara said sweetly. "Help is on the way."

Sirens rose into the night as if to underscore the promise. Ominous gray clouds rushed across the starry sky.

"Is she breathing?" Clara asked.

"I don't know. I hope so," I said, lowering my face to the strip of lace. I tipped my head to the material and listened for sounds of breath.

The broad beam of a flashlight bounced across the grass in our direction, and the brunette in tweed approached with a frown. "What's going on?"

"It's Aubrey," Aunt Clara said. "Good. She can help Fran with the group."

I looked up to see the woman in question. "We don't know what happened," I told her. "We found Dixie like this." The wind was too strong to hear her breaths, so I decided to try something else.

I set my lantern aside and pressed a palm gently to the dark dress, tracing Dixie's form. "Sorry," I said, dragging my hand over the curve of her waist, searching for her ribs instead. If I couldn't hear or feel her breaths in the wind, maybe I could identify the subtle rise and fall of her chest.

"What are you doing?" Aubrey asked. "Here use this. Those lanterns are for effect not utility. I'm not sure how anyone carrying one can see where they're going."

A wavering cone of light fell over me, and I reached for the object without thought.

My fingers curled around something narrow and cold.

I turned my eyes up to find the candelabra in my grip.

The heavy prop was smeared in blood.

And so were my fingers.

CHAPTER
THREE

Footfalls pounded the earth around me as first responders began to arrive. A pair of officers. A set of paramedics. A park ranger.

A fire truck parked in the distance.

Aunt Fran and Aubrey had relocated the tour participants to the reception area where they could wait for word on Dixie. But my great-aunts and I knew what that word would be.

Murder.

We'd been through more than our fair share of similar situations since my return to Charm, and we understood the protocol. All ghost walk participants were now potential witnesses to a crime. The police would want to talk to them. So, we couldn't let them leave.

Luckily, I'd delivered enough sweet tea and finger foods to the Wharf Museum today to keep everyone occupied for quite a while.

Aunt Clara had stayed with me, rubbing my

back and offering comfort, though I wasn't the one who'd known Dixie. She was. She sat beside me on the ground, neither of us willing to leave Dixie alone. Both of us knowing how bad the scene looked. Me with a bloody hand, blood-stained candelabra, and the motionless woman before me.

"I think she's dead," I whispered as the medics raced in our direction.

"What happened?" a familiar male voice asked. I recognized my favorite paramedic, Matt Darning, immediately. I'd seen him at other scenes like this one, and at various community events since I'd returned home. He was handsome, in a local surfer way, and genuinely kind to his core.

"Someone tried to kill her," I said grimly, hoping in vain they hadn't succeeded.

"We don't know that," Aunt Clara said. "We found her this way. We know she's bleeding from the torso. We were checking for signs of breath when we discovered the blood."

"Where's her head?" Matt's female partner squeaked.

The horrified young woman fell into step at his side. Her eyes were wide as she took in the dress sprawled before us.

Matt lowered easily into a crouch, already pulling a pair of scissors from his bag. "Under the costume. The island ghost walk was tonight, and this is Mourning Mable," he explained, positioning the scissors at the dress's hem. "Who's inside the costume?"

"Dixie Wetherill," Aunt Clara said. "She's from Kitty Hawk."

The female paramedic held a light while Matt cut the fabric, then set two fingertips against her neck, searching for a pulse.

"Any of her family around tonight?" he asked. "Spouse? Someone familiar with her medical history?" He rolled Dixie onto her back.

My gaze locked on the festive fall T-shirt she'd worn beneath the gown. A smiling pumpkin and pile of cartoon gourds, now soaked in her blood.

"No," Aunt Clara said. "She isn't married, and her daughter is grown."

Matt's expression fell as he continued to work over Dixie's still form. He looked up a few moments later and gave a small shake of his head.

"She's dead?" I asked, praying I'd misunderstood.

"I'm sorry, Everly," he whispered. Deep empathy wrinkled his suntanned brow.

I dropped the candelabra I'd been holding like a talisman, as if protecting Dixie's prop might somehow protect her as well. It was all she'd wanted before we'd left the museum. Before she'd met this awful fate. I slumped forward, emotionally wrecked.

Aunt Clara rubbed my back.

"How can this be happening again?" I groaned, wiping tears and fluctuating between stupor and outrage. "She was fine. We just saw her inside the museum! Who would do this?"

"I don't know, sweetie." The heartbreak and

compassion in Aunt Clara's voice sent tears down my cheeks.

I tried to imagine what I would do if someone brought me this kind of news someday, but I couldn't. My stomach cramped and roiled, rejecting the possibility. It was a scenario too painful to imagine, yet it was Dixie's family's reality.

"I'm sorry you had to go through this again," she whispered. "One time is too many. This makes"—she paused as if working up a tally—"five."

I'd found five bodies in two years. On an island that hadn't seen a murder in a decade before my return. I'd looked that up to confirm an earlier theory. My return to Charm had been magical for me and incredibly bad for the community I loved. I was a harbinger of death. The Grim Reaper returned. A plague.

"I would take the grief from you if I could," Aunt Clara whispered. "I know what you're thinking, and you're wrong. It's the shock."

"Everly?" the female medic said. "Everly S.?"

I raised tear-filled eyes to her. "Yeah?"

She swept the beam of her light onto the heavily shadowed ground at my side, where my name had been scratched into the dirt.

❧

Detective Grady Hays, the island's only homicide detective and my current crush, arrived dressed as Woody from *Toy Story*.

Aunt Clara and I had relocated to the base of a tree several yards away. From the small incline, we had quality panoramic views of the crime scene and everything else between us and the horizon. It was horrifying and surreal.

Grady extended a hand to Matt in greeting. "Sorry. Denver's school had a costume party," he said. "We went as a group. Denver was Buzz Lightyear. Denise was Bo Peep."

"I would've pegged her for Barbie," Matt said, accepting the handshake.

"Don't let her hear you say that," Grady said, probably only half-joking.

Denise was Grady's live-in au pair, a gorgeous, possibly lethal blond whom I'd thought of as a living Barbie doll more than once. Before that, I'd mistaken her as Grady's inappropriately young wife and mother to his son. These days, I thought of her as my friend. As an added bonus, she now helped me at Sun, Sand, and Tea each day while Denver was in school. It was a big win-win. Denise was getting to know the locals better, and I was getting more accomplished than I'd ever imagined, including extra baking and instructional videos.

"So, what do we have here?" he asked, crouching to scan the crime scene more carefully. He snapped on a pair of blue gloves from a black duffel I hadn't noticed him holding.

I paid close attention as Matt caught Grady up on the situation.

Both men were handsome to a fault, tall and lean with a healthy bronze glow, hard-earned by hours of working in the sun.

Matt had a youthful, untroubled look, complete with outgrown sandy hair and Atlantic-blue eyes.

Grady, on the other hand, was guarded and brooding. He'd been a hotshot U.S. Marshal until his beloved wife died of cancer when their son was only three. He told me once that he'd soaked himself in alcohol after her death, anytime he wasn't buried in work. It was how he'd tried to cope with her loss, and he'd stayed that way for nearly two years. Then, he got a case that had to do with a kid. He wasn't specific about the details, but whatever it was had shaken him. Sobered him. Reminded him that he wasn't the only one who'd lost Amy, and the realization had nearly leveled him with remorse. His preschool-age son had essentially lost both his parents, and he was too young to understand why.

Grady quit the marshal service, then found a tiny, rural island town in need of a detective. At half the pay and ten times the peace, he'd relocated immediately. Now, Denver was nearly seven. They'd been here about eighteen months, and the move had bonded father and son.

I was thankful for that, because they'd both become very important to me.

The female paramedic flashed a light on my name in the dirt, and Grady's head fell forward for a long beat.

He raised his face to Matt's a moment, then turned in my direction.

I lifted the fingers of one hand in a little wave.

Matt had taken a few photos of my blood-stained palms, then followed Aunt Clara and me to the tree where we were now. He'd dumped a bottle of water over my hands and rubbed my skin and fingernails clean with alcohol pads before returning to Dixie.

Eventually, Grady made his way to us. He stood hands-on-hips, looking like the world's most dangerous toy cowboy. He stared silently, brows furrowed.

I couldn't imagine the number of criminals he'd scared into confession with that expression alone.

He crouched, bouncing that intense gaze of his from me to Aunt Clara and back. Then he reached out, taking one of each of our hands in one of his and giving a squeeze. "You doing okay?"

"No," I said, fat tears welling in my eyes.

"It's been quite a night," Aunt Clara said, "but we'll get through it. We're the lucky ones." She patted his hand with her free one, then he released us. "There's something in your boot," she said, drawing my attention that way, despite an impending mental breakdown.

"It's a snake." He reached for the shrimpy-stuffed toy and freed the pin holding it in place.

I lifted my head. "There's a snake in your boot?"

"Yep."

I wiped my eyes and put my chin up. "I'm sorry you were pulled away from Denver's costume party."

"Me too," he said. "I'd planned to let someone else handle things here for another hour or so, while I finished at the school and drove Denver and Denise home. But your name came up." His lips twitched, fighting a smile. "Denver practically pushed me out the door then, and I don't think Denise would've let me back in if I'd tried."

"Oh, yeah?"

"They're protective of you," he said, gray eyes crinkling at the sides. "In case you haven't noticed, you're pretty important to us."

I pressed my lips together, enjoying his use of the word *us* more than I should. "It's good to have friends," I said, my voice too breathy for our situation.

"True." He handed me the little snake. "This place is good for finding support and acceptance. I'm not sure where else I could arrive at a crime scene in costume without losing respect."

I smiled. In Charm, folks would see the costume as evidence of how much he cared for his son. They'd see the uniform of a single father, and they'd see his dedication to our town because he prioritized our crisis over his leisure. Grady told me once that moving here was exactly what he and Denver had needed to heal and rejuvenate. And that he couldn't imagine ever wanting to leave. I knew the feeling.

"How's Denver doing?" I asked. His son had recently started having nightmares, and it had Grady on edge. I thought of them both every day. Denver for whatever he was going through. And Grady for how it hurt his heart to see his baby cry.

"He's struggling, unusually emotional and clingy. He's seeing a counselor who swears it's not uncommon for kids who experience a trauma like he did at three to recall the emotions later, when they begin to process the loss in new ways. He watched Amy battle long and hard. Then he lost her." Grady scrubbed a hand over his mouth. "He's able to understand all that now, even though the actual memories are mostly gone, and he's not emotionally mature enough to make sense of it." He frowned. "I still can't."

"We all deal differently," I said, speaking as someone who had, so far, lost two mother figures and feared every day that I'd lose another.

He pulled off the brown cowboy hat and twirled it in his hands, gaze traveling into the distance as a white cargo van stenciled with the county coroner emblem trundled into view. "There's the man I've been waiting for. Why don't I give you ladies a ride back to the museum where my guys are questioning the rest of the ghost-walk participants? We can talk more there, then I can drive you home."

"Thank you," Aunt Clara said.

Grady rose gracefully, then helped us each onto our feet. "I'm sorry about the loss of your friend," he told Aunt Clara. "She was a member of your historical group?"

Aunt Clara nodded.

He looked at me and sighed. "How did you know her, exactly?"

"I didn't," I admitted. "I've never spoken to her, and I saw her for the first time only tonight."

"But she knew you," he said.

"No." I felt my hackles rising as an earlier conversation flooded back to mind. "She knew who I was, and I'd heard of her too, but we'd never met." I rubbed my arms to quell the chills. My stomach rocked with too many feelings. Mostly guilt for my negative opinion of a dead woman.

He narrowed his eyes. "Any idea why she was writing your name in the dirt when she died?"

"Nope."

"You know how this looks, right?" he asked softly. "All things considered. At least until everyone's interviewed."

A dead woman had written my name in the dirt as her last earthly gesture, as if to possibly name her killer? And I was found with her blood on my hands. "Yes, but I was with Fran from the moment I arrived tonight." Except for a few minutes while she'd helped a woman with her wig, but Dixie had still been alive then. "There's no way I could've been the one who hurt Dixie. I have a continuous alibi." Even if my prints were on the candelabra. And she had a beef against my family.

My thoughts halted. "How did she die?" There'd been blood on her chest and torso.

"Looks like she was stabbed," he said. "My guys are looking for the murder weapon. Matt also noted a serious blow to the head, likely with the candelabra.

My best guess is that she was attacked from behind, knocked unconscious, then stabbed to finish the job. A premeditated crime. The coroner report will tell me more." He set a palm against my back as we moved away from the tree, Aunt Clara at my side. "I'm going to need you to tread lightly here. None of your usual snooping around. Anything you do, trying to save your reputation, will only make it seem as if you're trying to cover your tracks. People will speculate you hit her with the candelabra then hid the murder weapon. And they'll question whether or not your great-aunt would lie to protect you. Remember, Ms. Wetherill is from Kitty Hawk, where I presume the entire town doesn't know or adore you, and they will likely not afford you the same patience and leeway you find in Charm."

I scoffed. "Aunt Fran and I literally followed the tour group here."

He dropped his hand away from my back as we neared the workers gathered around Dixie.

"Detective?" The coroner motioned him closer.

I crossed my arms. "I'll wait here." A shiver rolled over me as the wind picked up.

Grady nodded, then reached for his vest and frowned, apparently having forgotten he was dressed as a six-foot stuffed toy. "I was going to offer you my coat."

"I've got it." Matt's voice carried through the wind. He hurried in our direction, stripping off the black EMT jacket with reflective silver letters and a stripe around the middle. His name was embroidered on the chest. "Here." He held the jacket open for me, and I obediently threaded my arms into the warm, sweet-scented material, then tugged it across my chest.

"Thanks."

Matt beamed.

Grady turned his eyes on me, then went to meet the coroner.

"You doing any better?" Matt asked.

"I think so."

Aunt Fran appeared on the trail, moving quickly, and headed straight to her sister. The women embraced and rocked back and forth a moment, unspeaking.

Matt smiled at them. "You guys make me miss my family." He folded his arms, probably frozen without his jacket. His biceps bulged with the movement, and I forced my gaze away. "My siblings are all over the country now, working, married, settled into grooves. My folks retired to a community in Florida that runs like a cruise ship that never leaves land."

"I'll bet they miss you too," I said.

He nodded. "Yeah. Mom calls a lot, but my hours are long and always changing. It's tough."

I remembered those days. Phoning in the love to Grandma while I'd been away. I could hear the longing and loss in her voice, willing me home, but I was on my own path, too busy to stop and too naive to understand our time was limited in this life.

Grady returned with a set of keys in hand. "Hey,

Fran," he said, greeting my newly arrived aunt. "How about a ride back to the museum, then home?"

"Please," she said, her arm thrown protectively around Aunt Clara.

Matt shook Grady's hand, then turned back for his partner. "Let me know if you need anything else," he called over his shoulder.

"Wait," I said. "Your jacket."

He turned, walking backward a few paces. "Hang on to it. Maybe I'll stop by tomorrow and pick it up."

I smiled, despite myself. "Okay."

"Okay," he echoed, looking unusually shy and at least a decade younger, then he spun and went back to work.

Grady stared at me, blank-cop expression in place. "Let's wrap this up and get you all home. It's been a tough night."

We rode in silence to the museum, a longer trip by road than it would have been on foot, but he was right. It'd been a tough night. Exhaustion was weighing on me and already visible on my aunts.

We moved stoically into the museum and gathered our things while Grady met briefly with a few of the officers, collecting the information they'd garnered so far.

A flash of pink tweed caught my eye through the crowd, and I hurried to tug on Grady's arm. "Excuse me," I said, butting into his time with an officer. "That woman in a pink Jackie O skirt and jacket. Dark bobbed hair."

Grady excused himself from the officer, then slowly scanned the room. "Yeah?"

"I saw her arguing with a man before the walk began. Her name's Aubrey. Then, a little while after that, she was looking for Dixie, who'd been looking for her candelabra."

"*The* candelabra?" he asked.

"Yeah. And she was the first person on the scene after Aunt Clara and me. In fact,"—I perked up—"she picked up the candelabra, which had been laying on the ground, and handed it to me when I wasn't looking, but needed more light. She didn't stick around to wait for the EMTs."

Grady's frame stiffened. "That so? We'll find her prints on the candelabra too?"

I frowned. "No. She had little white gloves on." They'd seemed to match the vintage suit. "She must still have them," I said. "She's part of Dixie's group in Kitty Hawk. Aunt Clara said Dixie wasn't very popular." I scanned the area, then I found what I was looking for. Tucked into a corner, looking pale and a little green, was the man. "There." I pointed. "That's the guy she was fighting with before the walk. Aubrey," I clarified. "Not Dixie."

Grady nodded, attention glued to the ill-looking man. "Wait here. I'll give you and your aunts a ride home in just a few minutes. I need written statements from you and Clara. Maybe you can work on those now," he suggested, already peeling away.

I considered his request as he wound through the

crowd, then followed him instead. I could write up a statement anytime. I could hear what this guy had to say about Dixie's murder only if I listened in right now. Plus, I reasoned, the victim had etched my name in the ground with her dying breaths. And I didn't even know her. Whatever Grady had to say about it, I had a dog in this race; and he was right, going on evidence alone, I looked sketchy as could be.

CHAPTER
FOUR

Grady stopped in front of the ill-looking man and introduced himself as a homicide detective. The words did nothing to improve the man's greenish complexion.

"Burton Chase," he said, eyes wide as he took in the six-foot Woody. "Did you say homicide?"

"'Fraid so." Grady watched Burton closely for several long beats, letting his silence wrap around the stranger like a noose before moving on. "You hadn't heard?"

I gave the busy room a disbelieving look. Even if this had been my first time at a murder scene, I was sure the number of lawmen would have tipped me off by now. People aren't corralled for questioning at the site of a heart attack.

Burton dragged a fingertip under the bottom edge of his glasses. The black, rectangular frames gave his large oval face a bit of an equine look, and the lenses magnified his beady brown eyes. I guessed Burton to be in his forties, same as Aubrey, and I wondered again about their relationship. "I heard the sirens," he said finally. "Saw the group returning early. People said she was down. Then that she was gone." His gaze flickered to mine, probably wondering why I was there.

I raised my hand in a sad hello, but the too-long sleeves of Matt's coat concealed every finger. "You didn't go out during the walk?"

Grady turned to frown at me, then refocused on Burton without bothering to ask why I wasn't writing my statement.

"I was here in case anyone needed anything," Burton said. "Acting as a runner for the actors and Charm Enthusiasts."

I made a mental note to ask Aunt Clara if that was a real job.

"How did you know Ms. Wetherill?" Grady asked.

"She's the Society's president. My wife, Aubrey, and I are part of her chapter in Kitty Hawk."

I cast a look at the woman in question, flipping through something on her phone. So, she and Burton were married. They could've been arguing about anything when I'd seen them earlier.

"Did you or Aubrey know Ms. Wetherill well?"

"Not really. As well as anyone from the Society, I guess."

"Is that Aubrey, there?" Grady tipped his head in her general direction.

"Yes. In the pink," Burton said. "Why?"

Grady stared again, waiting. Watching Burton

squirm in the silence. "Someone heard you arguing with her earlier. Then she went hunting for Ms. Wetherill. What was that all about?"

Burton frowned, then gave me a pointed look.

"Were the two events connected?" Grady asked.

Burton's knee began to bob. His gaze darted from Grady to Aubrey, halfway across the busy room. "Yes."

Grady rocked back on his heels. "Care to tell me about it?"

The sickly hue of Burton's skin flushed pink as he considered his answer.

I took a step in Aubrey's direction. "I can go get her, if you want," I said. "Maybe she remembers."

"No." Burton tensed. His jaw locked. "That's not necessary." He released a long sigh, then drew his attention back to Grady. "I'm an antiquities collector," he said. "Dixie has a book that was meant for me, and I want it. Aubrey doesn't understand why I'm so upset about the whole thing, and I don't know how she doesn't get it."

"How'd Dixie gain possession of your book?" Grady asked, head tipping slightly to one side.

"I won it in an online auction, but Dixie swooped in and paid more for it after I'd won. She made some kind of side-deal with the seller. So, even though I was the highest bidder, she won. Then the seller sent it to her." He rubbed his palms against his khaki slacks, pinching the material between his thumb and forefinger. "That's against the rules. They both knew it. The seller was greedy, and so was Dixie. That book is mine. I tried to buy it from her for what I originally offered the seller, but she said no. Then I offered her the amount that she swept in and paid, but she still said no." His knee began to bob. "She has a thousand books, and I only need this one to complete a collection, but she refused to give it to me. Even after I'd won it. I left a horrible review for the seller, but there's nothing I could do about Dixie."

"Wasn't there?" Grady asked, his expression chilly despite the cartoon cowboy getup.

"What?" Burton blanched. "Well, no. Of course not. I did everything I could." He rubbed the bridge of his nose, dislodging his glasses again.

"Must've made you pretty upset," Grady said. "What she did wasn't fair."

Burton swiped the glasses off his face and wiped his eyes roughly before resetting the frames. "Sure, but that's just Dixie. She does what she wants. And it doesn't matter who it upsets or offends. Sometimes, I swear she tries to cause problems. Puppeteering us. Like that's her idea of a good time or something."

"You mean was," Grady said darkly. "It *was* her idea of a good time."

Burton looked ill again.

I bit my lip against the swell of fast-forming thoughts. Most of which contained a pointed finger or the word *guilty*.

"Which book?" Grady asked.

Burton blinked, confused. "What?"

"What's the name of the book she bought?" Grady asked. "The one you wanted."

The middle-aged man opened his mouth, then closed it. He looked blankly at me, then back to Grady. "What's that have to do with anything?"

"You don't remember the title?" Grady asked. "The book sounded pretty important to you a minute ago. It completes your collection."

Burton cleared his throat. "*Coastal Lore, Legacies, and Legends*. It's the fourth book in the Barrier Island History Ensemble I've been collecting for a decade. The series was written at the turn of the previous century. The volumes are rare, out of print, and worth preserving. That's why I've been hunting them down all these years."

"Maybe Dixie needed it for her collection," I suggested.

Burton clucked his tongue. "She doesn't collect those. She likes maps and books on genealogy."

"How do you know?" I asked. "You said you weren't close."

"I know because we use the same auction site. She's on it all the time. Trolling. A benefit of being retired, I suppose. No pesky nine-to-five work hours to keep her from getting all the best stuff at premium prices. She's Island_Historian48. Was," he corrected. "Sorry."

"Interesting," I said, already dying for a look at Dixie's library and wondering how much her online book-buying nemesis had it out for her in real life.

Before I could ask any follow-up questions, Aunt

Clara waved me down, already hurrying in my direction. The crowd had thinned, and a pair of uniformed officers spoke with the final trio of potential witnesses near the door. "Everly!" Aunt Clara used her stage voice to be heard across the space. "We're moving the reception to Kitty Hawk. The Society wants to meet at their headquarters and spend some time together. We're packing up your food and drinks now, if you want to come with us."

A bubble of hope rose in my chest. Maybe talking to the people who knew Dixie best would help me make sense of what happened to her tonight. "I'll be right there."

I turned back to the men, now watching me. "I guess I'll see you later tonight in Kitty Hawk," I told Burton. "You and Aubrey will be there, won't you?"

Grady narrowed his eyes on me. "Don't."

"What?" I asked, my voice full of innocence. "I assume I'll see you there too. After you've had time to review the crime scene and Dixie's dressing room, then touch base with your men and the coroner again. Now you don't have to lose any time running us home."

Grady frowned. "I don't like how familiar you are with this process."

I forced a tight smile, agreeing silently with that sentiment, then nodded my goodbye to Burton and hurried for the door.

៚

The Society for the Preservation and Retelling of Unrecorded History, Kitty Hawk chapter, met in a beautiful historic mansion that had once been the local Women's Club. According to Aunt Clara, a generous donation had moved the Women's Club to new digs, and the Society now leased the mansion. However they'd come to call it headquarters, the place was phenomenal.

The residence had been built in the height of prohibition, when rum-running from Barbados was big business, and a wealthy northern family had taken advantage. I'd read about it in local history books, fascinated because our island didn't have a lot of historic structures. Fire had destroyed many of the older, wooden homes built inland, while the sea had taken those fashioned too close to the shore. Hurricanes were serious business in Charm and her sister towns. Still, my home, this one, and a handful of others had persevered.

I wheeled Wagon into the kitchen, admiring the Tiffany lighting, brightly colored paints, and stained glass at every turn. Surprisingly, my remaining refreshments filled the narrow countertops. Ghost walk participants had made short work of the desserts while waiting to be questioned by Charm police, but there were still plenty of finger sandwiches and appetizers to go around. And I'd found two untouched jugs of old-fashioned sweet tea as well.

"Hey," a vaguely familiar woman called. She was young, thin in the extreme, and gorgeous, despite the dark crescents beneath her eyes. "Swan, right?"

"Yes," I smiled.

She stopped before me, all shimmer and legs for days.

"That's a pretty dress."

"Thanks." She shrugged. "I got it in town." Her satin-gloved hands skimmed over the simple, black flapper dress. A sequined band circled the circumference of her head, onyx feathers standing tall above one ear. "I heard what happened to Dixie. You were there?"

"Yeah." My throat thickened, and I averted my gaze, forcing the gruesome images from my mind.

"I'm glad she wasn't alone at the end. I still can't believe she was bumped off."

I grimaced, both taken aback by the casual way she spoke about someone's murder and the incredibly old expression she used to describe it. Maybe she was in character? "Me either, I guess. Any idea who'd do something like that?"

"Probably lots of people," she said. "She was a bit of a pill."

The rest of the group made their way to the kitchen, talking softly and looking a little worse for wear.

"I'm Everly," I said, offering my new acquaintance a hand. "This is a beautiful home."

"Harriet." She squeezed my fingers and smiled. The chill of her frigid skin crept through her glove, and I shivered in response. "Want a tour?"

"Absolutely." I followed her from the kitchen and

onto a grand, gold-and-blue carpet runner stretching down a narrow hall, as if leading us back in time.

I wondered at Harriet's perfect porcelain skin, luminous, even in the subpar light. Did she ever go outside? "Are you from Kitty Hawk?"

"Originally," she said, trailing her gloved fingers over the hip-high wainscoting as she walked. "I've always loved this house. There's so much history here. Oh, the stories these rooms could tell."

I could only imagine.

I often thought about all the souls who'd lived in my house through the centuries. First my rumored ancestor, Magnolia Bane, the woman the home had been built for, had thrown herself from the widow's walk after discovering her lover's wife had learned of the affair before walking straight into the sea. Then Magnolia's lover, Lou, the wealthy businessman who'd commissioned the home for her, allegedly went insane inside it, grieving her loss and the passing of his wife. It was a tragic beginning, but the home had gone on to be a number of things. A boarding school and apartment house, among others. If my home could talk, I'd sit down and listen to every story.

"Dixie was obsessed with history," Harriet said. "I suppose she's officially part of it now. Her story will be told on the ghost walks of the next generation. Your kids will probably tell it."

"I don't have any children," I said, pushing the immediate thoughts of my family's alleged curse aside. *Swan women are cursed in love,* I heard my grandma's voice say. *Death befalls any man we dare set our heart on.*

"You will." Harriet stopped at a pair of intricately carved pocket doors, then pried them open. "This is Dixie's office. I hope you'll find the one who did this to her."

"Me?" I stared at her sincere expression as I shook myself back to the moment. "Why me?"

"It's what you do, isn't it?" she asked. "You were there when Mitzi Calgon died. You found her killer. And there were others." She flipped the light on inside the room, then turned to look at my stunned face.

"I'm just an iced-tea maker." Though I had gotten wrapped up in a few local investigations. And I desperately wanted to know what happened to Dixie before the Kitty Hawk newspapers painted me as a suspect, or worse, the villain. I could practically see the headlines forming.

Island native Everly Swan discovered at Willow Park with local historian Dixie Wetherill's blood literally on her hands.

Harriet chuckled. "You're far more than a tea maker." She pressed her narrow backside against the wall outside the open pocket doors. "I'll watch for incomers while you do your thing."

I examined the room before me. "I thought you were taking me on a tour."

She wrinkled her nose. "The others were coming, and I needed a reason to get you out of there before they started asking you questions. That would've taken all night, and I can't stay forever."

Considering I'd been the one to find Dixie, I supposed there would've been questions. And I didn't have any answers. "Good point."

"Besides," she said coyly. "This is what you really wanted to see. Isn't it?"

I hooked my hands on my hips and gawked at the floor-to-ceiling shelves stuffed with old tomes, and a window seat covered in them. The big mahogany desk in the room's center was barely visible behind stacks of books on the floor and polished desktop. "Yeah," I admitted. Dixie really did have a lot of books. Exactly as Burton had said. "What does she do with all these books?" I asked. "Is she starting a library?"

Harriet rolled her head against the wall and looked at me. "Dixie bought and sold antiques online. The profit margin was best with books, so she doubled-up on those, but maps and island families were her passion."

I circled the room, taking a closer look. The books were all old and covered topics related to the history of our area. Kitty Hawk, nearby towns, and Charm. There was plenty of material covering local legends and lore, but more surprisingly, not all the materials were published. In fact, many were handwritten accounts of island life. Journals, letters, essays, and numerous firsthand retellings of various times in local history. I lifted a few items carefully, unable to resist, then paged gingerly through the historic accounts of island life. Some of the ink had browned and faded drastically on the yellowed pages. Other stories were perfectly legible despite their age. The pages inside family Bibles listed the names and dates of weddings, births, and deaths.

So much for Dixie's obsession with preserving undocumented history. She'd obviously had a soft spot for detailed documentation as well. "It's a remarkable collection."

"Mm hmm." Harriet kept a careful watch on the hallway. "Have you seen the cloth-wrapped volumes on her desktop?"

"No." I made a trip to the room's center, then rifled through the stacks until I found a set of matching books swaddled in what looked like cheesecloth. "*Founding Families*," I read. "Is this about the Wetherills?"

Harriet slid her eyes in my direction, but otherwise pretended not to hear me.

I lifted the top book, then opened the tattered cover. I thumbed through aged photographs lying loose inside, all slightly faded and curled at the corners. I recognized images of a local historic church, the island's most famous lighthouse, and my home.

I nearly dropped the book. Someone had clipped an article about my house from the *Charm Register* more than a century ago, and slipped the brittle, folded section between the book's pages like a souvenir or cherished memory. A photograph accompanied the text, and I stared at the man in the foreground. Was it Lou? The home's original owner?

The sounds of sudden footfalls broke my concentration before I could read the article beyond the headline: "The Changing Face of Charm." I took a picture of the newspaper article with my phone, then returned it to the book and set the volume back on the pile. A receipt from Historical Pages in Hatteras was stuck to the cheesecloth.

I raised my eyes to check the situation with Harriet, but she was gone.

I beetled away from the desk, realizing Grady might show up at any moment. I snapped photos of everything in sight, then paused before a massive tapestry on the far wall. The image of a family tree stretched top to bottom, and dozens of Wetherills' names were stitched on the branches. The tree was impressive. Dixie's family lineage went nearly as far back as mine. I took a quick picture of the tapestry too.

The names and dates hadn't been updated in thirty years, but someone had recorded Dixie's marriage and her daughter's birth. A photograph on her desk suggested she also had a few grandchildren now.

I rifled quickly through a basket of old newspapers, then fanned through a stack of faded journals and maps. A shocking amount of the material was dedicated to unearthing buried treasure.

An uneasy feeling crept over me as I studied the room, packed to the gills with island history. I checked over my shoulders—in case someone was watching— recalling the earlier footfalls that had never arrived.

The urge to leave overcame me, but a collage of framed photos caught my attention. One image contained a line of ladies in flapper gowns, perched and posed on the window seat behind me. Men in suits filled the space along each side. The woman at the center held a sign announcing New Year's Eve 1923, and she could have been Harriet's twin, though a few years younger. I marveled at the similarities in their appearances, certain the woman from the photo must've been my new friend's ancestor. I scanned the names handwritten beneath, moving left to right, and started at the sight of the words identifying the woman: Harriet Wetherill.

I turned to stare at the place the young woman had been moments before, then forced myself to get moving. I had to get out of there before someone caught me snooping.

CHAPTER

FIVE

Business was slow but steady the next day, and I was thankful as always for Denise's help with customers. Partly because I was swamped with online orders for my family's rum cake. Mostly because I hadn't slept. Dixie's slack face had stayed just behind my eyelids all night, and I hated that she'd been lying there, only a few yards away, and I hadn't known until it was too late.

I chewed my bottom lip, unsure that was true. Maybe I hadn't known she was hurt, but I'd known something was wrong. So had Aunt Fran and Aunt Clara. All our instincts had been on high alert, but only I had heard the scratching. My stomach rolled in remembrance. While I'd been trying to place the unusual sound, a woman had been dying. And she'd written my name into the earth with her fingers.

What did it mean?

Not what it seemed, that was for sure. It seemed as if she'd been trying to identify her killer, but I hadn't hurt Dixie. Therefore, I could only assume she'd been trying to leave a message for me. I wished more than anything I knew what that was.

Movement on my rear deck caught my eye, and I smiled as the seagull who'd seemed to have come with the house landed on the railing, wings outstretched and head cocked to peer through the glass. I smiled, grabbed a bit of fish I'd saved in my fridge for him, and headed outside for a little fresh air.

"Hey, Lou," I said, enjoying the sun on my face. A briny wind rushed over me as I slid the plated treat onto a nearby table for his enjoyment. "What's shaking?"

He made his way to the food, and I gave him room. Lou was brave (for a bird) without being aggressive. He let me get close, but not too close, and seemed to enjoy listening to me talk. Maybe because the sound of my voice usually led to leftover fish and seafood.

"I'd stay and chat, but my life has gone sideways again. I've got another mystery to solve."

"Caw!"

"Back at ya," I told him as I retrieved the empty plate and headed back inside.

"How are the cakes coming?" Denise asked, sashaying behind the counter as I dropped the plate into my dishwasher. Her skinny jeans were fashionable and accented her fit physique. Her pale-blue V-neck T-shirt had the Sun, Sand, and Tea logo above the pocket and was a size small. I knew, because I'd ordered it.

My shirt was a clingy extra-large, and I'd long ago

ripped the size tag out of all my jeans. Not that size mattered, but it would be nice to zip my pants without having to lay on the bed and hold my breath.

"Good." I mixed enough batter for a pair of rum cakes then divided it evenly between two prepared Bundt pans.

I donned my favorite oven mitts, a shark on one hand, whose design made it appear as if the mouth was opening and closing when I gripped things, and a quilted red crab claw on the other. I loaded the future cakes into my oven and set the timer. "I never thought I'd say it, but I'm getting a little bored of making these," I said. I'd baked at least six every day for months. Once I'd advertised the dessert on my website, the orders had started coming, and I'd had to limit the number I was willing to fill. Six per day. Period. "I'm not sure if I own an iced tea shop or a rum cake factory."

She grinned. "Both. What do you put in them, anyway? They're addictive."

"Just love, rum, and some cake stuff." My family's rum cake recipe was one I guarded closely. Swans had been making the cakes since prohibition, and the process was a secret I wasn't ready to divulge. "I can't complain about the added revenue," I said. "It's nice to be paid for doing something I love. Not everyone gets to."

"That's how I feel about taking care of Denver," Denise mused. "Being his au pair is incredibly fulfilling. I'll be lost when he grows up."

"You won't," I said. "His life isn't the only one moving forward. Time has a way of putting us where we need to be when we need to be there." And as for the abundance of cake orders? The profits were slowly paying to spruce up my living quarters, so I decided to stop complaining.

According to county records, my home was about 170 years old, and while the previous owner had done a bang-up job on the first-floor renovation, his enthusiasm, funds, or both had run out before making it upstairs. I'd cheerfully picked up the torch, adding lots of aesthetic updates after moving in. The paint, throw rugs, art, and curtains were new, but the light fixtures, cabinets, and ugly laminate countertops were easily twice my age and in need of replacement. The baseboards needed to be sanded and refinished, desperately. The list went on.

Denise righted a pair of mason jars from the rack near the sink and filled both with ice. Her blue eyes narrowed as she watched me. "How are you holding up after last night?"

I wasn't. Dixie's murder had shaken me. I'd already seen too many deaths since my return to the island, and Dixie had carved my name into the ground with her final breaths. I had no idea how I'd heard the scratching over the sound of the wind, but the whole night had felt somehow surreal. Right down to the doppelganger flapper who'd led me to Dixie's office and pointed me to the book of island families on her desk. All in all, I was freaked out, feeling a tornado of emotions and wholly exhausted. "I'll be okay," I said, nodding in a lame attempt to support my answer. "You?"

She watched me a minute, probably seeing through my lie. Whatever she was thinking, she kept it to herself as she turned back to the jars of ice. "Denver had another round of nightmares last night, so no one got much sleep at our place. Breaks my heart to see him going through this."

"Mine too," I said.

She positioned one of the jars beneath the iced tea dispenser marked Apple Cinnamon, and the second jar under the dispenser marked Citrus Mint, then pulled the tabs. "Grady's working overtime to get Denver through this, but it's taking a toll on him too."

"Anything I can do?" I asked.

"I don't think so." She set the filled jars on a tray, then scooped chicken salad made with Greek yogurt and grapes into a pair of sliced croissants and plated each with homemade chips and a pickle. "We'll figure it out. Denver's a tough cookie. I just wish he didn't have to be."

I understood the sentiment.

She hefted the tray and ferried it across the café to her customers, then returned with an expectant look. "Did you ever decide on the special teas you want to feature for the ball and the election?"

I cringed. "Not yet." The Harvest Ball was a big event in Charm, an annual outdoor party with music, food, and boundless community spirit. Folks started talking about it the minute tourist season ended. I'd agreed to supply a large amount of my hibiscus tea, which was scarlet in color and worked well with the typical orange, red, and yellow décor. Once that was over, the town's election came next, and Aunt Fran was running for mayor. I wanted to create a special blend of teas for each event and give them catchy names. My little way of contributing to the celebrations.

"Halloween or Election Day?" Denise mused. "I can't decide which is scarier."

I grinned. "That'll depend on whether Aunt Fran wins or loses."

Denise laughed.

Truthfully, I was nervous. As the town's founding family, Swan women had held positions of every kind over the years, but if elected, Aunt Fran would be our first Swan as mayor. In fact, if Aunt Fran won the election, she would be the island's first female mayor. Quite an honor on all fronts and a feather for the family cap.

I wanted Aunt Fran to win because she wanted to win, but I worried about how the position would impact her relationship with Aunt Clara. I'd only ever known them as a set. How much time would Aunt Fran have for their little shop on Main Street? Would Aunt Clara be lonely? If so, would I be enough to bridge the gap?

Denise studied me from her position several feet away, wiping down the countertop. She glanced at the smattering of customers busily involved in their meals and conversations. "Do you ever wonder if the fact that you stumble onto all these dead bodies has something to do with your family's curse?"

My jaw dropped.

She raised her palms in apology. "I know you're sensitive about the curse, but it is curious, don't you think?"

My gaze darted erratically around the shop, hoping no one else had heard her. "Do you believe in curses?" I asked gently. She'd seemed incredibly level-headed to me, until she'd asked that question. "This is important, because you should know that, as your employer, I don't offer a mental health plan."

She snorted delicately at my disbelief, then gave up all pretense of work and moved in closer. "You're looking at me as if I just grew a second head," she whispered. "But your family business is widespread public knowledge. I wasn't always a believer, but I don't argue with facts. And the fact is that things work differently here. Moving to Charm has been a little like moving to Oz. Except instead of talking scarecrows and cowardly lions, I've met a charming but allegedly cursed tea shop owner who finds dead bodies several times a year. It's not exactly good luck," she said.

"Okay. Agreed, but I don't believe in curses. Those stories were designed to keep Swan daughters close to home in eras when it was dangerous for women to travel alone. Saying we had to stay here or bad things would happen meant keeping us safe. And saying any man that a Swan woman loved would meet an early demise was probably very effective at keeping unwanted suitors at bay. I'm sure that curse was actually a purity stunt put together by the dads."

"Dads?" Denise asked. "Tell me about those."

"What?" I stalled, seeing her expression slide from apology to challenge.

"The men in your family," she pressed. "What are they like?" She offered a sad smile, knowing my dad died before I was born. Sudden massive heart failure. He was twenty-eight. "Who are your uncles and grandpas?"

I couldn't answer because I didn't know them. Men didn't last when they married into our family, and Swan women didn't give birth to boys. Admittedly strong arguments for the curse's existence. Or, as I preferred to think about it, a series of completely unrelated and coincidental truths. For three-hundred-plus years. Swan women also didn't take their husbands' last names. Maybe it had to do with their fear of the curse. Or maybe traditions were just hard to break. But records showed a surprising number of husbands had taken the Swan name after marriage. I still got a kick out of imagining those requests being made at the courthouse, especially in generations past.

"I'm just saying," she continued. "Your family is different, and so is this island."

"And you're okay with that?" I asked. "I thought you were the only logical one left in this town." She and Grady, anyway. Possibly his mother-in-law as well.

Denise shrugged. "The stuff I've heard about your family is strange, I'll admit that, but people seem happiest when they stop fighting it, and I'm not here to buck the system."

I frowned. I tried bucking the system regularly, but so far it hadn't worked out for me.

"All I'm saying," she said, "is that maybe you left the island, and the curse was ignited for you. You're back now, and that's better than being away, but you've got a little baggage with you."

"I moved to the mainland for a few years, and my punishment is finding dead bodies?"

She lifted and dropped a palm. "I don't know, but you do find bodies. Did you do that before you left?"

"No."

Denise brushed invisible crumbs from the countertop, apparently resting her case. "I'm sorry I wasn't there for the ghost walk last night. Wyatt and I planned to come, but Denver's school had the party, and I needed to be there. Wyatt filled me in on some of the local tales last weekend when we walked on the beach. He knows a ton of them. I was really impressed."

Wyatt was the cowboy I'd chased across the Midwest on a rodeo circuit when I'd left Charm for culinary school. He lived here now too, and we were working on a new kind of relationship as friends.

"Wyatt's a sucker for Aunt Clara," I said with a smile. "He listens to all her tales at length and on repeat because he knows how much she loves it."

"Did you hear we're getting a blue moon this month?" she asked. "I thought it was still a few days away, but after what happened at the ghost walk, I'm wondering if it was last night."

I thought of the moonlight shining through the willows and shivered. Blue moons were rare, and not blue. Rather, they were the second full moon in a month and believed to impact the people they shined upon. There'd been a blue moon on the night Magnolia walked off my roof, so the phenomenon had always felt a little ominous to me. And imagining a blue moon in conjunction with Dixie's death raised gooseflesh on my arms. "I hadn't heard that," I said. But I could vividly recall the strange tug on my intuition and the creep of moonlight over the willows before she'd been found.

"Is it true the people in Charm believe the light of a blue moon causes lunacy?" she asked. "Wyatt told me about that too."

"I don't think people really believe it," I hedged, though they did say it.

"And that woman was killed in the moonlight. That's wild, right?"

"Wild," I agreed.

"Do you think the woman was a victim of blue-moon lunacy?" Her voice was flat, and her eyes narrowed.

"No, but I would like to know what happened and what it had to do with me."

Denise held up a finger, putting our conversation on pause, then she hurried to chat with a customer looking her way.

I thought again of Dixie and my name written

beside her body on the ground. She'd had a problem with my family, but I didn't understand why. Could we have been the Hatfields and McCoys of the island a few generations back? The Capulets and the Montagues? Were there answers in the book *Founding Families* that I'd seen on her desk?

All I really knew about Dixie was that she loved history. Her office was physical evidence of that truth, and I'd seen it with my own eyes. The endless stacks and rows of books on local lore, handwritten journals, diaries, and letters.

Then Burton, the rattled man I'd watched Grady interview, came to mind.

I hurried to grab my laptop, then flipped up the lid.

Denise walked to the register with the couple who'd gotten her attention.

I typed "Coastal Lore, Legacies, and Legends" into the search engine. It was the title of the book Dixie had allegedly swiped right out of Burton's hands, digitally speaking. I hit the enter key and scanned the results.

Printed in 1901, the book was fourth in a larger collection, as Burton had said. And according to the internet, *Coastal Lore, Legacies, and Legends* featured pirates, buried treasures, and sunken ships carrying gold bars and jewels. And tales of the ghosts who allegedly guarded them. The book included gorgeous hand-drawn maps and illustrations, a book collector's dream, as well as a treasure hunter's. I let that hamster of a thought run its wheel in my head while I contin- ued scanning the screen for information. "Holy crab cakes." Copies were selling for more than a thousand dollars, and they weren't in good condition. What would a nicely maintained copy cost?

Denise and a few customers looked my way, then went back to what they'd been doing.

I made a mental note to pull myself together.

I opened another window and clicked a link I'd saved in my Favorites, the *Town Charmer*, our town's highly accurate gossip blog. I had no idea who ran the site, but it was insanely popular and shockingly on the nose with its content. Charmers checked it daily and contributed under pseudonyms but downplayed their interest in person by claiming the site was useful for the tide schedules and weather. Which was also true.

The feature image was a collage. A larger photo of Dixie in her Mourning Mable costume beside smaller images of her in a pantsuit at a local charity event and me, hands covered in her blood. The headline below:

Has Charm's Local Sleuth Found Herself on the Wrong Side of the Case?

I scrolled past, mind scrambling over who could have possibly taken the photo of me, but not ready to read the blog post's content or the comments. The second article covered our upcoming election. Who would be Charm's next mayor? My incredible great-aunt Fran; Senator Denver, Grady's mother-in-law; or my lifelong nemesis, Mary Grace Chatsworth-Vanders and her new husband, Chairman Vanders, a self-proclaimed power couple planning to run the show together.

I considered moving every time I recalled the potential consequences of Aunt Fran losing. Senator Denver had bought a home in Charm last year, under the pretense of wanting more time with her grandson, when in reality, she'd come to corner Grady into doing something for her. She was highly educated, spent years in the military, and loved DC politics. I could only imagine what the rigid woman would do first to turn our town on its nose if she won the election. And sadly, whatever that was would probably be markedly better than seeing Mary Grace and her husband at the helm.

I scrolled back to the top of the screen and discovered the site had been updated with a new article.

A bold Breaking News headline informed readers of an age-old grudge between the Swans and the Wetherills. The content speculated I might have killed Dixie to finally end the century-old feud.

I guffawed.

Denise headed back in my direction. "Uh oh, what'd I miss?"

"The *Town Charmer* just gave me an idea," I said, stripping the half-apron from my waist. "Will you take my rum cakes out when the oven dings?"

She grinned as she passed me. "Absolutely. Enjoy your walk."

"Thank you!"

I grabbed a hooded sweatshirt with my shop's logo emblazoned across the back and zipped it over my matching T-shirt, then pocketed my phone and wallet. I hurried through the foyer, suddenly energized to get answers.

My ridiculous fitness bracelet flashed with its usual message. **BE MORE ACTIVE**.

I grumbled and gave it a flick with my thumb and first finger. "I am! Jeez."

A blast of chilly air rushed against me as I flung the front door open and jumped onto my porch. I nearly fell over an obstacle directly in my path.

A sword stood in the center of my porch, its tip plunged into the wide wooden planks that had been scattered with sand. A tattered scrap of material was tied to the handle and dripping in blood. A curled square of yellowed parchment was impaled beneath it. Beautiful black calligraphy instructed:

Return the map

CHAPTER

SIX

Grady's truck rocked to a stop in my driveway less than five minutes later. He'd been in town interviewing some of the Charm Enthusiasts when I texted him a picture of the situation at hand.

I'd texted Denise to let her know exiting guests should be escorted through the rear deck doors. The deck wrapped around, giving customers an alternative exit, so they wouldn't trample through the crime scene. I could only hope no new guests would arrive while there was a sword stuck in my porch.

Grady climbed out and stared a moment. I tried to imagine what the scene looked like from his perspective. Me in my usual jeans, ponytail, and hoodie, beside an antique sword, tied with a bloody scrap of fabric, and impaling a calligraphy threat on parchment.

I wiggled my fingers in greeting, and Grady shook his head.

His brown hair was a few weeks past a haircut, and

his face hadn't seen a razor in days. "This is new," he said, eyeballing the sword. He slung a black duffel bag over one shoulder, then stuffed a cowboy hat onto his head before shutting the truck door and making his way to me in long, confident strides.

"It's old, actually," I said, hoping to break the tension. "About two hundred years, I think. I was on my way to visit my aunts at their shop when I found it, but it's not for me." I stepped aside as Grady climbed the stairs.

"No?" he asked, sucking his teeth in disbelief before circling the sword. He snapped a few photos of the peculiar scene with his phone. "Not for you, huh?" He raised exhausted gray eyes to mine, an expression of mild amusement on his handsome face. "Who's it for?"

I raised my shoulders, palms, and eyebrows in an exaggerated show.

He smiled, and I relaxed.

This was exactly the sort of situation that would've sent him into a rant a year ago. I couldn't help wondering if that meant Denise was right and island life had changed him too, or maybe I was just wearing him down.

He squatted before the sword, the material of his jeans pulling tight across his thighs. "Is this supposed to be a pirate sword?"

"I think it's a captain's sword," I said. "I looked it up."

He slid the duffel from his shoulder, then stretched a pair of plastic gloves over his broad hands.

"What do you think it means?" I asked, inching closer, desperate to hover without contaminating the tiny crime scene.

He untied the scrap of tattered and bloody fabric, then stuffed it into a plastic evidence bag. "Looks like someone wants a map." He held the bag up, examining it carefully. "A bandana?"

"It's from a ship's flag," I said. I'd snapped a picture of the flag and sword's hilt with my phone and searched for matching online images while I'd waited for his arrival. Both returned results in a matter of seconds. "The HMS *Belvedere*."

Grady rested a forearm across his thigh and twisted for a look at me. "Her Majesty's Ship *Belvedere*?"

"Mm hmm." I chewed my lip. "It sailed between Charm and Great Britain in 1809. The captain's name was James Hudson."

"James Hudson?" Grady's brows pulled together, and I could see him working over the information. "The murderous sailor from the ghost story with Mourning Mable?"

"Yep."

"The Sandman?" he clarified, flicking his gaze to the abundant sand spread around the blade.

"Some believe so," I said. "Others think they're two different stories. The treasure is definitely part of the Sandman's story, and you know the legend of Mourning Mable. There's no definitive way to know if James Hudson was the Sandman or if the stories converged over time."

"Great." Grady tilted his head side to side, stretching his neck.

I inched forward, then tipped at the waist, speaking closer to his ear. "I think this is James Hudson's sword. The same one he allegedly used to murder Mourning Mable's husband, then lop off her head. It could be the same weapon used to kill Dixie last night."

Grady stretched upright, and I jumped back. "You believe in ghosts now?"

It took me a minute to understand his confusion. "No, but everyone on this island does. I think whoever did this and killed Dixie is trying to create a cover story to divert attention. Islanders are going to eat this up. I'm just giving you the narrative."

"So, where's the map?"

I raised my palms. "I don't have a map. That's how I know this message isn't for me."

Grady raised one arm and ran his jacket sleeve across his forehead. "I thought I'd seen everything during my time in the military. Then, I was sure of it during my time with the marshals. Then, I came here, and I don't think there's a limit to crazy anymore." He dislodged the sword with one hand, flipping it immediately up while dropping back into a crouch. He pressed two gloved fingertips to the note before it could blow away on a breeze. "Open my truck door?"

"Sure." I followed Grady to his truck and opened the door.

He set the antique weapon on his bench seat, then tucked the parchment into an evidence bag from his pocket as we made our way back to the porch. "So we're clear," he said, "the note is for you. People don't go around accidentally stabbing the wrong porch with antique weaponry."

"I don't have any maps," I argued.

"Someone thinks you do."

I watched as he scowled dubiously at the note. For a minute, I wondered if he saw something more on the curled parchment than I could. "What is it?"

"I think that unwritten-gossip society in Kitty Hawk is a little nuts," he said. "And I'm not thrilled to see the cuckoo is spreading."

"Aunt Clara's part of that group," I reminded him.

He shot me an apologetic look. "I can't understand how anyone believes the stories passed around a campfire as strongly as they believe the ones in reference books with supporting accounts and documentation. Legends, tall tales, curses. People have been lying since the beginning of time." He slowed to pin me with a pointed look. "I don't believe in that stuff."

"Me either." Mostly.

Something flickered in my gut, and I suddenly needed him to be specific. I wanted him to say he didn't believe in curses, especially the ones hanging over my family.

"I'm sure most local lore is based on some kernel of truth," he said, "maybe even enough truth to make the story seem legit, but that doesn't make it a fact. And apparent supporting evidence, no matter how imploring, isn't verification."

I crossed my arms, feeling the words hit home. "Well, true story or not, someone seems to think I have a map that I don't have, and they're trying to scare me into returning it."

Grady tucked the evidence bag with the parchment into his duffel, then used the contents of his official policeman crime scene kit to swab the floorboards for trace evidence and collect a sample of the sand.

A group of hikers in extensively pocketed, outdoorsy clothing and boots turned up my driveway, slowing when they saw Grady in the Charm PD windbreaker. His evidence-collection materials spread around the crimson spots on my porch. I didn't recognize any of them, but the binoculars hanging around their necks helped me peg them for birders, especially given the time of year. Their collective mouths opened and closed like baby birds in nests. Their gazes flickered to the carved-wood sign swinging from the eave above my steps. SUN, SAND, AND TEA. They were at the right place, but they fell back anyway, recollecting themselves before deciding against a trip to my tea shop.

I pursed my lips to suppress a sigh. I couldn't blame them, but I hated how quickly news of Grady's official presence would spread now and stoke the fire already lit beneath my reputation.

Grady stilled to watch the group disappear around the bend. His jaw set as he turned his eyes back on me. "I don't like knowing that whoever did this thinks you have something they want." He peeled the gloves from his hands and tossed them into the gaping mouth of his duffel before zipping them inside. "It means this is just the beginning. Whoever did this will come at you again, and I can't allow that."

"I don't have any maps, so this could be an attempted misdirect," I suggested. "A hope for chaos. Maybe you should ignore it and double down on the information you already have. You could be close to naming the killer, and this is a ridiculous attempt to break your concentration."

"It's not ridiculous," Grady said, leveling me in his heated stare. "It was effective. I won't ignore any threat made against you. So, you need to think about what this could mean and let me know. Everything else can get in line."

My breath caught as I took in his tone and the rush of emotion in his eyes. Grady and I had come a long way from the night we met, when he'd accused me of murdering an old man with my tea. We called a truce early on, and that had developed into an understanding that became appreciation. A friendship bloomed and blossomed. Now, whatever we had going between us was undeniably *more*. The problem was, I didn't know exactly what that meant.

A police cruiser motored into the driveway, effectively ending the moment. A pair of officers climbed out, dipping their chins in greeting as they made their way to my porch.

To our left, a group of my customers hurried into view with Denise on their heels. The patrons gaped at the incoming officers, then glanced to Grady and me before picking up speed across the porch and away from the crime scene.

"Have a lovely day," Denise called after them. "Come back real soon!" She watched until they were out of sight, then turned a deflated look in my direction. "Well, that's everyone. Their phones started dinging a few minutes ago, and suddenly they were all ready to leave at once."

"Birders," I said. I knew they'd looked like big mouths.

She wrinkled her nose but didn't ask for any further explanation. "Well, backup has arrived, so how about we move this trio inside for some tea?"

Grady exchanged a few words with the officers, then left his duffel bag in their care and followed Denise and me inside.

I took a seat with Grady at the counter.

Denise poured three jars of old-fashioned sweet tea, then distributed them. "Okay," she said. "Spill."

"Someone stabbed my porch with a two-hundred-year-old sword and an apparent bloody scrap of a ship's equally old flag," I said. "And there was sand. I think it was the same person who killed Dixie, and I think I'm supposed to believe it was the work of the Sandman."

Grady tapped his fingers against the sides of the jar in front of him. "First of all, we don't know any of that. There was a sword, some fabric, sand, and a note on what appeared to be parchment." He turned his eyes to Denise. "Whoever left the note seems to think

Everly has something he or she wants. So, as far as I'm concerned, Everly's in danger."

"I'm not in danger," I said, willfully asserting my denial.

Grady rubbed his forehead. "I'm heading back to Kitty Hawk this afternoon for another look through Ms. Wetherill's office. It was too much of a mess for me to make a decent catalogue of the contents last night."

"No doubt," I agreed. "It'd take a team six months to go through all her things."

Grady stilled, tea jar poised a few inches from his lips. "When were you in her office?"

"Last night."

His jaw locked, and he set the jar aside without taking a drink. "At what time last night and why?"

"When I got to Kitty Hawk with my aunts. Harriet offered to give me a tour of the home, and I accepted," I said. "But I was careful, and I barely touched anything."

Denise made a little snorting sound as she lifted her jar for a drink.

"Harriet who?" Grady asked. "I've been over the interviews. Mine and the other officers. No one spoke to anyone named Harriet."

"I didn't ask for an ID." Though the picture of Harriet Wetherill from nearly a century back came to mind.

He pressed a finger against the place at his temple where a blue vein throbbed. "How'd you get through the space without touching anything? I didn't see a path when I was there. Please tell me the lab isn't going to find your footprints on all those scattered papers. That'll just make it look like you were involved in this somehow."

I frowned, trying not to get hung up on how I must've looked with Dixie's blood on my hands. "What mess?" I asked instead. Dixie's office had looked like a set from an episode of *Hoarders* when I was there, but it hadn't been an actual mess. "There weren't any papers on the floor."

"Yes," he said. "There were. The place was completely overturned. There was sand and papers everywhere."

"Sand?" My mind immediately made the connection. Someone really did want people to believe the Sandman's ghost was back. "When did you get to her office?"

Grady rolled his eyes to the ceiling, thinking. "Must've been close to midnight. I had my hands full at Willow Park and the Wharf Museum. Add some commute time. It had to be eleven thirty or twelve. Why?"

I dug my phone from my pocket and swiped it to life. "I was there around ten thirty, and I took pictures."

Grady opened his palm in my direction, curling and straightening his fingers in the universal sign for "gimmee."

I placed the phone in his palm, and our fingers

touched briefly, sending a bolt of electricity through me.

He reviewed the photos while I collected my marbles. "So, someone came in and overturned the place in the hour or so window between your departure and my arrival."

A memory of feeling watched slithered down my spine. There had been a moment in Dixie's office when I thought someone might've been there with me, or nearby, observing me, but I hadn't seen anyone, and I wasn't sure it was worth mentioning.

Grady tapped my screen, forwarding my photos to himself. From there, he palmed our phones, side-by-side and one in each hand, using his long thumbs to swipe through the shots. He paused each time he found an image on my phone that was similar to an image on his. "Could've been this Harriet woman," he said. "She was there when it was orderly but gone when I arrived."

So was I, but there was no reason to point that out. "Everyone was probably gone when you arrived," I said instead. "It was midnight." I watched as he moved from image to image, comparing the vastly different scenes. "Wait." I lifted a finger to the screens. "Go back two on my phone."

He returned to a photo of Dixie's desk, arguably tidy compared to the similar image on his device.

I pointed to the empty spot in his photo. Papers spread over the floor where a basket stood in my shot. "The basket's gone."

He set his phone aside, then zoomed in on my photo, centering the basket on the screen. The image cleared, and Grady groaned. A basket of rolled maps.

Bugger.

CHAPTER

SEVEN

I stared at the basket in my photo, unspeaking as Grady shot off text messages, then went to talk to his team on the porch.

"You okay?" Denise asked, concern wrinkling her forehead.

"Kind of," I said. "Maybe." I didn't believe in coincidences, so I knew it was time to tell Grady about the eerie feeling I'd had inside Dixie's office.

He returned to the café as if on cue, looking amped up and uneasy.

"There's something else I should have told you," I said, drawing his eyes to my face. "I had a feeling someone was watching me last night after Harriet left. I didn't see anyone, and I didn't say anything sooner because I'd assumed I was wrong. I was shaken and on edge. It seemed logical to feel insecure in an unfamiliar place. But now that we know someone took the maps…"

Denise pulled in a sharp breath. "The killer could've been there with you."

"Maybe," I said. "Assuming the map in question was supposed to be in that basket and wasn't. But if it wasn't, I had nothing to do with that."

"Or," Denise said, "maybe the map was in that basket, and the Sandman thinks you took the basket, because he saw you in the room."

Grady dropped back onto the stool he'd recently vacated and rested his forearms against the counter, fists clenched. "So you are in danger." He groaned. "Again."

"Maybe, but,"—I gave a small smile—"this time it's a total misunderstanding."

He flipped his cowboy hat off and set it on the empty stool beside him. "If you hadn't been in her office snooping, there wouldn't be any room for this particular misunderstanding. So, you can't exactly claim innocence."

"I can because I am," I said defiantly. "How was I supposed to know this might happen? I don't have a crystal ball."

"You could have gone home instead of back to Kitty Hawk," he said, setting his jaw in challenge.

I guffawed. "I'd just been through an extremely shocking experience. A dead woman wrote my name on the ground." My voice cracked, and I took a beat to calm myself, horrified that I'd called Dixie Wetherill a dead woman, as if she wasn't also a person with a full life who'd been taken too soon. "I didn't want to go home and be alone. I wanted to be with other people who'd just experienced what I had. Once I got to the house in Kitty Hawk, Harriet took me to Dixie's office, and curiosity took over. I wanted to know something about the woman who'd left a message for me as she died. I still can't make sense of it. We'd never officially met, and she had some kind of grudge against my family. She died before I could ask her why."

Grady's features softened. "I was going to ask you if that was true. I read about it on the blog this morning." He laughed with a half-hearted smile. "I wore a costume to a murder scene last night, and I check a known gossip site for the latest scoop in my jurisdiction. It's like I fell through the looking glass when I moved down here."

Denise smiled at me. She'd recently said as much.

"And the crazy thing is," he continued, "whoever runs that blog deserves an award for the most spot-on journalism of the decade. I've never been steered wrong by the content. It's a little biased from time to time, but always on top of current issues."

"I read it too, and I was on my way to ask my great-aunts about the article when I found the sword. The thing is, there was only one person close enough to take that photo of me while I was still with Dixie, and that's Aubrey."

The door to my rear deck slid open, and a gust of wind rushed in with the sound of waves against the shore. "Hello," Aunt Clara called, closing the door behind her.

"Hi," Denise, Grady, and I answered.

Aunt Clara hurried in my direction. "Good. I

caught you," she said, dropping a kiss on my cheek. Normally, she and Aunt Fran stayed at their shop from open until close, aside from running errands or picking up lunch. It wasn't like her to come to my place until they'd locked up for the day, and I wondered if the birders had made it to Blessed Bee.

She smiled at Denise. "Hello, darling." Then moved Grady's hat and worked her way onto the barstool beside him. "Something peculiar happened, and I wanted to run it by Everly to see what she thought. This is better. Now I can collect three opinions." She leaned on the counter, peering around Grady. "There are policemen on your porch. They told me to use the back door, so I assume something's happened here as well. Are you all right?"

"Yeah." I gave Aunt Clara a brief rundown on what had happened this morning and the discrepancy between photos taken in Dixie's office.

Her eyes widened as I spoke. "Sand?" She clutched the strand of pearls resting on her collarbone. "Oh, dear." She looked at each of our waiting faces, a worried expression on her own. "So, it is the Sandman, then."

Grady cast me a curious look. "Everly and I were just trying to decide if he and James Hudson were the same man."

Denise perked, clearly understanding the question. "Wyatt says they are."

Aunt Clara nodded slowly, a genuine look of fear in her eyes. "I believe that too. And those missing maps are treasure maps of the island," she said. "Dixie collected them. So much has changed over the years, even the coastlines, that it's impossible to make heads or tails of the markings, but someone who'd known the island in its former state might not have any trouble at all." She tapped the tip of her pointer finger against her bottom lip. "The sand, the missing maps, the sword and flag, parchment and ink…" I wondered if she knew her stint as ghost tour leader had ended last night for the year. "Rumor has it that Dixie was knickers deep in research on something. What if she was close to finding the Sandman's treasure, and he found out? Maybe she'd found his map, and he wants it back." Her mouth fell open, and her eyes zeroed in on me. "And he thinks you have it."

"You know who else wanted something from Dixie?" I asked, unwilling to entertain her theory. "Burton. He wanted a book that I learned today was focused on local pirate lore, sunken ships, and other legends that could easily equate to 'buried treasure.'" I made air quotes around the last two words. "Maybe we should talk to him again," I suggested.

Aunt Clara looked relieved. "That's good. Better Burton than the Sandman, because, well, you know." She drew a thumb across the base of her neck, and I grimaced.

"So, we need to talk with Burton," I recapped to Grady. "Obviously, I'm not being stalked by a ghost sailor, and a ghost didn't kill Dixie, because ghosts aren't real, so Burton's our man."

Grady narrowed his eyes. "Mystery solved."

Clara jutted her chin forward. "Ghosts most certainly are real, and this is hardly the time to irritate them. It's a blue moon this week, you know."

"It might've been last night," Denise said. "Maybe blue-moon lunacy caused someone to kill Ms. Wetherill."

Grady lifted a palm to his au pair, then let it drop, in a silent, *Et tu, Brute?*

She smiled. "I'm just saying."

Aunt Clara shook her head. "The moon was big last night, but it wasn't full. It's also a supermoon this week, two things that never happen together. Now, ask me when the moon is officially full," she said, her expression going all mystical and woo-woo.

No one asked.

"All Hallows Eve," she whispered.

Grady balked. Denise gasped. I rolled my eyes.

Aunt Clara noticed my response and frowned. "Give me just a moment, and you'll all see I'm not crazy." She dug frantically in her giant Mary Poppins bag as she spoke.

Denise, Grady, and I exchanged looks. No one ever knew what would come out of that bag. She could've liberated a minor celebrity or a Volkswagen, and I wouldn't have been surprised.

"All the actors left their valuables with me for safe keeping during the ghost walk," Aunt Clara said. "I put them in a footlocker and left it inside my dressing room at the museum, then Fran and I hauled the locker back to Kitty Hawk after the event was busted up. Eventually, we brought it home with us, assuming it was empty, but when we were unpacking it at the shop this morning, Dixie's purse fell out. The contents spilled everywhere." She raised her eyes to Grady. "We didn't touch it, only the things that scattered on the floor." She hoisted a paper bag from her purse and held it between her thumb and forefinger. Blessed Bee's store logo was stamped in the center. She opened the top of the paper bag with a smug expression, then tilted the contents in our direction.

Broken shells and fragments of sea glass twinkled in a bed of dry sand. "See," she said. "Sand. Explain that."

Grady turned to me.

"Sand," I repeated.

He scratched his scruffy cheek. "It's like I left the U.S. Marshal service for a job on *Scooby Doo*."

I smiled despite myself. "Spoken like the dad of a first grader."

Denise delivered a jar of tea to Aunt Clara. "I'm glad you were able to find Grady and report this. Whatever the sand means, it can't be a coincidence."

"I was coming to see Everly," Aunt Clara said. "I wanted her opinion before I told anyone else."

Grady's lips twitched as he swiveled back to face Aunt Clara. "You wanted Everly's opinion? Not mine? After finding a murder victim's purse?"

She patted his hand. "You know how families are."

"I know how your family is," he said, reaching

across her to retrieve his cowboy hat. With a small grin, he popped it back onto his head.

Grady climbed off the stool and turned my way. "I'll be back to talk to you, so don't go anywhere."

He extended a hand to my great-aunt and flashed her a charming smile. "What do you say we go take a look at that purse. Where'd you leave it?"

She accepted his hand, confusion on her fair brow. "On the floor. We covered it with a bucket so no one would see it or ask about it. Fran's keeping watch until I return."

He set his hand on her back as they moved through the foyer, heading out the front door.

I stood and stared after them.

Denise grabbed a broom and rounded the counter to my side. "Go on," she said. "I've got this."

My heart leaped, and I stifled the urge to hug her. "Thank you," I gushed, already in motion for the door. "If you need to pick up Denver before I get back, just flip the dead bolt and the CLOSED sign behind you!"

CHAPTER

EIGHT

We made the quick trip through town in Grady's truck. He and Aunt Clara in the front seat, me in the extended cab. The town had undergone a massive visual change with the seasons, and the results were remarkable. The usual rainbow of summer decor had been replaced with a selection so classically fall it belonged on a Hallmark card. Piles of golden hay bales topped with generous numbers of pumpkins and gourds adorned the square. Baskets of richly colored mums in every shade, from scarlet to eggplant, lined storefronts and benches. Bundles of cornstalks loomed near doorways. Friendly scarecrows sat in Adirondack chairs.

I made a mental note to step up my decorating game at the tea shop.

I'd added a small, plastic cauldron filled with candy to the counter by my register and set out a stack of Harvest Ball flyers, but otherwise, I'd dropped the ball on decorating. If I wasn't careful, I'd soon see Sun,

Sand, and Tea on the *Town Charmer*'s Top Ten list of the town's Least Spirited Haunts, and I couldn't risk that. Some shops never bounced back. Charmers loved to spend money in places with enthusiasm, and they also loved to boycott the Debbie Downers. I couldn't risk rubbing anyone the wrong way. Not after a photo of me at another murder scene had shown up on the blog. This time with the victim's blood, literally, on my hands.

I wondered again who could've taken the photo, and how I could find out. But my money was on Aubrey.

Then today's article swept into mind. "Aunt Clara," I asked, recalling the pressing blog-related question I had for her, "did you read the *Town Charmer* today?"

"Of course."

"You mentioned that Dixie had something against our family, but the *Town Charmer* called it a feud between the two. Is that right?"

"Heavens, no," she answered. "Not a feud."

I relaxed a little at her words, but it wasn't like the site to miss the mark with its stories. "Where do you think the blogger got that idea?"

Aunt Clara dug into her purse, humming casually. She pulled out a mint and rubbed lint from the wrapper. "I suppose Dixie might've learned about the situation with Magnolia and taken offense. I can't say for sure," she said, separating the candy from the plastic, then dropping the former into her mouth and the latter back where it came from. "She and I weren't exactly friends, and I've already told you I explained to her about Salem."

"Magnolia Bane?" I asked.

Aunt Clara nodded, brows furrowed in thought. "It's possible Dixie realized Magnolia was a relative of ours and became upset about what happened between her and Lou."

Grady stopped at the light, confusion crowding his brow. "Lou, the seagull?"

Aunt Clara frowned back. "No. Well, maybe," she allowed after a moment of deliberation. "Before he was a seagull."

I rubbed my temple. "Lou was also the name of Magnolia's married lover."

"I know this story," Grady said, patting the steering wheel with one palm and frowning.

Aunt Clara's expression grew grim. "Magnolia was a Bane, not a Swan, but she's a cousin. And clearly covered by the curse, because her romance ended worse than any I've ever heard. Of course, it was a blue moon the night she died, so we have to account for that as well."

I tried to follow the logic. "Are you saying Lou was a Wetherill?"

"Maybe," she said. "I've heard it speculated, but never looked into it myself."

"Even so," I said, "isn't time supposed to heal all wounds? That affair happened more than a century ago."

"Nearly two!" Aunt Clara said.

I caught Grady's eye in the rearview mirror, and he smiled.

"Burton said he stayed behind during the ghost walk because he was a runner," I said, tapping Aunt Clara's shoulder. "He claimed to be helping actors and the Charm Enthusiasts as needed. Is that true?"

"Yes." She nodded. "He was perfect for that job. Quick on his feet and excellent at taking orders."

We cruised up Middletown Road at just under the speed limit. Grady seemed to scan the face of every pedestrian and fellow driver. Middletown Road was the belt that connected Ocean Drive to Bay View with historic downtown sandwiched in between. Ocean Drive ran along the boardwalk with scenic views of the Atlantic. Bayview boasted jaw-dropping views of the sound. He made a crawling turn onto Main Street, then took the first available space outside Blessed Bee, Aunt Clara and Aunt Fran's shop.

"So, Dixie might've been part of Lou's family tree?" Grady asked, settling the engine.

"I believe so," Aunt Clara said. "And it's my understanding that the lineage on that branch ended with him."

We all climbed out and headed for the sidewalk.

Blessed Bee was a yellow clapboard house situated between identical pink and blue houses. The pink shop sold ice cream; the blue shop sold books. My childhood friend Amelia owned the bookstore.

Aunt Clara had painted an array of fat honeybees flying cheerful loopy paths around the glass. She'd

recently added a few red, white, and blue SWAN FOR
MAYOR buttons among the bees and a flyer for the
Harvest Ball beside one about the upcoming election.
I ignored the tension in my gut as I stepped over the
welcome mat with a beehive on it. Despite my family's
centuries-old love of the little suckers, I'd been deathly
afraid of bees my entire life. I wasn't allergic, as far as
I knew, and I hoped to never find out, but I'd seen
firsthand what happened when bees stung someone
who was allergic.

The store's interior was adorable, with pale-yellow
walls and lots of white shelves and crown moldings.
A sky-blue ceiling stretched overhead, sprinkled with
fluffy, white cloud shapes. My great-aunts made and
sold everything from lip balm and face scrub to suckers and soap, all with pure, organic honey drawn
directly from the family hives.

Classical music drifted softly from hidden speakers throughout the store, and a smattering of shoppers gave me curious looks as I followed Aunt Clara
through the space.

She stopped at an overturned bucket with a sheet
of paper taped to it. Someone had scribbled CAUTION:
WET FLOOR in marker across the makeshift sign. A
circle of tiny orange cones had been erected all around
it, creating a miniscule barrier. I recognized the cones
from a presentation my aunts made regularly on
saving the American Honeybee. The cones were visual
aids for the section on navigating with caution near
their hives. For the bees' safety.

Aunt Fran appeared half a heartbeat later. Her expression moved from caution to surprise, then relief as she took us in. "Thank heavens." She leaned back, craning her neck for a look around the nearest set of shelves. "Do you know how many people have asked about this bucket? I hate lying. And I look like an imbecile for covering a fake spill with a bucket instead of just mopping it up."

"I told you so," Aunt Clara sang.

Aunt Fran pursed her lips. "I didn't hear you offer any better ideas."

"I had to go see Everly," she said, hefting the little bag of sand from her purse and giving it a shake.

Aunt Fran pressed a hand to her forehead, as if she were checking for a fever. "Who knew a bucket could draw so much attention in a beach town?"

Grady stooped for a closer look at the bucket. "May I?" he asked.

My aunts stepped back.

He removed the pail and photographed the beaded clutch before pulling a pair of gloves and evidence bag from his inside jacket pocket. He bagged the purse, then stood.

Aunt Fran looked to me; her gaze flickered briefly to her sister. "Did she tell you her theory about the sand?"

"Ghost sailor," Grady answered.

I smiled.

"You make jokes," Aunt Clara said, "but Everly found a captain's sword and note written on parchment today. Tell me that's a coincidence."

I felt my eyes widen, and I pressed a finger to my lips, warning her to keep her voice down. The store seemed to have stilled around us, and I was about eighty percent sure the shoppers were all eavesdropping.

Aunt Clara cringed, immediately contrite.

Aunt Fran tossed the tiny cones into the bucket, then motioned us to follow her. We stopped at a large, rectangular table near the front. The space was covered in supplies and freshly cut bars of soap. She tied an apron around her narrow waist, and Aunt Clara followed suit.

Grady and I took up position across from them.

Aunt Clara began cutting a roll of white lace trim into equal-length strips.

"I'm not normally quick to believe in ghosts," Aunt Fran said, "at least not as wholly and devotedly as Clara, but I can't deny there's something peculiar afoot here. And everyone knows these islands are a world unto themselves, most with a long, storied history of strange happenings." She heated a metal version of our family crest over a low flame, then pressed it against the finished soaps, leaving a shallow impression in each. "Considering the time of year, the supermoon, the blue moon, and All Hallows' Eve approaching," she said slowly, "it's not impossible to imagine that those who normally look on from the hereafter are able to reach across for a bit."

I felt my skin crawl and Grady stiffen beside me.

"I don't believe in that," he said. "No offense

intended," he clarified. "Just a different school of thought."

Aunt Fran shrugged. "To each his own, but something is definitely going on, and it clearly didn't end with Dixie's death."

"It probably didn't begin there either," I said. "Forget blue-moon lunacy. Someone made the active choice to end a life, and it didn't happen spur-of-the-moment during the ghost walk." The killer had approached Dixie already armed.

"Some folks think the Earth is flat," Aunt Clara said, wrapping a bar of soap with a piece of lace and tying a little bow. "Doesn't make it true. Other folks think the moon landing was a hoax. Doesn't make that untrue."

"I agree," Grady said, "but I'm going to follow my training and my instincts before I consider the culprit is someone who's been dead for two hundred years."

The soft snick of a camera taking a photo turned us around. The shoppers had gathered, blatantly listening as Aunt Fran practically declared the island as specter central.

A flutter of panic beat through me as I spun back to face my aunts.

Aunt Fran was running for mayor. She was supposed to be the level-headed Swan. Not the one sounding like a character on *Beetlejuice*.

She smiled confidently at the onlookers, dusted her palms together, then lifted her chin. "If only we could convince the spirits to vote!" She laughed heartily, nudging Aunt Clara to join.

"Ha ha ha!" I barked, trying to help, but sounding more like a hungry seal than intended.

Grady rubbed a hand across his lips, hiding a chuckle.

I fell silent, embarrassed and wishing for a sinkhole to swallow me or a giant cane to hook my waist and drag me out of sight.

Grady set a hand against my back and pressed his fingers against my hoodie.

I felt each tiny point of pressure, and they warmed me, settled me. I leaned against his side, silently thanking him for providing exactly what I'd needed at exactly the right time, without being asked. The truth was that I couldn't have asked because I didn't know what I'd needed. I'd wanted to hide. But this was much better.

Aunt Fran moved toward the little group of lookie-loos, pulling VOTE FOR SWAN buttons and honey candies from the pocket of her apron. She passed them into waiting hands. "Be sure to get out and vote. Preferably for me." She winked and shook hands and generally turned a potentially terrible PR moment around.

Grady lowered his head, speaking softly into my ear. "I can't tell if she just scared the snot out of them or endeared them to her."

"Maybe both," I said, feeling his breath against my cheek and enjoying it far too much.

"Well, I agree with her on one thing," he said. "This town is a world unto itself."

"True."

And at the moment, my silly heart was soaring somewhere beyond the moon.

CHAPTER

NINE

I left Aunt Clara at Blessed Bee and parted ways with Grady on the sidewalk. He needed to take Dixie's purse to the lab, and I needed to see my best friend.

Charming Reads was the town's only bookstore, but it was also so much more. Amelia had chosen the store's name as a throwback to the town she loved, and the place had lived up to its title.

I ducked inside, feeling instantly lighter.

The last twenty-four hours had been a whirlwind of awfulness, and once again, I'd landed smack in the center of the storm, but chatting with Amelia was sure to help.

"Hey, you!" she called, noticing me immediately. Her bright-blue eyes were wide with an appropriate mix of happiness and concern. "I didn't know if you'd stop by. I'd planned to come to your place if I didn't see you this afternoon."

I hugged her, crushing her petite frame momentarily to mine.

"Aww," she said gently, rubbing my back. "I'm sorry this is happening again."

"Thanks," I sniffled, pulling back to smile at her. "My life is bananas."

"Yes." She nodded, frowning. "Quite." She glanced around the quiet store, then tucked a swath of blond hair behind her ear and linked her arm with mine, pulling me to the front counter. "Did you see the blog?"

"I did."

Our new position gave us a panoramic view of the store. Faux spiderwebs had been spread across the tops of ornate cherry bookshelves and stretched over sconces on every wall. Cheery-faced jack-o-lanterns centered reading tables, and silk leaves in every shade from crimson to gold had been strategically placed around the room like confetti. Displays of favorite fall- and Halloween-themed books filled endcaps. Tiny wooden broomsticks and capes were piled in the children's nook, beside stuffed black cats and a bin of plastic "poison apples."

I smiled at the top-notch decorations and seasonal touches. She'd added hot apple cider to the complimentary refreshment bar, along with pumpkin spice coffee creamers and swizzle sticks shaped like magic wands. Everywhere I looked, the sights, sounds, and scents of the season were upon me, and it was one-hundred-percent Amelia.

No one would ever accuse her shop of lacking spirit or enthusiasm.

"You've outdone yourself again," I said proudly.

A former theatre nerd with a flair for the dramatic, Amelia had brought the place to life as usual, and she brought locals together regularly for book clubs, speakers, and events. I had no doubt the holiday lineup would be downright spooktacular.

"Thanks." She beamed back, taking a moment to admire her work. "Dad helped, and it took all night, but I think it was worth it."

"I agree." I surveyed the room again, an idea tickling the back of my brain. "Widow's brew," I said, turning my sudden smile on her. "For my specialty tea. I'll call it Widow's brew."

She grinned. "I like it. Sounds creepy."

I grabbed a pen from the mug on her counter and ripped a piece of receipt tape from the register, desperate to write down my idea before I forgot it. "Blood-orange tea with hibiscus is delicious, and they make a marvelous shade of red when blended together. I'll add rose hips and a light sweetener." I scribbled quickly, nearly illegibly, as my mind emptied faster than my fingers could take note. "I'll make it available exclusively through the night of the ball. After that, *poof*, it's gone." I wiggled the fingers of my free hand at the word *poof*.

"That's sheer marketing genius," Amelia said.

I performed a curtsy.

Her smile turned sad as she watched me reread the scribbles for legibility. "So," she said, catching my eye with her worried gaze.

"So," I repeated, running mentally through a list of optional natural sweeteners.

"The blog," she said, circling back. "Have you learned anything new about what happened last night?"

The question tossed me back to my bummer of a day.

I'd called Amelia when I got home last night and told her everything through tears as I choked down a pint of brownie batter ice cream. I sighed. "No, but someone filled Dixie's purse with sand and stabbed my porch with an old captain's sword."

Amelia cringed. "So that was true. I overheard someone saying as much, but thought I'd wait to hear it from you. It was one of the reasons I'd planned to come to you if you didn't stop by today." Her skin paled, and her eyes widened, as if something had just occurred to her. "Sand? And a captain's sword?" Amelia shivered. "That sounds like the Sandman. What are you going to do?" she whispered.

"I'm going to figure out who's trying to scare me and why," I said. "Hopefully, Dixie's killer will be unmasked in the process."

"Don't look into it," she said. "You know what happens when you do that. Bad things," she clarified. "Awful ones."

"I'm not sure what choice I have. Right now, it looks like I'm involved. I found her. Had her blood on me. Held the weapon used to knock her out." I sighed. "She scratched my name in the dirt as she died, and

I was in her office last night, a space that was found ransacked after I left."

Amelia looked ill. "I didn't know that last bit, but please leave it alone, okay? Grady will figure it out."

I didn't answer. I didn't want to argue.

"You know," she said. "Dixie was stabbed, and the sword was left on your porch. Do you think that's the murder weapon? If so, I hope you didn't touch it."

"I didn't touch it," I promised. "Grady sent it to the lab for testing."

"And you're sure it was a captain's sword?"

"Yep." I knew where this was going, and I reminded myself to be patient. Amelia was a believer.

She chewed her lip. "James Hudson was a captain. What if—"

"There aren't any ghosts," I said, shaking my head for emphasis. "None."

I waited, willing the statement to sink in. And be true.

"Then how do you explain the sand, and a two-hundred-year-old sword on your porch?"

"It was probably a replica," I said. "Grady's working on that. I'm going to talk to the other members of Dixie's unrecorded history group as soon as I can. Maybe someone will know something that points me in the right direction."

Amelia sighed. "And maybe you can figure out why she didn't like you?"

"It was my family she had a problem with," I said. "Not me. I never spoke to her."

"Yes, but you hate when someone doesn't like you."

She leaned a hip against the counter. "And now you'll never know why, so you can't try to change her mind. That must make you crazy."

"She didn't not like me," I said, bristling. "Fine, it bothers me a little," I admitted, "but more than that I hate that this happened, and that she was trying to leave me a message I'll never understand."

Amelia pulled her lips to one side, eyes scanning me slowly. "Just be careful, okay? I'm not sure how many more times I can survive hearing a killer had you in his or her clutches."

"Deal."

"Okay." She wiggled her shoulders and shook out her arms, as if to physically shake off the tension. "Now, about my book launch party. Any chance you'll have the Sandman bagged by then?"

I laughed. "Catch a ghost in a couple of days?" Considering the full and blue moons this week, I supposed it was as good a time as any for disproving the supernatural. "No problem."

Amelia smiled. "Great. Because I'm counting on your delicious teas and treats to make the night a hit."

I smiled back.

Amelia had embraced the challenge to write a novel almost two years ago, and quickly discovered her heart was actually in children's literature. She'd tossed the unruly adult manuscript aside and begun a fantastic early-reader book that I'd immediately adored. Her father, the island's most incredible painter, had handled the illustrations.

"I have something to show you," she said, perking.

I tucked the receipt into my pocket, then turned to watch her pull a box from under the counter. "They came."

I rose onto tiptoes for a peek inside. "What?"

She pried the cardboard arms back, revealing a stack of children's books with familiar, brightly colored art on the covers.

My heart jumped, the thrill for my best friend so strong, my eyes immediately stung with pride. "They're so beautiful. Can I hold one?"

She put a copy immediately in my hand, and I felt the familiar choke of emotion. *The Mystery of the Missing Mustang* was Amelia's creative retelling of one of our first adventures together. In her book, a boy named after Grady's son, Denver, searched for his missing plastic pony. He interviewed all the suspects, including another boy who'd admired the pony and wanted it for himself, a collector who didn't think the little boy cared for the pony properly, and a mean teacher who took kids' toys for fun. Then, the boy realized the culprit was the most obvious and overlooked suspect of all. The family dog. Denver followed the dirty paw print clues to uncover Fido's stash of items buried in the backyard. The combination of Amelia's words with her dad's illustrations was sheer perfection.

"This is hands down the most amazing thing I've ever seen," I said. "Can I buy this one?"

Amelia closed the book in my hands, then opened

the front cover again, turning to the dedication. She pressed a petal pink fingernail to my name. "This one is all yours."

I followed her gaze to the page.

> To: Everly, for our crazy island adventures, past, present, and future.

My eyes rose to meet hers. "You wrote a book," I said, reveling in the surrealism of the moment. "Holy wow! You did it, and it's here. And you dedicated it to us?"

She nodded, eyes glistening.

"I love it." I wrapped her in another hug. "You're the absolute best. You know that?"

She released me with a sniffle. "Don't make me cry. I'm at work." She laughed, dragging a fingertip beneath her eye. "My publicist is coming down from New York for the launch, and I'm a nervous mess. She's already talking to me about writing more in the series, but you'd be shocked to know how hard it is to write a mystery with less than two-hundred words." She laughed, and her entire body seemed to illuminate with the sound.

"I can't believe my best friend is a famous author now, who says things like, 'My publicist is coming down from New York for the launch.' I love it."

My obnoxious bracelet flashed and buzzed against my wrist, and I began to march in place. **BE MORE ACTIVE** blinked on the screen.

"I have to go," I said. "I have an epic menu of delicious, kid-friendly snacks to plan for my best friend's awesome book-launch-slash-costume-party this week."

Amelia clasped her hands in glee. "Thank you!" she called after me as I marched with exaggerated high knees through the door, making certain the bossy bracelet counted every step.

CHAPTER

TEN

Denise was on her way out when I returned to Sun, Sand, and Tea. Time to pick up Denver from school. I spent the rest of my workday serving iced tea and finger foods while dodging curious looks and pointed questions about British ghosts. Particularly one who might have a beef with me. I did my best to smile and pretend everything was completely fine while grumbling internally at the gossip blog for adding a new article on the topic. I could hardly blame the blogger. It was nearly Halloween after all, and news of a murderous, British sailor ghost, from one of the town's favorite legends no less, was bound to garner unprecedented page views.

In the moments between customers, I created a surplus of my newly imagined Widow's Brew, knowing it would be an in-demand item the moment folks took one look at the adorable black cat and witch's broom flyers I'd whipped up on my computer. I printed the ads, announcing the limited-time special blend, and slipped one into a clear acrylic stand near the register. I added the digital version to the tea shop's website, then printed more copies to peddle around town.

I put off making any plans for Amelia's book-launch party until seven sharp, then flipped the window sign to CLOSED and began to fret. Ideas for fun, child-friendly finger foods, desserts, and décor exploded in my mind like popcorn on a hot stove, but none of it seemed worthy of the event. My best friend had published a book. Was there a party good enough to celebrate that?

Denver's real-life love for horses paired perfectly with the book's mystery, so I wanted to go that route, but how? I imagined Denver and Grady in their matching cowboy hats, hand in hand walking the beach, and my heart melted a little. My favorite part of their walks was that they always stopped at my café for a sweet treat afterward.

I wiped down the counters, tables, and chairs. Swept the floor and scrubbed fingerprints off the windows and patio doors. Then, I loaded up the dishwasher and took my party-planning brain upstairs for a hot shower and a little downtime.

An hour later, my head was filled with dancing pastries and cowboy-themed décor. Cutout cookies shaped like horses, cowboy hats and boots. Haystack chocolates stuffed with shredded coconut. Red-and-white-checkered tablecloths lined in faux lasso rope. Tiny hay bale centerpieces with a copy of Amelia's book on each. Baked beans and little wienies. Mini cornbread muffins. Grilled cheese sandwiches cut into strips or quarter-triangles. A dessert I could top with brown sugar and horseshoe prints. And lots of magnifying glasses, cardboard standup question marks, and mystery-related additions.

I dressed in my softest hoodie and yoga pants, then scribbled the possible party details into one of my notebooks. Within seconds, haunting images from the previous night poked at my mind. I pushed the thoughts away, realizing belatedly that my subconscious had been working overtime to protect me from my recent trauma. Never one to willingly ruin a night of peaceful thoughts, I went to work baking rum cakes. I could fill internet orders while keeping my hands and brain busy with more calming things. At least until the sun rose and the massive, glowing moon stopped staring through my windows.

The cake batter came together easily. I'd made so many in the past month, I could practically do it in my sleep. I slid the pans into the oven and set the timer for an hour.

I marched across the room to pull the curtains across my patio doors and shut out the moonlight. The same moon who'd watched Dixie die and me stumble dumbly upon her, too late to do anything to help.

Lou cocked his head as our eyes met through the glass, a moment before the curtain shut him out as well.

"Sorry," I whispered.

I hooked my hands against my hips and tapped my fingers as I surveyed the space around me. The second floor of my home had a large, central living space with an open-concept kitchen across from a rear deck with broad windows and sliding glass doors. The master bedroom and en suite bath were on a third wall, with the remaining bedrooms and two additional bathrooms across from it, scattered down a narrow hallway. It was easy to imagine the property as a private school and boarding house in the last century. There was more than enough room, too much for me alone, but I loved it. Once I got the third floor cleaned out, I'd have more space than I knew what to do with.

For now, I scanned the space before me. My hand-me-down furnishings were positioned on an area-rug island that seemed to float in the center of an otherwise empty floor. The place was tidy enough. Nothing needed cleaning, but I was desperate for another distraction. Pronto.

My gaze caught on the row of built-in bookshelves across from my couch, and I sighed. It was a project I'd been avoiding, but one that needed to be done. The craftsmanship was exquisite. The wood was a mess, buried under endless layers of paint, hopefully none made with lead. I wanted to restore the piece to its original finish, whatever that might be.

I'd decorated with a neutral and airy pallet of blues and grays, creams and whites, so any woodwork was guaranteed to match perfectly. My new curtains were a delicate toile print. The rug colorful and braided by an ancestor's hands.

"Here we go," I told myself, heading for the bookcase.

I relieved the unit of my toppling stacks of cowboy romance novels, then wiped the entire case down, removing dirt and dust. Next, I needed to remove the paint. Sand the unit carefully, repair where necessary, then stain and seal. Intricate and scrolling details along the ceiling and floor would require cotton swabs and toothpicks to get into the grooves. Thankfully, I had plenty of both.

I checked the clock on my stove and decided I had enough time to gather supplies and get started, if I hurried. So, I did. I hauled everything I needed from a nearby supply closet, then covered a large area of carpet in plastic to protect it from solvents and reduce cleanup time. My gel paint stripper was safe for indoor use and went on easily with a brush. I coated every visible inch of the surface, careful not to miss any of the narrow crevices before removing my protective gloves and safety goggles.

Images of the books and overburdened shelves in Dixie's office rushed back to mind. And I thought again of Harriet and her hundred-plus-year-old doppelganger from the New Years' Eve photo on the wall. Then, Aunt Clara's words returned with a snap. She'd suggested the man who'd built my home was one of Dixie's ancestors, and I had a way to find out if that was true.

I washed up at the sink, then collapsed onto my couch and brought up the photos of Dixie's office on my phone. I swiped to an image of the enormous family-tree tapestry and stretched the image with my fingertips, zooming in on the branches closer to the ceiling than the floor. I held my breath as I searched for Lou's name, but the words were too blurry. I needed another look at the real thing to solve this mystery.

I switched to the dial pad and called Aunt Clara, then stood to pace while it rang. According to the clock on my stove, the cakes would be done in a few minutes, then I could go back to the kitchen and work out my anxiety there.

The paint had already begun to bubble on the bookshelves as I waited for Aunt Clara to answer. I put my gloves back on and crouched to lift the plastic putty knife from the protective drop cloth.

"Hello, darling," Aunt Clara cooed. "Everything okay?"

"Just checking in," I said brightly, already scraping the top layers of loose paint from the fixture's base. My mood instantly improved as I worked, wickedly thrilled with the long strips of wood becoming visible beneath the buckling paint. Exactly the sort of tedious and deeply satisfying work I loved, like picking off the remnants of a failing manicure. Entertainment for hours. "How are things?" I asked Aunt Clara, putting some extra elbow grease into my efforts.

"Good," she said. "Fran and I are tidying up

from card club. We hosted winner-takes-all Canasta tonight."

"Sounds like fun," I said, working the tip of my tongue between my teeth as the putty knife caught on a stubborn strip of paint. The instructions suggested waiting twenty-four hours instead of twenty-four minutes, but I had nervous energy to burn, and making the appropriate amount of small talk before asking Aunt Clara for a favor was about to kill me.

I leaned against the wall for leverage and dug in a little deeper.

"We served hot tea and scones. Both were a hit," Aunt Clara continued. "I got carried away selecting the honeys and jams."

My putty knife slid unexpectedly on a slick section of wood, and my weight fell against the wall.

Something clicked.

I froze, stunned and praying I hadn't caused any irreparable damage to the woodwork or wall. I settled back on my haunches, rubbing my hip where it'd collided with my baseboard and surveying the situation beneath my putty knife. Nothing appeared broken or cracked.

"Which did you choose?" I asked gamely, always interested in the popularity of our family's recipes. I wasn't great at cards, but refreshments were *my jam*.

"Rhubarb and an elderberry preserve blend," she said. "The ladies loved them both and made short work of our infused honeys too. Fran set out cinnamon and vanilla."

"My favorites," I said, returning the putty knife to the drop cloth. I ran my gloved fingertips over the progress I'd made so far, wondering if the sound I'd heard was actually one of my joints cracking.

"What are you up to tonight?" Aunt Clara asked. "I've been going on about Canasta and condiments. I haven't asked how you are."

"I'm okay," I said, frowning as my now misaligned bookcase came into view. I thought a nasty word and groaned. I'd broken my gorgeous, historic, hand-crafted bookshelves. All while trying to improve them. I set my phone on the carpet and pressed the speaker button, then gripped the built-in unit and attempted to drag it forward a quarter inch. Back into alignment with the baseboard.

No dice.

"Everly?" Aunt Clara asked, prompting a response to a question I hadn't heard.

"Sorry," I said. "I think I broke my house." I cursed the extra twenty-five pounds I'd been battling since returning to Charm. Apparently, these days putting my weight into something meant permanently denting it.

"What?" Aunt Clara asked. "How?"

"I'm not sure," I said, deflating.

"I'll take a look at it the next time I'm there," she said. "I'm sure you haven't broken your house."

"I hope not." I dusted my palms together and refocused on my reason for calling. "Any chance you're going back to the Society headquarters in Kitty Hawk soon? I'd like another look at the family-tree tapestry inside Dixie's office. I took some photos when I was there, but the writing is blurry, and I can't make out the names. You've got me wondering if Lou was Dixie's ancestor. Could the world really be that small?"

Aunt Clara laughed. "Darling, yes! We live on an island. Our world is very small. When would you like to go?"

I grinned. "Soon?"

"I'm meeting the Society members for a late breakfast tomorrow morning. We're planning a small memorial for Dixie and need to hammer out the details. You're welcome to come along."

"I'd love to."

"Wonderful. I wouldn't mind getting a look at that tapestry too," Aunt Clara said. "Maybe we should have one made for the Swan's family."

"Maybe," I said, wondering how large a Swan family tree would need to be. The redwoods in California came to mind.

I thanked Aunt Clara, then said goodbye.

I gave my bookcase another enthusiastic pull, but it didn't budge.

Behind me, the oven dinged. I looked over my shoulder, thankful my rum cakes were done. I preferred to pass my time in the kitchen, where I didn't normally break things. It was time to make the secret drizzle, then pour it over the cakes when they cooled. It'd become part of my routine to poke holes in the cakes then use a basting brush to assure every rum cake leaving my care was fully saturated in sweet, rummy goodness.

After that, it would be straight to bed for me.

Maggie, the fluffy white Houdini cat appeared as I liberated the cakes. She lifted her chin and worked her nose through the air. Maggie was an ageless feline who, like Lou, had seemed to come with the house. I'd happily claimed her, or rather, she'd claimed me, once we'd officially met. Now, I kept her food and water bowls full, and she did what she wanted, coming and going as she pleased. I had no idea how she got in or out without being noticed, and I tried not to think about that.

"Hey, there," I said, smiling. "I missed you."

Maggie slunk forward, green eyes luminous, and bumped her head against my calf.

I set the cakes on a cooling rack and stripped off my oven mitts so I could pet her. "Have you had a nice day?" I asked. "Want to try my tuna tarts?"

I moved to the cupboard where I kept her treats. "I baked these just for you," I told her. "I used a new recipe, and if you stick around, there's peanut butter and bacon muffins for dessert."

She pranced delightedly to the mat with her bowls, then waited to be served. "You would tell me if you were the reincarnated ancestral spirit of my distant cousin, wouldn't you?"

"Merowl," she said, beginning to purr.

"My aunts think Lou is the reincarnated spirit of your adulterous lover," I explained, delivering a scoop of homemade tuna tarts, "so don't feel bad."

"Merowl," she repeated, more loudly this time, and glanced briefly at my closed patio curtains before shoving her face into the bowl.

Outside my deck doors, the motion light flashed on, and I jumped.

The shadow of a pterodactyl-sized bird appeared on my curtains.

I looked at Maggie. "Are you talking to Lou? Or was that a coincidence?"

She didn't answer. Which was probably best.

I went to see if it was really Lou, still sitting there an hour after I'd closed the curtain, or just a random bird. I took a handful of tuna tarts with me either way. I was an equal opportunity animal feeder.

I pulled the curtain back and smiled, then opened the patio door as well.

"Hey, Lou." I stepped onto the deck, leaving the glass door ajar behind me. "I can't say I'm surprised to see you, but I'm sure that says more about me than you."

I lined a row of tuna tarts along the handrail before me like ants on a log.

The moon was unusually bright and big in the sky, illuminating everything beneath it and giving an eerie sheen to the blackened sea below.

Lou sidestepped his way to the treats and gobbled them up. He kept one beady eye on me as he went.

"You're welcome," I said, wishing for the thousandth time I could stroke and pet him the way I sometimes could Maggie.

The moon's ominous shine cast a strange aura over

Lou's white feathers and everything else in sight. I blinked in an attempt to clear my vision. When that didn't work, I turned tail to run.

Not at all because I was afraid of catching the blue-moon lunacy.

"I'll see you tomorrow," I told Lou, darting back inside.

I shut and locked the deck door, then pulled the curtain once more. I nearly collapsed against them in relief when I saw Maggie and straightened.

Maggie sat on the plastic drop cloth's edge, staring at the place where I'd accidentally cracked my baseboard.

"No, no," I said, shooing her away and gathering my supplies. "This is all very bad for you. Don't lick anything, and try not to inhale too deeply. I'll have it cleaned up in a minute."

When I returned from putting away my supplies, Maggie was back on the drop cloth, staring blankly at the misaligned baseboard and built-in bookcase.

"Excuse me," I said, lifting the plastic from the floor and using painter's tape to secure it over the bookcase. "There," I said, affixing the final strip of hot-pink tape. "Now you'll be safe. Carry on."

Maggie took her seat again. "Merowl," she called, watching Lou's silhouette on the curtains.

"Caw!"

I looked back and forth between them, and for a minute, I wondered if anything really was possible in Charm.

CHAPTER

❧

ELEVEN

Aunt Clara picked me up at nine the next morning in the family car, which like everything else she owned was a relic. The 1959 Chevy Bel Air was roughly the size of a cruise ship, with the modern appeal of a tugboat. The vehicle had been in the family since it was purchased new by Aunt Clara and Aunt Fran's mother. It was in mint condition, but not original. Aunt Clara had commissioned seat belts be installed when I was young, much to the dismay of the auto shop that mournfully complied. The mechanic warned that a change of such magnitude would depreciate the car's value, but Aunt Clara told him the car's ability to maintain my safety was where it got its value. And she refused to budge.

I smiled as I jogged down the porch steps to where she waited behind the wheel. The car was immaculate, with low miles, not surprising, since we lived on an island and the car was rarely driven. Aunt Clara took it out a few times a year just to make sure it still ran, but nothing more. Black with an abundance of chrome and fins that stretched out in back, the Bel Air was a sight to behold, especially for collectors and folks who remembered when people, other than my aunt, actually drove one. I liked knowing that if my aunts were ever in a car accident, they'd be safe inside their enormous tank.

I climbed into the passenger seat and buckled up, still smiling. I waved goodbye to Denise, who was sweeping the front porch as we drove away. "Thanks for doing this," I told Aunt Clara.

She patted my hand, then shifted into drive. "How could I resist a road trip with my favorite great-niece?"

There was something off in her tone, and I eye-balled her grip on the wheel. "Everything okay?"

She shot me a sad smile. "I just hate taking this big girl out, that's all. She's terrible for the environment." She shook her head. "A real shame."

I relaxed against the tan leather seat, thankful that was all that was wrong. "Well, if it's any consolation, you don't take her out often."

"Not normally," she agreed, pulling in a long, steadying breath. "But this is my second trip to Kitty Hawk in three days, and I'm thinking of trading her in."

"What? Why?" Sure, the beast was terrible on gas, but it wasn't as if my aunts ever left the island. How much damage could one car do in an hour of use three or four times a year?

"For starters, I'm not getting any younger," she

said. "I'm able to walk or ride my bicycle almost anywhere I want to go, but that won't always be the case." Her cheeks pinked, and I saw how much it'd cost her to confide the fact. "I know this car has been a part of your life from the start, and you've said goodbye to too many things already, so if you'd rather I hold onto it, I will."

"No," I said, relaxing against my seat. "I completely understand. Don't keep it on my account. How will you sell something like this?" It wasn't as if the local dealership was in a position to flip it, and there weren't any collectors on the island that I knew of.

"Amelia's dad has been helping me negotiate with a man on the mainland," she said, turning onto the highway connecting the island towns. "He's offered a fair price, and I've been looking at a Prius."

A bark of laughter ripped through me. "You could park a Prius in the Bel Air's backseat."

"Exactly," Aunt Clara said. "They're good on gas, economical, and environmentally friendly. A Prius will be easier to park, and I won't feel as if I'm personally ruining the ozone every time I drive it."

"True." I agreed. Then the other side of the story rose between us, tense and uncomfortable. The Bel Air had been her mother's car. "What does Aunt Fran think?"

She rolled her eyes. "The only person more sentimental than me is Fran. She's not thrilled but understands."

"For what it's worth," I said, "I'm glad you're getting

older. All the lucky ones do." Too many women I'd loved had never gotten the chance.

"Oh." She glanced my way, then set a soft palm on my cheek, steering one-handed for a beat. "I miss them too, you know. All of them. Every last soul who's gone before me. You and I are the same that way. And you're right. Aging is a privilege." A tear slipped from beneath her sunglasses, and she pulled her hand away from my cheek to wipe her own.

We passed the WELCOME TO KITTY HAWK sign a few minutes later, then turned into the neighborhood where the Society kept its offices. She slowed as a familiar black pickup came into view. "Dear," she said, "I believe that's Detective Hays's truck."

"It is," I said, feeling butterflies of anticipation take flight beside the black moths of dread in my gut.

"What should we do?" she asked, looking nervous as she parked, then re-parked, and finally fit the Bel Air into a space in the lot across the street from our destination.

"Nothing," I said. "You're here because you have a meeting this morning, and I came along because I wanted to." Grady wasn't the boss of me.

I climbed out on noodley chicken legs and put my chin up. Grady would take issue with my presence, but he'd have to get over it. Just like I had to get over the fact that I hadn't spent more time on my hair or makeup this morning. I pulled a tube of my aunts' homemade lip balm from my hoodie pocket and drove it over my lips a few times, enjoying the warm, minty tingle. Then, I finger-combed my ponytail until the brave digits got stuck knuckle deep in unruly curls.

"Look," Aunt Clara whispered, winding her arm around mine. A pair of Kitty Hawk police cruisers lined the street at the end of the block.

"Uh oh. What do you think that's about?" I asked.

"Maybe they're here to make an arrest," she suggested. "Maybe Grady figured out who hurt Dixie, and he's hauling the killer in."

I cast a wary look in her direction. It'd only been a few days since the murder, and Grady would've brought his own men to collar the culprit, not called in the Kitty Hawk PD.

I opened the beautifully crafted door to the historic home and held it for Aunt Clara to pass. We moved in tandem through the cavernous foyer and into the den, where a group of people stilled and stared at us.

Grady and two Kitty Hawk officers stood shoulder to shoulder before a collection of seated society members. Everyone in a chair looked distinctly uncomfortable.

The beefier officer broke from the pack and moved in our direction, his sagging utility belt forming a dilapidated smile beneath his middle. He had thick, gray hair and a nose that appeared accustomed to punches. His smarmy expression hinted at the reason. "Ladies," he said, addressing Aunt Clara and me with raised brows. "Can I help you?"

Aunt Clara flipped her attention from him to

Grady. "I'm here for a planning session," she said, "to honor Dixie with a memorial."

"You're a member of this group?" he asked, tipping his head to indicate the seated members. He flicked his gaze my way, including me in the question.

"Yes," Aunt Clara answered as I said, "No."

Grady sauntered over, looking intensely unhappy, as predicted. "This is Clara Swan, a Society member, and her great-niece, Everly Swan, who has no reason at all to be here."

I stifled the childish urge to stick out my tongue.

"The woman who discovered Ms. Wetherill," the officer said, clearly recognizing my name. He rocked back on his heels and gave a low whistle. "Well, I'm glad you've made a surprise appearance, Miss Swan," he said, narrowing his eyes. "Your prints were on the candelabra found next to Ms. Wetherill in Charm, and at a crime scene here as well."

Images of Dixie's overturned office flashed into mind, and I bit my tongue as the phrase, *anything you say can and will be used against you*, ricocheted in my mind.

"According to your written statement, you'd never met Dixie Wetherill, yet you were the one to find her body, handle the weapon used to render her unconscious before she was fatally stabbed, and your prints put you in her private office. Odd, no?"

I turned my chin slowly left, then right.

The room was silent, raptly awaiting my response. Which they weren't getting without my lawyer present.

And since I didn't have a lawyer, or money to hire one, I kept my mouth shut.

The officer looked to Grady when I didn't respond.

"A word?" Grady said, his voice low and thick with warning.

I nodded quickly and moved to his opposite side, putting him between myself and the officer.

Grady excused us, then swept an arm in the direction of the kitchen. I hurried ahead, his heavy footfalls echoing behind me. I stopped at the island, but Grady took my hand and towed me around the corner into a small room, then closed the door.

"Holy hotcakes!" I squeaked. "Is this a pantry?" The answer was obvious. Floor to ceiling shelves on three walls nearly bowed under the weight of their bulk food and dessert contents. A gorgeous stained-glass window illuminated the space in rainbows of tinted light. "I have dreams that start like this."

"What are you doing here?" Grady asked, hands braced on narrow hips.

"You dragged me," I said, forcing my attention away from the overstuffed shelves. "What are you doing here?"

"I'm investigating a murder and cooperating with local authorities on a related break-in." He leveled me with a pointed stare. "Why are you in this house with Clara?" he asked, impatience thick in his tone.

"I wanted another look at the family tree tapestry in Dixie's office," I admitted. "Aunt Clara got me wondering if Dixie was really related to the man who commissioned my house."

Grady narrowed his eyes. "And?"

"And nothing." I crossed my arms. "Did you ever find Aubrey's white gloves?" I asked, the question popping into mind. "The ones she wore when she handed me the candelabra?"

"Yes. And I didn't have to ask. She'd already tucked them into a plastic bag and delivered them to arriving officers."

I pulled my lips to the side. "I guess she had to. She would've known I'd tattle."

Grady rubbed his stubbly cheek. "The lab rushed the results on your recent delivery for me. Curious?"

"About my porch threat?" I asked, trying not to let the intensity of his gaze or general nearness buckle my knees. "Of course."

"The dried blood on the swatch of material was real. The wet substance on your porch was not."

"Fake blood?"

"Stage blood."

"Interesting." Given the abundance of Halloween costumes and makeup at every store in town, I doubted it was much of a clue. I mentally moved on. "Whose blood was on the cloth?"

Grady avoided my gaze, then pushed his hands into his pockets. "I'm not sure. The lab technician found evidence of antibodies that don't exist anymore."

I hiked a brow. "Anymore?"

His gaze caught mine again, and he shifted his stance. "It's likely the cloth is from the early nine-teenth century. Possibly the blood as well."

The pantry door creaked open, and I nearly swallowed my tongue.

Aunt Clara stepped inside. "Oh!" She pressed a hand to her chest, looking as startled as I felt, both by her sudden appearance and the news of two-hundred-year-old blood on my porch. Plus, some fake stuff from a costume store.

"You're in the pantry," Aunt Clara said, pointing to bulk boxes of pancake mix.

"It's kind of marvelous," I said.

"It is," she agreed. "It's where I come to hide when things get rowdy at the meetings." She pushed a case of minute-rice aside and retrieved an open box of salted caramels. Her nimble fingers made short work of the wrapper, then pushed a candy into her mouth. "Mm." She sighed. "Takes the edge off."

"The meetings get rowdy often?" Grady asked.

I helped myself to a caramel and felt my insides cheer. I needed this recipe.

Aunt Clara winked at me. "See?"

"Clara?" Grady nudged.

She smiled sweetly, unwrapping a second caramel. "Dixie liked to argue. Didn't matter what about. Most recently, it was the ghost walk content. She hated when anyone wanted to retell unrecorded stories with a paranormal edge, as if nothing unexplained by modern science could be real. We'd been discussing a lot of unexplained things lately, in preparation for the ghost walk, and she hated it."

I frowned. "Yet, she played Mourning Mable."

Aunt Clara shrugged. "Nothing paranormal about a jealous sailor. It's one of the most popular stories. I told her the fun of the ghost walk is the speculation and wonder. No one was forcing her or this group to help. She'd volunteered them. It was nice having the extra hands, but we've put on that show for ages without them. She relented, of course. I always pick the walk's content. Then she took the role of Mable. Probably because everybody else wanted it, and she liked a good show of power."

That sounded in line with everything else I'd learned about her so far. "Well, someone's working overtime to make it seem as if Mourning Mable's killer is back from the dead and coming for me."

I turned to Grady, and he nodded, clearly sharing my thoughts on the matter.

"I'll keep you posted," he said.

"Fair enough. I don't suppose you'll let me back in Dixie's office for another look at that tapestry before I go?"

"We're thinking of making one," Aunt Clara said, neatly folding the empty wrappers from her caramels.

Grady huffed a quiet laugh. "Is there enough material on the island to make your family tree?"

She smiled. "If we stitch it right. Maybe."

"So, that's a yes?" I asked.

His smile faded. "No."

"I just need a picture," I said. "I won't touch anything."

"That's what you said before." His jaw clenched.

"You told me you didn't touch anything, and now I have local PD telling me prints pulled from a book on her desk match prints on the candelabra at the murder scene. Your prints."

I made an exaggerated frown. "I forgot about the book." *And the receipt*, I realized. I pictured the narrow strip of paper, the inky blueprint, but I couldn't recall the store name. Maybe it didn't matter.

"Anything else you've forgotten to tell me?" Grady asked, seeming to read my mind.

"How would I know that?"

We locked eyes like two kids in a staring war.

I was the first to cave. "There was a receipt with the book on the desk, but I can't remember where it was from." I shrugged. "Will you at least take photos of the tapestry for me? I'm looking for Lou's name. Somewhere mid-1800s or just before."

Grady scratched his head, then hooked his palm around the back of his neck. "Maybe, but the room's a crime scene, and not mine. This is Kitty Hawk's jurisdiction. They're allowing me here as a courtesy until they find evidence to prove our suspicions that the murder and break-in are related."

"Okay." I nodded. "I'll be patient and take what I can get."

"Good."

"Do you know if anything was stolen besides the basket of maps?" I asked.

"Not yet. There's too much to go through, and the only person who could say for sure is dead."

"Clara?" A woman called from somewhere outside the pantry.

Aunt Clara jumped into action, pocketing a few caramels, along with the neatly folded empty wrappers, then she hid the box again, back behind the rice. She took the only glass from a shelf beside the door and pressed it to the barrier, listening. In the next instant, she'd returned the glass and slipped out.

"That's quite a routine," Grady mused.

"She hates confrontation," I said. "And those are really good caramels."

Grady laughed, and it reached his eyes. Grady's smile was the stuff of billboards and toothpaste commercials.

"So, how are you?" I asked. "How's Denver?"

"Struggling," he said.

I wasn't sure if he meant him or his son, but I suspected it was true for both. "If you ever need to talk," I said, letting the invitation hang.

"I know." His gaze became intent and purposeful as he looked into my eyes.

The space around us seemed to shrink.

I wondered briefly if he could sense how much he and his son meant to me, or how important their happiness was to my own.

"We should probably get out here," he said, opening the door for me with one long arm.

"Right." I shook myself back to the reality of being on the Kitty Hawk PD's possible criminal list, then proceeded with caution.

We followed the low rumble of arguing voices around the corner to the kitchen, where Burton and his wife glared at each other.

They stilled at the sight of us, stepping apart immediately.

"Everything okay?" Grady asked.

Aubrey smiled. "Of course."

Burton gave her one last dirty look before glancing our way. "I'm just waiting for my turn with the other interrogators."

Aubrey scoffed. "They aren't interrogators, and neither am I, if that's what you were implying."

"Burton?" An officer waved from the doorway, and Burton shuffled off, looking glad for the escape. I wasn't sure I blamed him.

"You're all right?" Grady asked, advancing on Aubrey. "Sounded as if the two of you were fighting."

She dropped her crossed arms to her sides and straightened her spine. "I knew this would happen, and I told him we should've stayed home today, but he insisted we come. We weren't here ten minutes before the cops showed up. Now there won't be any memorial planning accomplished, and our entire day will be wasted, when I had things to do at home." She shook her head, clearly infuriated. "Dixie Wetherill's dead, and she's still causing me trouble."

I hoped Grady had Aubrey and Burton on his list of suspects, because they both seemed extremely shady to me. I just wasn't sure why. All couples argued, but these two pricked at my instincts.

Her gaze jerked to meet mine. "I heard them talking about you."

I froze. "Me? Why?" *And who?* The police? The Society members? Someone else?

A smug expression curved her lips and narrowed her eyes. "Apparently Dixie had some old photographs of your house. From the same decade it was commissioned. The police can't understand why, and they think you might've been in her office to collect them, though they can't make sense of that either. There's nothing to make sense of. That's the problem. She was obsessed with your family. I don't know why Clara put up with her snide remarks and attitude as long as she did. I certainly wouldn't have." She cocked her head, examining me. "I don't think you would've either."

"Aunt Clara loves history," I said, mystified by everything Aubrey had just said. "What do you mean Dixie had pictures of my house? I didn't even know her." And did she have photographs of *my house*, or my family homestead, where Aunt Clara and Aunt Fran lived? I'd owned my place fewer than two years, but the homestead had been housing Swans for nearly two hundred.

"Who knows," Aubrey said. "But trust me, Dixie had her hands on something of everyone's."

Burton reappeared in the doorway, sweat peppering his brow. "Your turn," he told her, mopping the droplets with a handkerchief. "I said I'd send you in."

Aubrey squared her shoulders and marched past her husband without another look at Grady or me.

And I was left to stare after her. Wondering why Dixie had photos of my house, and what Aubrey had meant about her having her hands on something of everyone's.

My gut said the answer wasn't good, and someone had had enough of Dixie's meddling ways.

CHAPTER

TWELVE

An hour later, Aunt Clara and I headed out. Aubrey had been right. No memorial planning had occurred. Instead, the police had questioned everyone about the night of Dixie's murder, their relationship with the deceased, and their general knowledge of her life. They'd asked me infinitely more questions than I had answers to, then eventually dismissed me at Grady's insistence. Afterward, the officers had lingered, "observing," until the group disbanded, too rattled to make any decent plans.

I waited until we were locked safely inside the Bel Air before turning to Aunt Clara. "Do we have time for another stop before heading home?"

"Why not?" she asked. "I'd like to be able to say we've accomplished something after bringing the car out for the day. Where to?"

I opened a search engine on my phone. "I'm not sure. I saw a receipt on Dixie's desk before the place was ransacked. It might be nothing, but maybe we should check the place out."

"I thought you couldn't recall the name of the store."

"I can't," I said, searching the internet for antiquities shops and bookstores on the islands.

"Dixie ordered a lot of books online," Aunt Clara warned. "The receipt could've been from anywhere in the world."

"Not this one," I said. "Shipped things come with packing slips. The receipt I saw was like the ones generated by my register." I turned my phone to Aunt Clara. "There are three stores claiming to carry antique books and collector series on the islands."

She smiled. "Where should we start?"

I perused the websites of all three shops, spending an extra moment on the homepage for a place called Historical Pages in Hatteras Village, a neighboring town on the island. Not only did the name feel distinctly familiar, but the website banner proudly announced an extensive cartography selection. Since there was a map at the center of this mess, Historical Pages seemed like a good place to visit.

೧

Historical Pages was housed in a single-story, coral-colored house near a marina. The home was trimmed in white with a black roof and door. A simple polyester sign waved from a flagpole on the porch, declaring the business OPEN.

"What a lovely display," Aunt Clara said, hurrying up the front steps to admire an arrangement of welcome and directional signs nailed to the clapboard beside a bay window.

I opened the door and ushered her inside.

The space was filled to the rafters with books, set up like a small library with shelves on every wall and more standing in rows down the room's center. The scent of aged paper clung to everything.

"Can I help you?" an older man asked, emerging from the stacks.

I recognized him from the ghost walk. More specifically, as the priest Aunt Fran and I had discovered in Aunt Clara's dressing room.

"Oh!" He closed the book he was holding and headed our way with a broad smile. "Clara, hello there." His thick, white hair was clean and tidy. His jeans were loose and belted above his navel. "What are you up to? Out joyriding?" he teased.

Aunt Clara blushed. "I didn't know you worked here, Tony. I thought you were retired."

I watched the pair ogle each other and trade flirtatious niceties a few minutes before I butted in. "Hi." I offered a hand. "I'm Everly, the great-niece. We met briefly the other night. You were on your way to church."

He laughed. "I recall. Tony Grayson," he said, giving my hand a firm pump. "It's nice to see you again, and this time I don't have to rush off. Your aunt talks about you all the time."

I eyed Aunt Clara, who was still blushing at my side. She'd never once mentioned Tony. Not before or after I'd first seen him in her dressing room.

"I missed you at the meeting," she said. "We've just come from the Society. Local police broke it all up. We'll have to meet again, possibly somewhere else, or make memorial arrangements by phone. I assumed you were under the weather when I didn't see you."

"Nah," he said. "I'm a hearty old goat, and I am retired, by the way. This is my grandson's place. Finn took over when I was ready to sell. Smart as a whip. He's got degrees out the wazoo. Complete history buff. I hang around a few days a week to help out and keep him company. I suppose I miss the place."

"Is Finn here?" I asked. Maybe the owner of this operation could tell me more about Dixie and what her last few purchases or sales were like. At the very least, maybe the owner of an antique bookstore could tell me more about the book Burton had argued with Dixie about.

"He ran out for a pair of those fancy, overpriced coffees," Tony said. "He won't be long if you want to look around." He sidled up to Aunt Clara and offered his arm. "I'd be glad to give you the tour. Finn makes maps. You should see some of his work. Amazing."

"Yes," I told Aunt Clara. "Have a tour."

She pressed her lips together and turned scarlet as she slid her hand around his elbow.

With Tony occupied, I got to work exploring. Looking for what, I had no idea. But I started by locating the collections section and searching for

Costal Lore, Legacies, and Legends, book four in the Barrier Island History Ensemble Burton couldn't stop talking about.

I didn't have any luck with that, so I explored the shelves dedicated to island families. The book I'd seen on Dixie's desk was on that topic. I didn't find any direct references to the Swans or Wetherills, so I moved on.

The cartography section was tucked neatly against the rear wall. There was a felt-topped table for unrolling and examining the materials and several pairs of white cotton gloves for handling them.

My gaze danced over the stacks of rolled maps and apparent blueprints.

"Can I help you?" a man asked.

I jumped, my wrecked nerves screaming inside my head. I worked to catch my breath and smile. "Hi," I puffed. "Sorry. I didn't hear you."

He smiled, a disposable cup of steaming coffee in each hand. "It's the boat shoes," he said, wiggling one foot. "Grandpa keeps telling me to switch to cleats, or a cowbell." He set the cups on a nearby shelf and offered me his hand. "I'm Finn Grayson. I own the store and am addicted to really great coffee. Not the stuff I make."

"Everly," I said, accepting the shake.

Finn wore a plaid button-down and tie, with tan pants and boat shoes. He had a schoolboy haircut and round, gold-framed glasses, circa the *Where's Waldo* cartoons.

I'd seen him before, I realized. The night of the

ghost walk. I'd thought he was part of the museum staff, but he must've been there with Tony, the way I'd been there with my aunts.

"I'm visiting with my great-aunt Clara," I explained. "She knows your grandpa."

"Right," he said, nodding. "From the ancient gossip society in Kitty Hawk."

I laughed. He sounded a lot like me. "That's the place."

"Well, is there anything you want to see while they visit? Maybe something I can help you with?"

I considered him and my insurmountable questions, then decided to go for it. "Did you know Dixie Wetherill?" I asked. His grandpa had known her, and Finn was close to Tony, so it seemed possible. And hadn't Burton told me Dixie liked maps?

"I did," he said, a sad smile tugging his lips. "She stopped by at least once a week to see the newest books I'd gotten in. And she loved to talk about maps. I make them, so she posed questions, and I did my best to answer. We had fun trying to figure things out if I didn't know."

"You had fun with Dixie?" I asked, confused and certain I'd misunderstood.

"Sure." He looked surprised by my apparent disbelief. "She was smart and loved to talk about history. She reminded me of my grandma. Except Dixie fancied herself a treasure hunter." He smirked.

I bit my tongue against the urge to ask if she was hunting the Sandman's treasure. "Do you know

Burton Chase from the unwritten history society too?"

"Yeah. He and his wife shop here sometimes. Well, he shops," Finn corrected. "She tags along. I'm pretty sure she's physically attached to his side like a barnacle. I always wonder if it drives him crazy, but the guy clearly married up, so I guess it can't be all bad for him." He paused, mid-ramble. "Was that sexist?"

"A little." But he wasn't wrong. Burton was plain and a little lumpy. Aubrey was shiny, apparently fit, and well put together. A mismatched set from the outside for sure. "Do you know if Burton and Dixie got along?"

"They had common interests, so sometimes, yes. Other times, it gave them grounds to argue."

"Over books," I said.

"Yeah. Burton's a collector, but Dixie only bought to resell. She took a few things out from under him online. Ticked him off. I ordered what I could to help him out when that happened. Sometimes I can get a heads-up when things come available on the message boards between independent bookstores."

I considered that a moment. "That was nice of you."

He grinned. "It wasn't bad for my sales, either. Dixie loved nabbing deals Burton thought should be his. They were the same that way, both feeling entitled. But it's like I told him. Possession is nine-tenths of the law. Once it's hers, it's hers."

I thought of the stolen maps from Dixie's office

and wondered if Finn thought they all belonged to the thief now. "And Dixie was also into treasure hunting?"

He nodded, and the sad smile returned. "She told me there was a thrill in the hunt. Seeking treasure was as good as finding it, because until it was found, anything was still possible." He shrugged. "It sounds silly, but it gave her purpose and a sense of adventure."

I smiled. "And if she ever unearthed a chest of Blackbeard's gold, she would've been filthy rich. Possession being nine-tenths and all."

Finn pushed his glasses higher on his nose and laughed. "Actually, I believe pirate treasure falls under the *finders keepers* rule."

"Ah. Of course."

Finn shifted, eyeing me more carefully. "You're the one who found her, aren't you?"

"Yeah." I winced at the flash of unbidden memory. "I hate that she'd been alive when I got there, but I couldn't save her," I said, the words flooding free and choking me.

Finn's expression softened. "It's not your fault. You can't blame yourself."

I blew out a sigh. I knew he was right, but it didn't feel that way. "I just wish I knew what happened." I lifted my eyes to his, a flicker of hope growing. "Do you have any idea why she'd write my name with her last breath?" They'd been friends, kind of. Maybe he could shed some light. A theory. A guess. Anything.

He seemed to consider, then shook his head. "No."

"She didn't like my family," I said. "Did she ever tell you that?"

"Not directly. She didn't like a lot of things, but she usually made the point with a roll of her eyes. I rarely got any details."

I deflated a bit but wasn't ready to give up. "I saw some books about island families on her desk. Do you know anything about those?"

"Yeah." He smiled. "She was looking into some kind of family treasure. Something hidden by one of her ancestors, but I'm not sure what. I don't think she really knew either."

I leaned against the felt-covered table, processing. It was an interesting revelation, considering our families were possibly intertwined.

"We should get together sometime," Finn said, a puff of energy seeming to course through him. "Maybe we can pick up where she left off. Honor her with a final treasure hunt."

I felt my brow wrinkle, then tried to rearrange my expression. "I don't really believe in that stuff. Buried treasure," I clarified. "Or treasure hunting. I think if someone buries something, it should stay that way."

He covered his heart with his hands and pretended to be crestfallen.

I laughed. "But if you're ever in Charm, you should stop by for some iced tea. I have a shop on the beach." And if I had any additional questions, I'd have someone to bounce them off.

"Finn?" Tony called, stepping around the end of

an aisle with Aunt Clara still on his arm. "I thought that was you."

Finn lifted a cup of coffee and passed it to his grandpa. "Plain black, your favorite."

Tony accepted the cup, then offered it to Aunt Clara.

She shook her head. "I prefer tea."

The three-letter word reminded me. "I have to get back." I turned wide-eyes on Aunt Clara. "I completely lost track of time."

She detangled herself from Tony and came to a stop at my side. "No problem. Finn, it's lovely to meet you, though neither of these rude people introduced us."

He laughed and waved. "You too. I guess I'll see you around sometime, maybe."

I smiled. "Maybe."

I thanked the men for their time, and with plenty to think about, climbed back into the Bel Air.

CHAPTER

❧

THIRTEEN

I waved goodbye to Aunt Clara from my front porch, feeling uneasy, as she drove away in her mother's giant Bel Air. I hoped, sentimentally, that I'd see it again someday. The car was a part of my childhood and my history. My mother and father had ridden away from the church in it after their wedding, tin cans and old shoes tied to the bumper. The photographs were beautiful. A year later, the car had taken Mom to the hospital to have me, then brought us home to the most warm and loving place a child could be raised. Decades of perfect memories had been made in the Bel Air. And it felt, illogically, as if all that history was about to be stripped away. Traded for a Prius.

A lump grew in my throat, but I reminded myself that sentimentality was what created hoarders, and it was impossible to hold on to everything. Memories lived in our hearts and minds, not necessarily in the things collected along the way.

I gave the world around me a careful scan, then

shook off the feeling of being watched. It wasn't as if I was being followed already. I'd just gotten home.

I went inside and worked on Amelia's party prep until three, when Denise went home for the day, then I turned on the shop-owner charm and took over waiting tables.

At quarter past four, Burton arrived.

"Welcome to Sun, Sand, and Tea," I said carefully, settling a logoed napkin and glass of water on the table before him. "What can I get you?"

He glanced at the enormous chalkboard menu hanging behind my counter. "What do you recommend?"

"The Widow's Brew," I said smoothly, pushing my specialty blend automatically, as I had all afternoon. "Can I get you something to go with it? The jerk chicken tacos are spectacular."

"Sure. I could eat."

"Coming right up." I spun on my heels, glad to put some distance between us and wondering what had brought him back to Charm. More specifically, what had brought him to Sun, Sand, and Tea?

I filled a jar with ice, then set the cubes afloat in a flood of my crimson Widow's Brew, imagining multiple sinister reasons for Burton's appearance.

"Care if I sit here instead?" Burton asked, taking a seat at the counter.

"Not at all." I forced a tight smile. "Here's your tea." I set the jar on a napkin and scooted it in his direction while he made a show of looking around.

"This is a fun place. I like the music and the vibe here."

"Thanks." I dabbed a bit of coconut oil into a skillet and turned on the burner beneath it, then pulled ingredients from my fridge. Chicken. Mayo. Lettuce. Homemade tomato and corn salsa. I lined the ingredients on my prep counter, then grabbed a pair of taco shells from the pantry and set them on a plate.

Burton watched as I washed up, then selected a few strips of chicken and rubbed them with my dry Jamaican jerk seasoning before delivering them to the heated skillet.

I added my secret jerk seasoning to a dollop of mayonnaise and beat it together while the meat cooked. Mouth-watering scents rose from the skillet as I layered shredded lettuce onto the taco shells, then spooned the mayo mixture into a pastry bag and flipped the chicken.

"I didn't know you worked here," Burton said. "In case that's what you're thinking."

I smiled politely, not sure I believed him, especially since he knew Aunt Clara, and she loved to tell people everything about me, including where I lived and what I did here. Also, I couldn't ignore the feelings I'd had of being watched, both in Kitty Hawk, where he'd been, and more recently, after Aunt Clara had dropped me off. "I own the shop," I said. "I opened it about a year and a half ago."

Burton lifted a finger toward the stove. "Smells delicious. You must be pretty good to run your own café."

"I serve mostly family recipes," I said, turning off

the burner. I removed the chicken from the skillet and arranged the strips over lettuce before piping a generous zigzag of seasoned mayo across the top with my pastry bag. I gave the tacos a dash of coarsely cut cilantro, then presented them to Burton with a set of silverware. I filled and delivered a small bowl of homemade corn and tomato salsa on the side. "The tomatoes and corn were grown in the family garden."

He spooned salsa over the tacos before rolling the tortillas tight. "I needed this," he said. "I love tacos." Burton took a bite and reveled in it, his eyelids fluttering shut.

I smiled. "Good?"

His eyes sprang open, his expression one of disbelief. "Good? I think I just found religion."

I laughed. "I'm glad. Let me know if I can get you anything else."

Burton took another bite and chewed reverently. "Can I get another order of these to go? I want to have them again for dinner."

"No problem," I said, grinning. The look on his face was the reason I'd gone to culinary school. All I wanted in life was to feed people and make them happy. Was that so much to ask?

"I don't suppose you saw my book when you were in Dixie's office," he said, dotting the corner of his mouth with a napkin. "I heard the cop say your prints were in there. She hated people in her office."

"Sorry," I said. "There were hundreds of books in there. I didn't see the one you mentioned."

He sipped the tea and nodded. "I figured, but I had to ask. I guess it's time I try to find another copy and let this one go." He lifted the taco again, less happy this time. "It just stinks. I was so close to finishing my collection. Why do some people have to be greedy and rotten?"

"I don't know," I said. But his question put another one in my mind. "Why do you think she wanted the book so badly?"

Burton polished off the first taco, looking pensive as he chewed. He sipped a little tea to wash down the bite. "She just liked having whatever someone else wanted."

Maybe, but Dixie also liked maps, and the book in question included several. And she'd forged a friendship with Finn, a local cartographer.

"What do you think happens to all her stuff now?" Burton asked. "Will it be sold? Like at an estate sale? Maybe I can find the book there and buy it back."

I raised my shoulders. "I'm not sure. Depending on the will, Dixie's estate will probably go to her next of kin. I think Dixie had a daughter. Maybe she'd be willing to let you have a look at her mom's collections."

Burton gave me a long, piercing look, but didn't voice whatever he was thinking. Instead, he finished his tacos and tea, then paid for a second order to go and left me a generous tip on his way out.

I sagged with relief in his absence. Burton liked my food, and he didn't seem homicidal, but I couldn't discount the fact that Dixie had done him wrong, and

CLOSELY HARBORED SECRETS 151

she'd refused to make it right. That gave him a motive to be angry, and he was present for the ghost walk, so he'd also had opportunity. He was desperate to find a book he believed was his among her things, giving him motive to search her office, and being a member of the Society provided opportunity for that as well.

I checked on my other guests, then went onto the rear deck to clear my head.

Cool autumn wind struck me in a blast as I parted the glass doors. I wrapped my arms around myself on instinct and leaned against the railing. I squinted at the glistening sea, absorbing its peace and beauty while breathing in the salty air. Couples and families walked the water's edge as a fling of sandpipers raced the surf. All my favorite sights, scents, and sounds. And I felt myself becoming centered once more.

The itchy sensation of being watched ruined my zen. I scanned the area instinctively for signs of Burton. He'd just left, and it made sense he'd still be nearby.

Burton might not have been the only Society member present at the ghost walk and headquarters, but he was the only one in Charm at the moment, and that bugged me.

I made a mental note to see what I could learn about him online tonight, then went back inside and closed the door tightly behind me.

❧

Amelia called at closing time, and I hurried upstairs to grab my notebook. I wanted to tell her all my fun, kid-friendly recipe ideas and see which were her favorites. I hoped there would be at least a few. By the time we hung up, nearly an hour later, I was on my second batch of cutout cookies. Half were on a cooling rack, fresh from the oven. The others were mostly decorated and shaping up to be amazing. I snapped pictures of little black and brown horses mid-gallop, manes of piped frosting flowing down their necks beside narrow licorice reins.

Inspiration struck, and I accessed my live stream phone app, a tool I was still getting used to but had proven to be a real lifesaver once. Unlike the tutorial videos I often made of myself baking, then edited and uploaded to my blog, the phone app allowed me to share what I was doing in real time with my followers. Drops, spills, flubs, and all. Strangely, my audience seemed to enjoy watching me do all those things. And I found the option kind of fun, like inviting people over on a whim, then simply saying goodbye when I was done.

I propped my phone up on the counter, then angled the camera to keep my hands in frame as I worked, narrating the process as well as ways to clean or cover up frosting faux pas. "And since I have an abundance of these little guys," I told viewers, "you can pop into Sun, Sand, and Tea tomorrow and pick one up for a small fee. I'll leave the amount up to you and forward all pony-cookie proceeds to the drive for restoration of barns and facilities damaged by the summer hurricane."

My phone rang, and I smiled at the camera. "Life is calling," I said. "I've got to go, but the cutouts will be available tomorrow. Until they're gone." I closed the app, then reached for the phone, propped against my backsplash.

Aunt Fran's number lit the screen below an image of her on the beach. "Hello," I chirped. "How's everything going?"

"Poorly," she returned. "Mary Grace has launched a new commercial for her ad campaign. Have you seen it? It's ridiculous."

"I haven't," I said, though I wasn't surprised to hear anything related to Mary Grace was ridiculous. She'd been my nemesis since elementary school, when she'd spread the rumor my mother wasn't dead, but had run away to be a circus clown rather than raise me.

"It's running on the town's official website," Aunt Fran continued. "Her puppet of a husband and stand-in mayor must've approved it. Now, the *Town Charmer* has picked it up, and it's only a matter of time before every registered voter in Charm sees it. No one will vote for me after this."

"I'm sure it's not as bad as you think," I said, trying to sound hopeful as I ran for my laptop.

Aunt Fran growled into the phone.

I flipped the laptop lid and accessed my favorites bar, where I kept the *Town Charmer* site at the ready. "I've got it," I said, easily spotting the blog's newest post.

ELECTION DAY IS ON THE WAY. WHO WILL YOU BE VOTING FOR?

I clicked the video and waited as "Hail to the Chief" began to play. The camera panned across a section of pristine beach and landed on Mary Grace, dressed in a white skirt and suit jacket over a soft red blouse, billowing in the wind. Her bleach-blond hair was twice its usual size and flapping around her face as she smiled at strategically placed actors. The men and women fell into step behind her as she passed, increasing her numbers. Young adults, grandparents, and children quickly joined the pack.

A female voice, that most definitely wasn't Mary Grace's, engaged as the music quieted. "Mary Grace Chatsworth-Vanders grew up in Charm, North Carolina. Her family moved away before she was ready, but that didn't stop Mary Grace from returning as soon as she could, back to the town she loved. The people she loved. And those who love her in return." The video image gave way to a slide show of Mary Grace at community events. Picnics. Parades. Parties. Raising money to repair lighthouses, restore historic properties, and rebuild docks along the bay. "If you love your town, you've surely met Mary Grace Chatsworth-Vanders."

I rolled my eyes. Everyone in town did most of those things throughout the year. It was part of belonging to this community.

A record scratch cut through the peppy music, and an ominous tune began. "If you follow local crime news, you've seen the competition around town too." A photo of Aunt Fran appeared, distributing tea samples outside my shop while emergency lights colored the background. It was the first murder scene I'd been to when a man's body was discovered along the boardwalk. My aunts had tried to put the crowd at ease with the tea, but the picture made it seem as if she was serving refreshments at a celebration.

"Uh oh," I said.

"Keep watching."

The photo appeared to spin on screen, revealing a backside with another image that quickly filled the screen. Aunt Fran at a massive buffet on the beach as authorities carried a gurney with a body bag up the hill behind her. A friend's beach reception. A murdered groom.

Then Aunt Fran outside my home at Christmas. A broken garden gnome in an evidence bag, an imprint of a body in the snow. And an array of gnomes outside a yellow, clapboard shop on Main Street. The Blessed Bee sign in clear view.

My stomach dropped, and my heart ached as the commercial continued.

Aunt Fran in her beekeeping gear, calming the colony that had just stung Grandma's best friend countless times. Her body unveiled before a crowd, at a luncheon to celebrate my aunts' love of the American honeybee.

Finally, an image of Aunt Fran dressed in a flowing black gown for the ghost walk, the image taking on an eerie feel against a backdrop of the giant moon and blackened sea. Emergency lights colored her pale skin at Dixie's murder site.

"Five murders," the voiceover began again, a heartbreaking drawl in each word. "Five victims. One common denominator." The ugly images returned in a parade, smaller and circling a central photo of Aunt Fran in black, the Grim Reaper's scythe obviously photoshopped into her hand.

Then, back to Mary Grace and her collection of lemmings on the beach. "Vote Mary Grace Chatsworth-Vanders for a brighter tomorrow. Unless you'd like a visit from that other candidate."

I stared, open-mouthed, at the closing image of Mary Grace at the head of a table set for twenty, breaking bread with the people who'd followed her. Her new husband standing proudly at her side, one hand on the arm of her chair. And the image of Aunt Fran as the Grim Reaper looked on from behind them.

"Is it too on-the-nose for me to say I want to kill her?" Aunt Fran asked.

I laughed, the comment snapping me out of my shock. "A little."

"She portrayed me as the Angel of Death. How do I come back from that?"

"With an answering video," I said, pushing my laptop aside. "We'll create a commercial that supports your campaign without smearing hers. Remind our town that you always take the high road. I'm sure she's expecting you to hit back and planning to use the anger she incited against you."

"That husband of hers will never agree to air anything from me on the town's official site," Aunt Fran said. "As the town council chairman and stand-in mayor, he controls everything about our website."

"Yes, but according to the campaign regulations book, the town has to support each candidate equally. By approving Mary Grace's commercial for the website, he's committed himself to approve yours as well. The *Town Charmer* will run it too. They'll use the two of them as fodder for days. Making comparisons and asking viewers to vote on their favorite ad."

"I have a name I'd like to submit for her ad," Aunt Fran said.

I didn't blame her, but I knew Mary Grace well enough to see the new ad for what it was. A trap. "Why don't I swing by in a few minutes, and we'll work on a commercial promoting your campaign? We can use photos from the family albums showing you in Charm since birth. Remind folks that Swans settled the island and founded this town. You *are* Charm, Aunt Fran. No one can deny that, and no one loves this place more." Plus, she was right, Mary Grace's commercial would be poisoning the minds of half the town before breakfast. Time was of the essence, and I liked helping my aunts. "Only fools would vote against you," I told her, hurrying to my room to change out of my jammies. "So, get ready. I'll take a few candids while I'm there."

"Fine," she said, sounding slightly appeased. "Should I look for my scythe?"

"That won't be necessary."

CHAPTER

FOURTEEN

I hurried down the staircase to my foyer, then flipped the lights on inside the café. I'd changed into my most comfortable pair of jeans and a white, long-sleeved shirt with lace at the hem and cuffs as well as covering a keyhole cutout up front. The loose A-line design flattered my figure, and the soft cotton material made me feel pretty without being uncomfortable. I wished I had the shirt in six other colors. I'd zipped tall brown boots over my feet and calves and released my wild hair from the ponytail that had started to give me a headache.

Fresh air and time with my aunts were exactly what I needed, but first, I had to make a stop in the café. I'd nearly forgotten about the container of shrimp in my refrigerator. The shrimp had been defrosted all day and gone unused. I didn't like to serve defrosted shrimp a second day, so a friend of mine was in luck. I smiled brightly as I ferried the container to the rear deck and swept the door open.

"Lou?" I removed the lid on the little container,

then gave the shrimp a shake before dumping them onto a tabletop for my favorite seagull. I searched the inky sky for him, admiring the countless stars. My eyelids fell shut as I took in the moment, allowing myself to be still when my week so far had demanded continuous action. The air was brisk, bordering on cold. I missed the blistering southern sun and suffocating humidity. I missed the sounds of music pouring through portable speakers on the beach and laughter mixing with the waves.

I sensed a shift in the air around me and opened my eyes.

Lou stretched his wings on the rail at my side. He did a little hop when I smiled.

"Hungry?" I asked rhetorically, having never met a gull who wasn't.

I stepped back to give him space to dine. "I'm going to visit my aunts," I told him. "Mary Grace is at it again." I thought I saw him roll his eyes, and I nodded. "I know. Now, we have to remind her, politely, that being a spiteful, self-obsessed power-monger isn't the kind of behavior that's considered acceptable in Charm."

Lou gobbled up my shrimp, one beady eye on me, and made no comment on Mary Grace. Lou was a gentleman that way.

"I wish you could talk," I said for the thousandth time since I'd met him. I was sure Lou saw and heard everything that went on in this town during his daily flights around the island.

I pressed the lid back onto the empty shrimp container, then gave the view from my deck another long look. "You're welcome to follow me to my aunts' place, if you want. It's dark, and I'm feeling a little intimidated about the trip, to be honest. I wouldn't mind having the company."

I waited, for what, I wasn't sure. After a moment more, I went back inside.

I grabbed my bag, keys, phone, and last sliver of bravery, then headed for the door. I stared briefly down the long, shadowy boardwalk, then hooked a right across my property toward the carriage house where I kept Wagon, my bicycle, and Blue. I told myself the trip would be faster and safer in a golf cart, and that Grady would approve, then picked up my pace.

I relaxed behind the wheel a moment later and buzzed away. Blue was by far the coolest golf cart in Charm, which was saying a lot, because there were so many. Blue was vintage. A classic. I'd discovered her in someone's front yard with a sign claiming she was "good for parts" and "cheap." It was love at first sight. I gave her the TLC she needed, plus a thorough once-over by the local golf cart mechanic, some new tires, and a paint job. Now she was running, painted blue, and stenciled with my shop's logo. Perfect for making deliveries in the rain and advertising Sun, Sand, and Tea anytime I took her out.

I rested my head against the headrest where she'd once been stabbed. Grady had patched her with silver duct tape cut into the shape of a star. Considering his former position with the U.S. Marshal, I knew how much the star meant to him, so instead of removing the patch to fix the damaged material properly, I cherished it.

I motored away from the carriage house at triple the speed I could've walked, enjoying the view as Blue carried me along.

The shops on Ocean Drive were closed at this hour, but the restaurants were packed and filling my world with the scents of grilled seafood and cheeseburgers. White twinkle lights hung in sweeps and bows from store fronts, mixed with orange and purple for now. The colors would move to red and green in a month or two as Charm prepared for the holidays.

My mind wandered over the awful week I'd already had and the seemingly countless commitments immediately ahead. Creating a proper campaign ad for Aunt Fran, planning and executing Amelia's party menu, choosing a gown for the Harvest Ball, fixing my busted bookcase—or wall, I wasn't sure which was actually broken—*and* I needed to know who was masquerading as a two-hundred-year-old ghost sailor. Because my gut said that was also the person following me, the one who'd left a threat on my porch, and the one who'd murdered Dixie Wetherill.

I hadn't come up with any new guesses by the time I turned onto my aunts' street, so I tucked the worries aside and parked Blue in the gravel driveway beside the homestead.

The property had belonged to a Swan since my female ancestors had claimed and settled the land hundreds of years before. The original home had burnt down once or twice in the early years when dry summers, wooden structures, and the reliance on indoor fire for light were a dangerous but necessary combination. The home standing before me today, however, had been there for generations.

Neat black trim lined the windows, accenting the dark-gray clapboard face and sides. A matching black roof and door gave the home a stern and oddly gothic appeal, despite an interior bursting with love and joy. The wildflowers that normally pressed against the scalloped wooden fence were gone, replaced with neatly bundled stalks of corn and cheery, decorative scarecrows.

I climbed out, mesmerized by a colony of bats swooping past the oversized moon. Silvery sleeves of light stretched across the gardens and through the trees, shimmering in patterns over a neatly cut lawn.

I grabbed my bag and jogged up the walk to the historic colonial saltbox where I'd grown up. Where my mom, grandma, and great-aunts had also grown up, and their mothers before them. And so on. A smile parted my lips, the way it always did when I returned home.

I'd barely landed on the front porch before the door swung open, and my aunts welcomed me inside. I loved the way Aunt Clara and Aunt Fran always seemed to know I'd arrived before I knocked, as if they'd been eagerly awaiting my arrival.

We spent the next two hours catching up on things, questioning what had happened to Dixie, and muttering about the campaign's competition. I laughed at Aunt Fran's comments on Mary Grace's commercial, and cried over photographs of my grandma, who I missed so much it hurt. Aunt Clara insisted on midnight pancakes at ten, since I wasn't planning to stay until midnight, and I was reminded how nice it felt to be served and cared for. One of the many reasons I'd made feeding people my life's work.

Aside from pancakes in the kitchen, we'd spent the bulk of our time in the family archives, a room at the back of the home where Swan journals, cookbooks, and records were stored. The collection was extensive and required shelves on every wall as well as rows in between. I snapped a dozen or more pictures of Aunt Fran, then selected a stack of photo albums to take home and examine more thoroughly.

By eleven, I was yawning and unsure how much progress I'd be able to make on the commercial before bed. Fatigue had come from nowhere, tugging at my limbs and threatening to pull me under against my will. I said my goodbyes, and my aunts walked me to the door.

"Call us when you get home, so we know you arrived safely," Aunt Clara said while Aunt Fran attempted to turn on the porch light.

"Bulb must be burnt out," Aunt Fran said, flipping the switch uselessly several times. She slipped outside and squinted into the shadows overhead.

"It was working when I got here," I said, joining her on the porch. "If you have another bulb, I can swap them for you."

"I'll get the ladder," Aunt Clara said.

I stepped back, and something crunched beneath my shoe.

Aunt Fran accessed her phone's flashlight and aimed the beam at my feet.

Shattered bits of glass glinted around my sneakers.

She raised the phone overhead, illuminating a broken bulb in the socket. "Something shattered the bulb."

Or someone.

Ice ran down my spine, into my gut, then lower, curling my toes inside my shoes. I scanned the quiet world around us, listening intently for an indication we weren't alone.

There was only the massive moon and quiet har-rumph of hidden frogs.

Aunt Clara returned with a step stool and broom, then locked her arm with mine as Aunt Fran swept up the glass. "Maybe you should stay here tonight," she suggested, "or at least let me drive you home. You can come back for Blue tomorrow."

Enticing as her offer was, and as much as my chicken-self wanted to stay, I couldn't work on the commercial for Aunt Fran without my laptop, and that was at home. Also, I didn't like the idea that who-ever had killed Dixie and was threatening me might be here, on Swan property. I didn't want to endanger my aunts by staying. And I didn't want Aunt Clara to take the Bel Air out again just to drive across town. "I'll be okay," I said. "Will you watch me until I get Blue started?"

"Of course," my aunts answered together.

I hurried down the stone path to my ride, cell phone poised in front of me, flashlight app illuminating the way.

I stopped short when something moved on Blue's roof. My arm jerked instinctually upward, raising the beam of light and tightening my stomach.

A black flag had been erected there, waving lazily in the breeze. The white skull and crossbones emblem jeered down at me.

"A Jolly Roger," I whispered.

My aunts arrived at my side seconds later, pulling me back toward the house as I fumbled to snap a photograph and send it to Grady.

The Jolly Roger was a warning shot given by pirates to their intended prey. A final opportunity to surrender.

Or be forcefully taken.

CHAPTER

❧

FIFTEEN

I drove home in the safety of Grady's headlights. I didn't want to leave Blue at my aunts' place, and she wasn't a crime scene, so Grady met me there, collected the flag, then followed me home. I was thankful for the time to think, and I felt invincible, untouchable, in the beams of a big, protective truck. A truck piloted by my favorite not-to-be-messed-with lawman.

He met me at the carriage house doors when I parked, and he set a palm on my back as we walked to the house together. I waited in the foyer while he checked the first floor for intruders, then I followed him up the narrow, interior staircase to my living quarters and waited on the threshold as he performed another sweep.

All clear, Grady returned with his hat in his hands, then dropped it onto the kitchen counter. He'd seemed unusually distracted since arriving at my aunts' house, and at the moment, he looked blatantly miserable. The blank cop stare was completely gone. And he opened his arms.

I fell against him easily, eagerly, pressing my cheek to his chest and tightening my arms around him as he curled me into his embrace.

"I'm sorry this is happening to you again," he whispered, his cheek resting on the top of my head.

"Thanks. I hate that I'm the one calling you away from Denver again tonight. I wasn't sure what else to do." I held onto him a moment longer, then stepped back and worked up a smile. "Tea?"

"Yes, thank you. And you did the right thing. Always call when you need me."

I popped a pair of mugs under my two-cup instant brewing station, an apple-cinnamon tea pod on each side, then pushed BREW and waited for the mugs to fill.

Grady watched. "Tell me about the Jolly Roger. You said it marked intended victim ships?"

"Not exactly. Pirates used them as warnings," I explained. "They sometimes flew fake flags to make other ships think they were friendly, so they could get near enough to make a run at them or fire on them without them getting away. Then they'd put up the Jolly Roger, as a way to announce their intentions. Sometimes they'd throw in a warning shot."

"Then what?" he asked. "The ships would battle?"

"Sometimes," I said. "If the other ship had a big enough crew, was carrying enough weapons, or had a cargo worth dying for. If not, the captains told their men to stand down and let the pirates have their way. Live to sail another day."

I collected the filled mugs of tea, then passed one to Grady. We carried the drinks to my couch, and each of us took a cushion. I curled my legs beneath me and pushed the hair behind my ears.

He nodded, thoughtful. Grady was a fighter, trained and capable, but his goal was always peace. And he was never rash. "The flag left on Blue looked pretty old," he said. "I'm thinking the lab will say it's as old as the other stuff left on your porch."

"Probably," I said. "But I can't figure out why whoever is masquerading as a British sailor ghost used a pirate flag tonight."

Grady rubbed the stubble across his jawline. "I think it's because your stalker is playing a role, and the Jolly Roger is a message James Hudson would have understood. I've been reading up on him. He died in a fight with pirates."

I grimaced. "I didn't know that." Though, in truth, I knew very little about any of the individuals mentioned in our ghost-walk stories, beyond their roles in the legends themselves.

Grady shifted, leaning forward as he sipped his tea. "This was a second demand for the map. A follow-up to the note on your porch and apparently a warning shot. Surrender what he or she wants, or it will be taken from you by force."

"That's a real problem, because I don't have any maps."

Grady sighed. "Yet, someone is going to great lengths to make you believe they're the ghost of James

Hudson. They want to scare you into compliance, and it worries me more than your run-ins in the past, because this nut is using valuable relics to support the narrative. If it's all part of a role they know they're playing—fine. If it's someone who's had a mental break…" He trailed off with a frown.

I didn't like the sound of that. Regular stalkers and murderers were bad enough. I couldn't bring myself to think about the lengths someone who was actually out of their mind might go to get something from me that I didn't have. This investigation needed a kick in the breeches before I was pillaged. "We should find out where all these old things are coming from," I said. "I can help. There are a dozen maritime museums on the islands. Surely a curator somewhere has made a police report for the missing relics. If not the flags, then the captain's sword. I can make some calls tomorrow."

"I've already put in a few calls," he said. "I don't need any more help than I already have. The Charm PD is capable of following up on my inquiries."

He leveled me with a pointed stare.

I bristled. "Fine."

"Fine."

I set my mug on the coffee table and went to collect a small container of the pony cookies I'd finished before going to see my aunts. "I baked some trial cutouts for Amelia's book launch," I said, returning with the container. "How about something sweet to go with your tea?"

His eyes widened at the sight of my cookies, and

a smile bloomed on his lips. "You made these?" He selected a brown and white pony, then raised his clear gray eyes to mine. "Is there anything you can't do in the kitchen?"

"Not really," I said, completely bragging and thrilled with the compliment. I nabbed a cookie and returned to my seat.

Grady licked crumbs from his lips, clearly in love. With the cookie. "These are amazing."

"Thanks. They're made using a standard cutout recipe with homemade icing." I'd found the recipe in a cookbook from the archives. Amelia's guests were sure to love it. "Are you and Denver planning to be at the book launch?" I asked, already dying to see what Denver would think of the cookies and the party.

"We are. He tells everyone we meet, very humbly, that he's the boy in the book and therefore famous. We wouldn't miss the launch."

"Well, he's not wrong," I said, laughing. "How's he doing? Any better?"

Grady's shoulders rolled forward. He finished the cookie, then cradled his mug between giant palms. "I don't know. The therapist says he's going to be okay. That he's working through the loss. She thinks there's already been progress, and the outlook is good, but it doesn't seem good from where I'm standing."

I offered a small smile, imagining what it might feel like to see my child hurting and unable to make the pain go away. "How about you? How are doing?"

He laughed, his gaze jumping to mine. "You know you're the only one who ever asks me that?"

I shrugged. "That's because you're the big, tough hero of everything and everyone around here. People forget you're human under all those intimidating looks and blatant brawn. You put up a good front, Hays, but I see you."

"You do, don't you," he said softly, expression going serious, searching.

"Absolutely."

Grady selected another cookie, averting his gaze from mine and giving the room a long look that settled on my bookshelf. I'd removed the plastic and as much paint as humanly possible before breakfast. "What's going on there?"

"I'm trying to restore it. I used a stripper on the paint last night and finished scraping off as much of it as I could this morning. I was supposed to wait until tonight, but I couldn't. Good thing, because it's not like I've had any time," I rambled. "I still need to sand off the paint I couldn't get with the stripper, then stain and seal the wood."

Grady stretched onto his feet and moved closer to inspect my work.

"Caw!" Lou yelled outside my deck door, and I jerked around to see him flapping. He was on the arm of my deck chair, head cocked and peering through the glass like a maniac.

Grady looked from Lou to me.

I laughed. "I don't have any more shrimp, you

walnut." I waved. "I'll see you at breakfast." Lou and I liked to watch the sunrise together.

Grady frowned. "Your relationship with that bird is weird."

"You're weird."

Grady laughed. "I'm getting there," he said. "This island's got me chasing British sailor ghosts. Everywhere I go, people are asking if it's true you're being haunted." He ran a finger over the intricate scrollwork on my bookcase. "Incredible craftsmanship. I hadn't noticed before."

I ignored the bit about being haunted and focused on the beautiful woodwork. "That's because the paint had globbed over the finer details. It wasn't easy getting all the gunk out of the crevices. I'd say it was worth it, but I think I broke the whole thing trying." Heat flushed through my cheeks at the recollection. I stepped back and pointed to the quarter-inch split at the base, where the bookcase met the wall.

Grady crouched with a frown. He ran his hands over the trim.

"Caw! Caw! Caw!"

I gasped as Lou bounced and beat his wings on the deck. "Jeez Louise!" I said, glaring through the glass. "Knock it off already. There's no more shrimp."

Grady grabbed ahold of the bookcase, ignoring Lou's outburst, and leaned back, attempting to pull the bookcase into alignment with my room's baseboards.

"Caw!"

"For goodness' sakes." I marched across the room

and yanked the curtain. Normally, I enjoyed Lou's rants, but I was spent.

Grady stood and dusted his palms. "It won't budge. The house has probably shifted. No one will notice. I hadn't until you pointed it out."

"Thanks for trying."

He nodded, then stepped away from me. "I should get back. Check on Denver."

"Okay. I appreciate you following me home."

He smiled, but there was a weird sadness in his eyes. I couldn't make sense of it, and I didn't know what to say to fix it.

I spun for the kitchen. "You should take some cookies to Denver."

Grady watched as I collected a shallow container and wax paper. "I meant what I said about letting Charm PD follow up on the artifacts," he said. "I'm going to talk to the Society in Kitty Hawk again too, so no need for you to head out there either. I'll figure out who had access to the sword and flags and where they came from. Then I'll find the one following you and shut that down."

I lined the container with wax paper, then added two carefully selected ponies. My thoughts and emotions battled for attention. "Someone stole all the maps from Dixie's office," I said, "and I felt someone watching me while I was there. What if whoever saw me is the one threatening me, because they assume I took the maps? But someone else went in after me and stole the whole bin. Now that person has what the first person wants, and the first person thinks it's me." I felt a bubble of panic swell as I fumbled to seal the lid over my cookie container.

Grady gripped the back of his neck, looking more exhausted by the minute. "That's complete speculation. I'm not dismissing the possibility," he warned, pinning me with another heavy stare. "I'm saying, *I'll* figure it out."

I pursed my lips, another question rising in me. "What do you think Aubrey meant by saying Dixie had her hands on something of everyone's?" I asked. "Do you think she had something of Aubrey's? Aubrey was the first person to arrive at the murder site after Aunt Clara and me. And she handed me the candelabra. Plus, I'm certain she's the one who took that picture of me with Dixie's blood on my hands."

"Stop," Grady said firmly, drawing me up short.

My eyes widened.

"Everly," he said softly. "The candelabra wasn't the murder weapon."

"But Dixie was struck with it," I said. "So, tricking me into getting my fingerprints on it, while she wore gloves, was dirty."

"Everly." He repeated my name, more firmly this time, breaking it into syllables.

I froze.

He heaved a sigh and dropped his hands to his hips. "We need to talk."

I pulled back. Nothing good started like that. "About?"

"You and I have been getting closer for a while now."

My insides tensed. He hadn't said anything bad yet, but I felt it coming. The air had changed. His posture had changed. Everything had changed. It was only a matter of him saying so.

"Denver's counselor asked me if there was someone else in Denver's life that he feared losing. She suggested that maybe, the possibility of suffering a second loss of that magnitude had set him off with the tears and the nightmares. She assumed that person was me, because of my job. Maybe it is," he said. "I don't know, but—"

"You think it's me," I said, my insides twisting painfully. "Because I'm the one who's been nearly killed multiple times a year since you moved here. And I'm being threatened again now."

Grady pressed his lips tight. "I was going to say I don't know if there's more to Denver's nightmares than the loss of his mother, but I'm working with the therapist however I can to find out, and I need to be there for Denver as he heals. Every minute I'm not on the job. My life has to be about him. It can't be about me."

Or me, I realized, the truth a vise on my chest. "You're breaking up with me?" I asked, smiling slightly to ease the mood. Of course, we weren't breaking up. We weren't a couple.

Grady searched my face with a solemn gaze.

I waited, desperate for breath. Arguing with myself for caring this much. For being overly dramatic. For the tears I felt forming and the confusion still circling. "Grady?"

His jaw set, and his expression turned grim. "I'm giving all I have to my son and this investigation right now."

My world tilted, and I pressed my palm to the counter for support. He was breaking up with me. "As you should," I said. "Work and Denver are your top priorities."

"There isn't time for anything else," he continued. "I want you to know I value your friendship."

I imagined collapsing. Or screaming. Grady had used the *F* word.

Instead, I stood there dumbly, attempting to look strong and unfazed.

"I'm thankful for what we have, it's just that you and I…" He cleared his throat. "We can't."

"Got it." I fixed what was surely a maniacal smile to my face. "I never thought we could." I mentally gathered my aching heart into a little ball and locked it into a vault for protection. "Did you have a chance to take pictures of the tapestry in Dixie's office?" I asked, abruptly changing the subject.

Grady stared.

I raised my brows. "Any chance you saw the pictures of my house that Aubrey mentioned? I'm not sure if she meant this house or my aunts', but I'd like to see either."

He was silent for so long I wondered if he'd heard me.

"Grady?" I prompted. "The pictures?"

"Yeah." He cleared his throat. "Kitty Hawk PD is finished with Ms. Wetherill's office as a crime scene, so the Society members can get in there now. Clara can look at the tapestry for as long as she wants, but I have the pictures of your home in my truck." He stuffed his hat back onto his head. "I'll grab them now, on my way out."

I pushed the container of cookies in his direction, and he scooped them up.

"Denver will appreciate these."

I followed Grady stoically down the steps and onto my porch, then waited while he dropped the cookies into his truck and returned with a manila envelope.

"I meant to get these to you sooner, but that Jolly Roger sidetracked me." He handed off the envelope, then headed back to his truck.

He opened the door and paused, watching me before climbing inside. "I'm sorry if I upset you."

"You didn't," I said, though I wanted to kick sand at him for bringing it up again. "We're friends. It's all we've ever been and all we'll ever be, and that's exactly what we both thought. I was only joking about us breaking up. I shouldn't have said it. Now everything's weird."

"It's not," he said. "I just wanted to be sure we were on the same page, because with what Denver's going through right now, I—"

"Need a friend," I said, cutting him off. "And I'm your only island friend. So, come by anytime, and we can talk. You don't owe me anything for it."

Heartbreak worked over Grady's handsome face in the moonlight, and I began to believe in blue-moon lunacy. Because I clearly had it.

I couldn't breathe, I missed him so much.

He'd never been mine, but I'd officially lost him. How was that for irony?

Tears manifested without warning, hot and heavy in my eyes. "Goodbye, Grady," I said, then hurried inside as tears began to fall.

CHAPTER

SIXTEEN

I popped into Sun, Sand, and Tea feeling exhausted but hopeful the next morning. After wrapping myself in a blanket and sitting on the deck with Lou last night, I'd gotten the perspective I'd needed. Grady and I were friends, and I treasured that. Nothing had actually changed, and everything was good. I was fine. Absolutely. Fine.

Lou had whole-heartedly agreed, so I'd straightened my ponytail and gone to bed.

After several hours of fitful sleep, I'd decided to make rum cakes and get a jump start on my day. I'd pondered Aunt Fran's comeback commercial while I prepped food for the café, then shot off a flurry of emails in search of help. Staying busy kept my mind off things I couldn't control, like my recent threats and the way things had been left between me and Grady. Not that I'd been replaying and over-analyzing his words in my head all morning. That would've been ridiculous. And I was *fine*. I was also running on sheer adrenaline by the time my shop opened.

Denise waved goodbye to a set of customers just before noon, then came to greet me at the counter. "You're Miss Productive today," she said. "Makeup on. Hair down. Cakes baked. What lit a fire under your behind?"

"Probably that bananas commercial Mary Grace put out yesterday," I said, deflecting. "I was up late, working on a video for Aunt Fran, then had trouble sleeping."

Denise leaned her hip against the counter. "I wondered if you saw that. Did Fran?"

"Yes, and she nearly blew a gasket."

Denise nodded in full understanding. "What are we going to do about it? Can we petition the town council to take it down?"

"We can, but everyone's probably already seen it," I said. "I'm nearly finished with an ad for Aunt Fran that will remind people of who she really is. A woman with roots in this town deeper than most trees."

Denise grinned. "I like the sound of that. Can't wait to see what you have up your sleeve."

"I hope to have it all finished and uploaded tonight. I've already sent a teaser to the *Town Charmer* to get some early buzz going. I learned that trick from Amelia's pre–book launch agenda." I climbed onto my step stool behind the counter and erased the daily menu from my chalkboard. "I also came up with a fun way to promote Aunt Fran from here." I scripted a red, white, and blue chalk outline around the words: VOTER'S DELIGHT. "We officially serve a trio of Aunt Fran's favorite family recipes, for one patriotic price. Passionfruit and ginger tea, a small charcuterie board, and blueberry cobbler. All things I can prep in bulk and have consistently at the ready until Election Day. And every Voter's Delight comes with a Vote for Swan button." I motioned to the glass gallon jar I'd tied a red ribbon around and filled with Aunt Fran's swag.

Denise clapped.

I took a bow, then climbed down.

"Have you looked at the blog recently?" she asked.

"No." I flattened my step stool and tucked it away. "Why?"

She wrinkled her nose. "People are starting to report ghost sightings around here. Always a sailor. Usually somewhere near your property."

I groaned. "I am not haunted."

Her phone buzzed on the counter, and she flipped it over, then smiled at the screen. "Oh, my goodness. Look at all this cuteness."

I went to see, hoping shamelessly it was a photograph of Denver. I hated that he was so unhappy, and it made me ill to think I might be the cause of his nightmares. A photo of him smiling would go a long way to heal my heart.

She turned the screen to face me, and an image of Wyatt surrounded by pint-sized cowboys centered the screen. "He started a new session of Cowboy Camp today. They're grooming the horses, talking about respect for animals and nature, then having a snack before the moms come to pick them up from the Nature Center."

My heart softened looking at all those big-cheeked cherub faces and wide, hopeful smiles. "I love that he's teaching these classes." Wyatt had recently given up his pursuit of the rodeo completely and settled in Charm to work full time at the Nature Center. The cowboy classes for kids were a brainstorm of his that had a wait list a mile long. Rightly so. There was no one more qualified or more passionate about the proper care of horses. The tots under his tutelage were luckier than they knew. "Wyatt should bring the kids here for snack time," I said. "I have tons of cold drinks and healthy food."

Denise bit her lip and smiled. "He told me you'd say that."

"Who?" I asked. "Wyatt?"

She nodded. "They're on their way here now."

I rolled my eyes and grabbed a tray of jars from the counter. "The man knows me well."

Denise helped me fill the glasses with ice. "He asked me to the Harvest Ball last night," she said, rocking onto her toes then down. "I said yes, and now I have no idea what to wear." She made a bunch of crazy expressions and mimed her head exploding.

"Whatever you wear will be perfect," I told her. "It's just a lot of fun to get together and dance."

"What are you wearing?"

An excellent question. One I'd asked myself many

times in the past month without finding an answer. "I'm not sure." I normally used the ball as an excuse to dress up, because there weren't a lot of occasions for that in a beach community.

"Are your aunts going?" Denise asked. "What are they wearing?"

I turned a goofy smile in her direction. "Aunt Clara and Aunt Fran always go as seventeenth century witches." And their costumes were perfectly Puritan, complete with narrow wisps of red and yellow fabric along the hems to resemble flames licking over the dark dresses.

Denise smiled. "I remember that now. They were dressed that way last year."

"Every. Single. Year," I said.

"A nod to your ancestors?"

I slid my eyes at her, then smiled as I began to fill the jars with old fashioned sweet tea. "What do little cowboys eat?"

"Between meals, Denver likes peanut butter and jelly. Fruit. Cheese. Yogurt. And anything with enough sugar."

I snapped my fingers. "I'm hearing fruit and yogurt parfaits sprinkled with mini chocolate chips."

Denise's blue eyes widened. "I want some of that."

"You've got it." I pulled ingredients from the refrigerator while Denise lined up the parfait cups.

"Have you decided what you're making for Amelia's book launch?" Denise asked, grabbing napkins and spoons to go with the cups.

"I have a loose idea. I made sample menus for Amelia to review and give feedback. Those cutouts at the register are one of the dessert options."

Denise smiled. "Those pony cookies have been gone since about five minutes after we opened."

I went to check the display case, and my heart bounced with glee. "People must've seen my live stream." And they'd come for my cookies. I pressed a hand to my heart, overwhelmed with love for my community.

"People were donating five bucks a cookie," Denise said. "One guy gave me a fifty, then handed his cookies out to people in line behind him. A couple of those people gave me money anyway, even though they already had a cookie. It was fantastic."

"I'm sorry I missed it." I'd been a little late coming down with the finished rum cakes I'd started upstairs. It'd taken several trips to carry them all safely. Then I'd been tied up on the telephone, making a multitude of calls to locals who'd placed an order, as well as to schedule a postal pickup for cakes headed out of town.

My seashell wind chimes jingled, and a herd of preschool-aged boys and girls appeared. They wore jeans, boots, cowboy hats, and matching T-shirts that said Cowboy Club across the front. Wyatt brought up the rear. Tall, lean, and handsome to a fault, Wyatt winked at me, then smiled broadly at Denise.

He helped the kids onto counter seats and nearby chairs, then sidled up to the blushing blond at my side. "It's good to see you," he said, a little too slow and breathy.

Denise's cheeks went from pink to crimson. "You too."

I beamed at the crew of tiny ladies and gentlemen. "Welcome to Sun, Sand, and Tea," I said. "I heard you might be visiting, so I made you all a special treat. Are you hungry?"

I received a hearty round of "Yes, ma'ams," then began distributing the sweet tea. "Any allergies to fruit or dairy?"

Wyatt shook his head, jumping in with Denise to hand out napkins and silverware. "We've got some pollen and bee sting issues, but we're clear on dietary restrictions."

"Perfect!" I filled the parfait cups with yogurt and fruit, then Denise delivered the finished treats.

I shook my half-gallon container of mini chocolate chips, then moved kid to kid, lighting up their day. I sprinkled a little pile of chips onto each parfait and basked in the glow of wide-eyed faces.

Wyatt stooped to kiss Denise on the cheek and squeeze her hand before taking a seat among his crew. He'd put on a little weight since returning home, and his face had filled out, no longer gaunt from hiding injuries and managing pain. He was happy. He made Denise happy. And I was happy for them in a way I hadn't originally expected.

Wyatt had broken my heart once, and I'd held onto that hurt for too long, only realizing recently that the experience was necessary to bring us both back to Charm, where our futures awaited.

Before I could dwell on my hope for the future, five-and-a-half feet of immediate bad luck strolled through the door.

Mary Grace Chatsworth-Vanders led her new husband to a table with four chairs and a stunning view, then sat in the seat beside his.

I made a quiet gagging noise that earned some laughter from the Cowboy Club. There was only one reason Mary Grace would be in my shop the day after putting out a commercial portraying my great-aunt as the Grim Reaper. She wanted to gloat.

Denise grabbed two place settings and headed over to greet the newcomers.

I grabbed a towel and went to clean the handful of available tables.

"Welcome to Sun, Sand, and Tea. What can I get you?" Denise asked, sliding napkins and silverware in front of the couple.

Mary Grace smiled smugly. "I'm off carbs, so I'll take an unsweetened iced tea and house salad with salsa on the side."

I tried not to stare as I processed her new look. She'd teased her normally sleek hair to within an inch of its life and sprayed it to stay that way. Ruby-red lips and tarantula lashes accented the appearance. She was dressed all in white again, like on her commercial, and I wondered if she was in costume as a television evangelist's wife.

"My husband will have the Voter's Delight, hold the Swan pin," she said, staring at me as she ordered.

"Fran will need it to hold her frown upside down when she loses."

Vanders, her thick-headed husband, looked confused. "Got any baklava?"

"Sorry," Denise said. "Only what's on the menu."

He shrugged, and sunlight streaming through the windows glinted off the gallon of product he'd used to slick down his dark hair. The strands looked wet, but I was confident they'd crunch if I pressed on them. "Thanks, anyway."

Denise bowed away to prep their orders, and I wiped smudges off windows with my towel.

"Your aunt is tanking in the polls," Mary Grace called. "No surprise, really. She means well, but this town is ready for some young blood, and Fran Swan doesn't know the first thing about politics."

A dozen retorts piled on my tongue. Aunt Fran had been on the town council for years. She knew this place and these people better than anyone, and she cared. Bottom line: she was more qualified than any mayor we'd ever had, but I wasn't going to be baited into a public squabble.

"I'm not trying to be rude," she lied. "I'm just a fan of facts, and most Charmers appreciate honesty. Even if it's hard to hear."

The chimes over my front door jingled, and I inhaled deeply, thankful for the distraction.

"Welcome to Sun, Sand, and Tea," Denise and I sang in near unison.

Matt Darning appeared with a grin. He raised a

hand in greeting to Wyatt, then Denise, before heading my way. "Hey, Everly."

"Hey," I said. "Here for lunch?"

"Yes, ma'am," he said with a charming grin.

I led him to a tall bistro table, away from Mary Grace, then leaned against it and beamed. "How's it going? I don't get to see you too often outside a crime scene."

He smiled back. "I was thinking the same thing."

"Yeah? Well, I'm glad you came in," I said. "What can I get you?"

"Everything. I'm starving." He unsnapped his uniform jacket and set it on the back of his chair. "I'll have to eat fast. I'm on duty, but that's the job." He smiled brightly, unaffected by the demands of a career he loved, and I appreciated that.

Backlit by the beautiful day and gleaming sea, I also appreciated how handsome he was. He had good guy written all over him, and a heart of gold pinned to his sleeve. I'd seen him caring for patients and soothing loved ones as he worked. Matt was sweet, kind, and genuine. His lips parted when he caught me staring.

I blushed. "Sorry. I was lost in thought for a minute. What can I get you?"

He looked past me to the chalkboard. "Definitely the Voter's Delight. Supporting your aunt?"

I warmed to him for asking. "Absolutely."

"Tell her she has my vote."

"I will."

The wind chimes jingled again, and I let Denise handle the welcome.

"Hi, Matt," a female voice said. The new EMT, who'd been with him at Dixie's murder scene, appeared and took the other chair at his table. Her hair was down today, long and wavy across her shoulders. The embroidery on her coat said her name was Jane.

I cleared my throat and stepped back, realizing too late that I'd gravitated unnecessarily close to Matt's side, and suspecting he had something started with his new, beautiful young partner.

"I love this place already," she said. "Good choice."

Matt looked from Jane to me, then back. "The menu's over the counter. I ordered the Voter's Delight, but everything Everly makes is exceptional."

"So I've heard," she said. "I'll have what he's having."

I nodded, unable to find my tongue.

"How are you holding up after the other night?" she asked, her eyes warm with concern.

"Okay. I'll be right back with your meals." I excused myself with a smile and went to make their adorable matching orders.

Denise met me at the counter. "Don't look now, but that cute EMT is watching you," she said.

I definitely wasn't looking. At anyone.

I concentrated on prepping the meals while Mary Grace glared holes through my forehead.

"I think they're talking about you," Denise added.

I raised my eyes to the couple in high end suits and dress shoes.

"Not them," Denise said. "The EMTs."

Wyatt slid off his stool and smiled at me. "Time to get the crew back to the Nature Center for pickup. Thank you for a delicious treat, Miss Everly." He turned to the little ones.

"Thank you, Miss Everly," they repeated.

I smiled brightly back. "Anytime."

Wyatt handed a couple of twenties to Denise, then kissed her cheek before glancing back in my direction. "Good luck with that." His gaze flicked in Matt's direction, and my face grew hot.

I loaded two boards with salty meats and savory cheeses, then added bunches of olives, pickles, berries, and apple slices, ignoring him. I prepped their drinks and arranged them on a tray with the charcuterie and headed out to deliver the goods.

Matt and his partner were on their feet before I reached the table, cell phones in hand. "We just got a call," he said, looking deeply apologetic. "What do I owe you?"

"Nothing." I turned on my heels and rushed back to the counter, where a stack of carryout containers waited. I swiped two from the top and transferred the charcuterie quickly. "On the house," I said. "It's the least I can do for someone who's kept me alive more than once this year."

I stacked the containers on the counter, then overturned the tea jars into disposable containers and pressed lids on top.

His partner took the containers and smiled. "I'll go start the bus."

Matt's tan cheeks flushed a bit as she walked out, blue eyes searching mine. "Confession. I stopped in for more than lunch. I wanted to ask you something. I didn't expect to be interrupted. I mean, there's always that chance when I'm on duty…"

I puzzled at his words. "What did you want to ask?" Then, I remembered. "Oh! I have your coat. From the other night." I looked instinctively toward the foyer, where steps led to my private quarters. "I can grab it, if you have time."

"No." He shook his head, then moved toward the door. "It's not that." He tipped his head, encouraging me to walk with him.

I followed, curiosity aflame. Did he have news about Dixie's death? Had he heard something during one of his stops?

We paused on the porch as the ambulance idled several yards away.

Matt turned his back to his partner, looking unusually pale.

I raised my brows. I'd never seen him frazzled, but it was kind of adorable.

"Do you want to go out with me sometime?" he asked. "We can do anything you'd like. I just want the chance to get to know you, when I'm not on the run or patching you up at a crime scene."

I laughed. My head nodded before I had time to think the answer through. Then my mouth started running. "I'd like that. A lot, actually." And I was surprised to realize I meant it. "Call me?"

"I will." He ran for the ambulance, smiling widely as he leaped inside.

I felt lighter as I turned for the door, then froze as Denise, Wyatt, and a crowd of little cowboys and cowgirls smiled back.

They all began to clap.

CHAPTER
SEVENTEEN

I spent the afternoon and next day prepping the recipes Amelia selected for her book launch. It was a busy but threat-free time that I appreciated immensely. I had hours to mull over what was happening in my world. Who was following and threatening me? Who killed Dixie? And why? And less importantly, exactly which map was my stalker looking for? I didn't come up with any answers, but I'd baked my heart out, and Amelia's buffet was going to be the talk of the town. As a bonus, I'd also finished Aunt Fran's commercial.

I closed my shop promptly at three for Amelia's party and put a sign in the window directing anyone who stopped by to visit Charming Reads instead.

Amelia planned the timing of her launch brilliantly, to coincide with the town's trick-or-treat. Meaning families were already out in droves, and her bookstore was likely on their route. Amelia had kid-crafts and games, plus food and drink for everyone.

And if guests stuck around, they could get a signed copy of her new book!

I left home for the second time at seven. After helping Amelia and her dad set up the event, I'd gone home to get into costume. Trick-or-treat in Charm was one of the most popular events, and almost everyone participated. As expected, the streets were alive with goblins, Ghostbusters, and ice-making princesses on my return to trip to Charming Reads.

I slid Blue into a nearby parking space, then adjusted my red velvet cape as I climbed down. My Little Red Riding Hood costume seemed fitting for a party at a bookstore, and as a bonus, there was plenty of room in my basket for treats. I'd baked and iced dozens of pumpkin-shaped cutouts, then tied the bags with red curling ribbon and smoothed a logoed Sun, Sand, and Tea sticker across the bags' backs. A shameless but delicious plug for my store that doubled as trick-or-treat sweets.

Music and chatter burst from the store with every opening of the door. I slipped inside, elated by the massive turnout.

Amelia waved immediately from her place at a little table topped with books. Images of her story's pages played on a big white screen behind her. The houndstooth coat, cape, and hat she wore made her the cutest Sherlock Holmes I'd ever seen. She laughed and raised her oversized magnifying glass to each child arriving at the table.

I mingled with the crowd, thanking everyone for coming and handing out cookies from my basket.

The "Monster Mash" played quietly on hidden speakers. Friends and neighbors noshed cheerfully on my treats, and there was happiness in every bone of my body.

Mr. Butters caught my eye from his place in the children's section, where a sign indicated he would soon lead willing participants in a pony-themed craft. He ducked away, heading for me with outstretched arms and a wide smile. "Look at you." He pulled me against his chest in the warmest of fatherly hugs.

I'd met Amelia when we were young, and Mr. Butters had welcomed me into their home with enthusiasm. I'd marveled at the concept of being raised by a man, while Amelia had been enamored with my trio of mother figures. We'd all become a sort of loose extended family from there. And since I'd returned to the island, our little team of loved ones had grown even closer. It was one of my favorite parts of being home.

"You look great," he said. "This costume is fantastic."

"Thanks." High praise coming from a theater geek like himself. I returned his squeeze before releasing him for a better look at his ensemble. "Zorro?" I grinned. "You know I love Zorro."

"Who doesn't?" he asked, standing taller and flapping one side of his cape. He spun, then struck a pose to complete the show. Hands-on-hips, chin up, and staring into the distance.

I clapped.

He bowed. "Thanks for all your help today. I know your life is a little"—he searched for the right word "challenging at the moment."

"I'm doing okay," I told him, putting on my bravest face. "And my best friend is having a book launch party." I stepped back to wave my hands around like a nut. "Where else would I be right now?"

He chuckled. "Well, if I was being haunted by a killer-ghost at Halloween, I'd be on a fast plane to Timbuktu, but you were always braver than me." He smiled. "If there's anything I can do for you, you let me know. I'm a whiz with those online airfare sites."

I laughed, feeling the familiar wave of emotion that always hit when he stepped in to look after me. "I will."

A group of kids began to pound their fists on the pint-sized craft table, and Mr. Butters frowned. "I'd better get over there and start this craft before we have a mutiny on our hands."

I wished him luck, then scanned the room in search of Denise or Grady. I spotted Denver at the craft table and knew his caretakers wouldn't be far.

Denise smiled at me from an alcove, where she was stealthily keeping an eye on Denver as he worked. "You look amazing," she said as I approached. "Way to work that hourglass figure."

I blushed. If there was a clothing style that my newfound curves did well in, it was anything vintage and A-line. My costume had come with an embroidered black corset that went on the outside of a long-sleeved, off-the-shoulder red blouse. The corset laced below my bra line and did all sorts of favors for my waist and my bosom. The flared satin skirt hung in red waves over layers of black crinoline that accentuated my calves. A nice reminder that despite my scale's infuriating reports, those daily walks were good for me.

"You're about to turn Oz on its head," I said, skimming her perfect costume.

She'd French-braided her hair into pigtails and tied little bows at the ends. Her blue and white gingham dress was a flawless replica of Dorothy's costume from the Wizard of Oz, right down to the glittery red pumps and stuffed Toto in her basket.

Denver was, of course, a cowboy.

"Is Wyatt running around here as a flying monkey or member of the Lollipop Guild?"

"He's the Tin Man," she said, digging into her basket. "I have his heart right here." She pulled a big red heart from underneath Toto.

I laughed. "Does that make Grady the Scarecrow?"

"He's not here," she said, sliding her gaze back to Denver. "He had something to take care of, so Wyatt and I brought Denver."

"Oh." I ignored the pang of disappointment and worked up a smile. "I'm glad you made it. This is a great turnout, right?"

Denise swung her attention back to me, evaluating.

I shifted and cleared my throat, searching for a subject change. "I finished Aunt Fran's commercial this morning. Everyone I'd reached out to got back with me, and I was able to do what I'd hoped. I've already uploaded it to my shop's website, sent my request to the *Town Charmer* and the official Charm website, asking for the ad to be made available ASAP."

She perked. "Can I see it?"

"Sure!" I dug my phone from my basket and accessed the commercial, feeling my chest swell with pride. "I haven't checked to see if it's live yet, or if I've had any comments. I've been here most of the day." I pressed Play with intense anticipation, and the room fell away as I waited for the ad to roll.

A sweet classical tune played softly as an array of Aunt Fran's photos arced across the screen, each pausing momentarily in the center before making room for the next. The images arrived in chronological order, changing from black-and-white to color over time. Photos of Aunt Fran as a child, then as an adolescent, a teen, and an adult. With her mother and grandmother. With her sisters. And with me. The shops on Main Street changed along with her as years went by. She held babies that were now grown, many older than me, and those folks would see themselves on the screen and remember how she'd touched their lives from the start. They'd recognize loved ones who'd long passed, homes and businesses that had come and gone. And understand the one thing that has been consistent in this town over the last six-and-a-half decades was my Aunt Fran.

The narration started a few seconds into the slide

show. A collection of community voices, fading in, then out as the next voice began. Charmers reading their own words, from cards and letters they'd sent to Aunt Fran over the years.

"Thank you for your help with the bake sale... for bringing me groceries when I couldn't get out last month...for watching my baby so I could go to work...helping me plan my wedding...daughter's birthday...mother's surprise party. It meant so much...meant everything. Your kindness...generosity...faithfulness to this community...is the reason I stayed...set down roots...have hope again. You... you...you...Fran Swan...have made all the difference. Thank you." I let their voices come together on the final sentiment and felt my eyes sting with the pride I felt each time I watched the piece.

Denise covered her mouth, her eyes glistening. "That's beautiful. How did you put that together so quickly?"

"I had help," I said, spotting many of the people who'd shared their voice in the crowd. "I got the idea from one of Aunt Fran's photo albums. There wasn't a single photo inside, just a thousand Thank You cards she'd kept through the decades. For gifts and acts of service. For listening and for seeing them when they felt invisible. Anything and everything, and I realized, the best way to remind people why Aunt Fran is the right person to lead this community, was to let the community say it themselves. So, I emailed the people from the cards and asked them to leave me a voice mail reading their card. I'd hoped to get three or four willing participants. I got thirty-five." I batted my still stinging eyes. "This town loves Aunt Fran. I need to remember that and stop worrying about Mary Grace and Senator Denver. I know Charm will do the right thing at the polls."

I pressed the pad of my thumb to the corner of my eye, trapping a renegade tear before it wrecked my makeup. "Sorry," I laughed. "I get choked up. I don't think I've ever been so proud to be a Swan."

"As you should," she said. "Your family is lovely."

"What's Senator Denver been up to?" I pried. Mary Grace had been openly over-the-top for the past month, gathering enthusiasm from her supporters, but I'd barely seen Grady's mother-in-law, and that worried me. She was the candidate with all the experience.

Denise sighed. "She's been locked in her study for the past week, collaborating with colleagues in DC to create a last-minute push for votes. She loves to win, and I appreciate her devotion to the cause, but between you and me, I think she'd be happier back in the city, surrounded by hustle, bustle, and political drama. I don't think this is the right place for her. The sad thing is, I think she knows it, but she's a junky on the campaign trail, seeking the adrenaline rush of a victory."

I chewed my lip. "Do you think she'll leave town if she loses?" I asked, hating to think of Aunt Fran not winning the election, but also wanting Denver's grandma to stay, especially considering what he'd been going through lately.

I gave the crowd a quick look, hoping no one was listening to our candid discussion.

A man in an old-timey sailor costume caught my eye from across the room. Large gold buttons lined his navy jacket, and tall black boots met his trousers at the knees. The big hat on his head cast a shadow over his eyes, and a black bandana hid the bottom half of his face, like a bank robber or Old West bad guy. He appeared to be looking directly at me, and a shiver rocked down my spine.

"Look," I said, lifting a finger in the man's direction. "Do you see him? Could he be the one the locals are reporting as a ghost sighting?"

She inched forward, squinting at the sailor in question. "That costume is seriously creepy. And incredibly authentic."

"Do you think he followed me here?" I asked.

The sailor bowed slightly, then turned to leave, swinging a sword onto his shoulder. A crimson stain lined the silver blade, glinting and gruesome beneath the fluorescent store lighting. A moment later, he vanished through the front door.

"Watch Denver," Denise said, clutching her basket tightly in one hand, then giving chase.

I gaped after her.

"Everly!" Denver called, running to catch me around my legs. His pale-gray eyes were a perfect match to his father's, underscored by chubby, ruddy cheeks and a brilliant smile. "Look what Mr. Butters helped me make!" He held up a construction paper pony with a yarn mane, tail, and reins. "If I blow on the tail like this, it moves." Denver blew across the paper, and the yarn fluttered. "Cool, huh?"

"Yeah," I said, no longer able to see Denise or the man with the bloody sword. "Very cool."

"Can I have a cookie now?" he asked. "And some soda?"

"I only made sweet tea and lemonade," I told him, "but yes. Let's get a snack."

Denver led me to the buffet table near the front wall of windows, where I had a good look at the darkened street teeming with folks in costumes. I didn't see anyone dressed as Dorothy or a two-hundred-year-old sailor. I wasn't sure who to worry about more, the man who'd possibly killed Dixie and threatened me, or Denise. I didn't know anything about the possible killer, but Denise was fast, fierce, and likely lethal if necessary. She'd been handpicked by Senator Denver to protect Grady and Denver.

Actually, the more I thought about it, the more I feared for the sailor.

"Hey!" Amelia bounded into view, a willowy woman in her wake. "Everly Swan, I want you to meet Macy Hilliard, my publicist."

Macy smiled and offered me a hand. "It's lovely to meet you. I've heard so many interesting things."

I smiled back, accepting the handshake and hoping my palm wasn't sweaty. "It's great to meet you," I said. "The party seems to be a hit." My gaze moved from

the woman's sincere brown eyes and flawless sandal-
wood skin to the window and street beyond, eager for
Denise's return.

"It is," she agreed. "I'd suggested Amelia launch
in New York, but she insisted we do it here, and I've
got to say she was right. The setting and costumes
alone are going to make great social media material.
Speaking of, your costume is fantastic. Amelia said she
made hers. Don't tell me you did the same."

"No." I dragged my attention back to Macy. "Amelia
was a theatre kid. She can make anything. Costumes,
props, entire sets with enough time and materials. I
bought the pieces for this at a thrift store, then paired
them up. The cape was originally a velvet curtain," I
admitted. "So, technically, I made the cape."

"It's magnificent," she said. "Where'd you learn to
sew?"

"My grandma."

Macy wasn't in costume, but she looked fabulous
in a professional black dress and pearls.

"Have you met Denver?" I asked, moving closer to
the little cowpoke in my charge.

He turned and beamed on cue. "I'm the boy from
the book. Mr. Butters drew me."

Macy crouched and offered him her hand. "Hmm.
I think you're bigger and taller than the pictures."

"That's cause I'm growing like a weed," Denver
said seriously, adding a third cookie to his tiny dessert
plate.

Macy stood with a broad smile. "Charming. Like

everything else in this town." She tilted her head and pressed her shiny red lips together. "I hear you help solve local crimes, and your family's been here since the founding. Is that right?"

Amelia waved to someone over my shoulder. "Correct, and here they are now. The one in black is running for mayor."

Aunt Clara and Aunt Fran arrived with Denise trailing behind.

Denise shook her head, and I breathed easier. She hadn't caught the sailor, but she also hadn't confronted him. No one was injured. Or worse. "He vanished," she whispered, cheeks pink from the brisk autumn air. "I circled the block, but he was gone."

"I'm sure it was nothing to worry about," I said. "It's trick-or-treat tonight, and I probably overreacted, but thank you." I smiled, and Denise patted my back.

"Anytime."

Macy shook my aunts' hands as Amelia introduced them. "I love your costumes," Macy said, admiring my aunts' everyday wear. "They're amazing. So authentic. Turn of the last century?" She narrowed her eyes at the cuffs on Aunt Clara's blouse. "Is that hand stitched?"

Aunt Clara smiled. "My mother made it."

Amelia caught my eye and smiled. My aunts hadn't actually dressed up tonight. They'd come from work in their extremely vintage, but typical everyday wear.

Macy blinked.

Aunt Fran turned pointedly to face me. She took my hands in hers and squeezed them.

"Everything okay?" I asked, a thread of panic coiling in my chest.

"Your commercial is the most amazing thing I've seen in all my years," she said, a slight quiver in her normally steadfast voice. "A tribute like that, to this island and its people, means absolutely everything to me. And I want you to know that whether I win or lose this election, I'll carry the words of that ad in my heart until my very last breath."

My heart expanded proudly, filling up my chest and lodging in my throat. "You know it was supposed to be a tribute to you, right?"

Aunt Clara moved closer, a bright smile lighting her features. "People came into Blessed Bee all afternoon to pledge their support for Fran. They enjoyed seeing images of themselves and their loved ones over the years. They adored that Fran made the island, and not herself, the center of her campaign. And bless whoever is behind the *Town Charmer*, because they've featured your work all day as the main story. The comments are a mile long, and all good as far as I can see."

Bless the *Town Charmer*, indeed. I yanked my phone from my basket for a second time and hurried to the local gossip blog.

"Read the headline," Aunt Clara encouraged.

I waited impatiently for the blog to load, then beamed as I read the headline. "When integrity counts."

Aunt Fran hugged me quickly, then stepped back with her chin held high. "I'm starving. Let's eat."

I excused myself from Amelia, Denise, and Macy, following my aunts to the buffet.

Denver was struggling to add another sweet to his precariously piled plate, so Aunt Fran stepped in to give him a hand.

Aunt Clara turned to me with a little cat-that-ate-the-canary grin. "I hear you have a date with Matt Darning. That ought to be interesting."

Denver froze and turned to stare.

"Nothing official," I said, feeling senselessly guilty.

Denise reached for Denver's shoulders and steered him away from the desserts. "Let's find a table before we drop Miss Everly's treats all over the floor."

Aunt Fran frowned. "I thought you and Grady Hays were an item."

"No," I said. "Not really. And he made that very clear the other night. I told him I understood, and Matt asked me out the next morning."

"Perfect timing," Aunt Clara said. "One door closes; another opens."

Aunt Fran's frown deepened. "Hogwash."

"I like Matt," I said defensively. "He's sweet and kind. And he makes me laugh."

Aunt Clara nodded. "Easy on the eyes too."

Aunt Fran grabbed a plate. "I'd like to have a word or two with that detective. The oaf must've broken your heart with that nonsense. It's obvious how much you two mean to each other."

"Do not—" I began before Aunt Clara cut me off.

"I suppose it's for the best," she interjected.

"Detective Hays is clearly your soul mate, and given our curse, that wouldn't have ended well for him. He has a son to raise," she added in a whisper. "So, this is better."

Aunt Fran frowned. "I suppose that's right."

I grabbed a plate and got in line. It was going to take a lot of chocolate to help me forget she'd just said all of that.

The door to Charming Reads opened near the end of the buffet, and Burton walked inside.

Aunt Clara straightened. "What on earth is he doing here?"

I thought of the disappearing sailor and the way Burton kept turning up in my path. "I think he's looking for a book." And I was pretty sure he thought I had it.

The door opened again while we were staring, and Aunt Clara's friend, Tony, walked in.

"Oh!" she peeped. "Excuse me." She passed me her plate and hurried in his direction.

Aunt Fran rolled her eyes.

"What's going on with them?" I asked, watching in amusement as Aunt Clara bebopped to his side.

Aunt Fran bit into a cookie. "I don't like him."

"Why?" He seemed nice enough to me. How bad could a guy who loved his grandson and wore his jeans around his navel really be?

"He's a chronic dater. Apparently, he can't stand to be alone. He even went out with Dixie Wetherill for goodness' sakes." She pulled her lips to one side. "I wouldn't spend time with a man who doesn't like his own company, and I don't trust anyone with such bad taste in women."

I gaped. "Tony dated Dixie?" Why hadn't anyone mentioned that to me sooner? Did it matter?

A moment later, Finn stepped into the store, scanning the room, then headed toward his grandpa and Aunt Clara.

My gaze swung from Burton to Tony and Finn. All three men had various personal relationships with Dixie. All were in Charm the night she'd died.

And all had appeared in Amelia's bookstore a short time after I'd been visited by a sailor with a bloody sword.

CHAPTER
EIGHTEEN

Matt stopped in to see me on his lunch break the next day. This time, to arrange our date. Seven hours later, I was on my third glass of iced tea and stress sweating. The idea of going out with Matt at some point in the future had been heartwarming. The idea of going out with him tonight was terrifying, and I was taking it out on Lou.

"What do you think?" I asked, balancing poorly on one foot, then the other, as the wind worked on wrecking my hair. "Cute canvas sneaker, or"—I shifted, switching feet to hide the sneaker and reveal option two—"simple black flat?"

Lou stared at me, focused on my feet as I repeated the process.

"Come on," I begged. "This is the last thing I'll bother you about tonight, I promise, but you've got to help me."

So far, I'd shown him hairstyle photos on my phone, roughly every outfit in my wardrobe, and six necklaces. He'd provided a definitive "Caw!" eventually, for each set of choices, but he was holding out on me with the shoes. I was beginning to wonder if the other caws had been to state his preference or send me away, because I always left afterward.

"The sneaker is more comfortable, but the ballet flat is fancier," I explained. Both shoes coordinated perfectly with my sleeveless, teal silk blouse and black dress pants. So, there was no way I could decide.

Maggie trotted onto the deck through the open sliding glass door. She moved in close and rubbed her face against the leg with the black flat.

"This one?" I asked, thrilled by her weigh in. "Are you sure, because I don't know what we're doing tonight, and there might be a lot of walking."

"Caw!" Lou flapped his mighty wings without going anywhere.

Maggie bumped me again, purring this time. She rubbed the length of her fluffy body along my right leg then flopped across the shoe, rolling onto her back and stretching her tiny paws into the air.

"Caw!"

I laughed. "Okay. Okay. I guess you're sure. Simple black flat it is." I crouched to stroke her fur and give her a thorough pet. "Thank you, too, Lou," I said, feeling a little bad that she'd stolen his show. Though, admittedly, he hadn't been much help on the footwear.

I went inside and toed off the sneaker. Maggie followed. I slipped into the second black flat and checked the cat bowls for fresh food and water. "Looks like you have everything you need, so I'm going downstairs to puff into a paper bag and try not to pass out before Matt arrives."

I grabbed my bag with a wallet, phone, and keys, then locked the door to my private staircase when I entered the foyer.

Matt rapped on the door before I finished twisting the key.

"You're early," I said, opening the front door to greet him.

He smiled, and I was momentarily stunned at his appearance. He'd traded the usual navy EMT uniform for nicely fitting khaki pants and a long-sleeve, blue dress shirt he'd unbuttoned at the cuffs and rolled up his forearms. His sandy hair looked soft and mussed from the wind. His eyes twinkled as he took me in. "I was nervous, and I didn't want to be late," he said, his nose wrinkling immediately. "That didn't sound very manly."

I lifted a palm, smiling widely back. "It sounded honest, and I like honest."

He shook the tension from his shoulders. "Good, because I am excellent at that skill."

A laugh bubbled from my chest. "Perfect." I lifted my arms out at my sides, unsure what to do next. "Can I get you something before we go?"

He wagged a finger at me. "I know you love to serve, but tonight, I want to give you a break."

I pulled my lips to the side, fighting a smile. I did love to serve, but I absolutely adored the sound of a break. "Well then." I shouldered my bag and stepped onto the porch, locking up behind us. "Where to?"

Matt walked me to the passenger door of his Jeep Wrangler, then offered me a hand climbing inside. "How do you feel about fancy, candlelight charity events and seaside museums?"

My heart skipped. He'd said nearly all my favorite words in one sentence. "Love them. Why?"

He grinned and shut the door, then rounded the hood and climbed behind the wheel. "I had a feeling." He gunned the engine to life and pointed us out of town. "It's going to be a nice night, and there's a little shindig going on at the Roanoke Island Festival Park in Manteo."

I squelched a squeal, doing my best to be cool. "How on earth did you get tickets to that? I've always wanted to go, but they sell out so fast, it's impossible, unless you belong to one of the groups that sponsor it or make a blood oath to Neptune."

He slid his eyes my way. "I didn't think anyone knew about my deal with Neptune."

I laughed, and whatever tension had remained in me fell away. "It's what I do," I said. "I make tea and know things."

Matt's grin widened. "I'm a friend of the museum, so I volunteer from time to time, and I helped the curator's wife a few years ago when she went into pre-term labor with their twins. The family still sends me holiday cards. I have a lifetime membership to the park and an open invitation to this event. I never miss it."

"I guess saving lives really does pay."

He looked at me, eyes alight once more. "It really does."

Heat crept over my cheeks, and I glanced away, admiring the view from my window. A velvet sky arched overhead, a billion stars visible without obstruction in the inky night, and little towns blurred past as we jetted along the highway connecting the islands.

"Tell me something I don't know about you," Matt said. "Anything you want, then I'll do the same."

I thought about the question a minute, then rolled my head against the seat back to face him. "I went to culinary school in Kentucky for a few years, then dropped out a semester before graduation." I wasn't sure why that bit of trivia had come to mind, but it felt suddenly important, paramount even. It had been a turning point for me, and a catalyst for the life I had now.

"That's when you came back to Charm, right?"

"Yeah. I was dating Wyatt, but that wasn't working, then I lost my grandma, and I realized it was time I came home."

"I'm glad you did," Matt said. "And I'm sorry about your grandma."

"Thanks."

"I'm not sorry you and Wyatt didn't work out," he added, smiling to lighten the mood. "He's a good guy, but you know."

I laughed. "Tonight probably wouldn't be as much fun if we had to bring him."

Matt lifted a hand from the steering wheel. "Exactly."

"Okay. Your turn."

Matt chewed his lip and narrowed his eyes at the road. "I'm the youngest of five siblings. Raised by a single mom and four older sisters."

I laughed. "That explains a lot."

He smiled. "Should I ask what that means or be glad I don't know?"

"It means you're compassionate and kind," I said, ticking attributes off on my fingers. "Thoughtful and attentive. You made a career out of caring for people. All things traditionally associated with moms."

"You mean with women." He laughed. "It's okay, you can say it."

"I think it's nice." I stared at his cheek until he looked my way again. "You should thank them. They raised the perfect gentleman." Probably the perfect spouse, father, and friend as well.

He nodded. "All right. Your turn."

"I changed my outfit eleven times tonight," I said. "I spent longer getting ready than I will ever admit, and I'm still not sure I chose the right things. Though, if I didn't, I blame Maggie and Lou."

Matt laughed. "That's your cat and a seagull, right?"

"Yes, and they weren't as helpful as you'd think."

He laughed again. "You have an interesting life, Swan."

"I do," I said. "And I'm having a lovely time on this date."

Matt slowed to take the exit to Roanoke Island, glancing at me as we turned. "Just wait until we actually get there."

He was right.

I'd never been to Festival Park at night, and my jaw dropped when he turned onto the entrance road. The entire property seemed to be lined in tiki torches or draped in twinkle lights. People in fancy attire walked the grounds and cobblestone paths, carrying wine glasses and small plates with cheeses and hors d'oeuvres.

I gave my outfit a long look as Matt settled the engine of his Jeep.

"Have I told you I think you look beautiful?" he asked.

"No." The word arrived more breathlessly than intended, and I mentally thanked the cat for not letting me wear sneakers.

I climbed out and linked my arm with Matt's as we explored the grounds. The buffet was extravagant. The views, astounding. And the clusters of guests chattered about all my favorite things. Island history, delicious foods, and raising money to repair hurricane damage throughout the area.

Matt and I sipped wine and enjoyed finger foods from a table overlooking the sea. We took silly selfies and traded stories about our lives before we'd met, and I liked everything I learned. Not surprisingly, Matt had been a semi-professional surfer once. I'd seen him surf, and he was good; plus, he had that look about him, kind of wild and free beneath the uniform and uber-serious job. A career he'd moved into after witnessing a shark attack at a surf competition. The experience had curbed his enthusiasm for the sport and ignited his interest in emergency rescues.

I told him about my life in Charm, past and present, and he marveled at my determination to renovate a six-thousand-square-foot Victorian home on my own. "In my defense, the previous owner did most of the work on the first floor before I got there," I said, polishing off the last bite of my manchego and tomato crustini.

He rolled his eyes and laughed. "Yes, and you've only turned the space into a successful iced tea shop. Nothing amazing about that."

"I had a lot of help and encouragement from my aunts. And plenty of luck."

The lights flashed off and on in the distance, like a theatre announcing intermission's end.

"What's happening?" I asked.

Matt moved to my side and offered a hand. "Tour time."

I curled my fingers around his and let him lead me to the main building. A man in a navy jacket and tie welcomed us all to the special charity event, then invited us to begin a short stroll through history. He winked at Matt, then led us inside.

We moved casually through exhibits on the Roanoke Voyagers, the Civil War, and Freeman's Colony before stopping at a display on eighteenth-century pirates.

The group leader began his speech, and I checked the area for signs of danger. An icky sensation had crawled across my skin somewhere between the discussion of Virginia Dare's birth and the disappearance of her colony. I was familiar with the story but couldn't seem to shake the heebie-jeebies.

Virginia was the first English child born in the New World, right here on Roanoke Island, and possibly the area's first unsolved mystery. Virginia's grandfather, John White, returned to England for additional supplies a few days after her birth, planning to be back as soon as possible. But circumstances delayed him by three years, and when he arrived, the entire colony of Roanoke had vanished. The word CROATOAN, carved into a tree near the water's edge, was the only clue left behind. White searched, but never found his granddaughter or any of the missing colonists.

A light beneath a nearby doorway caught my attention, and I paused to consider who else was in the building tonight.

Matt popped up before me, wearing a child's pirate hat and eye patch from the cardboard treasure chest. He brandished a plastic hook in one hand. "Argh!"

"Ah!" I gasped, then lost my footing as I broke into laughter.

Thankfully, Matt caught me before I toppled and took out a pamphlet display.

I waved apologies to the group while I regained my composure and pressed a palm to Matt's chest for support.

He covered my hand with his. "Sorry." He chuckled softly near my ear. "I thought you saw me coming. I'd hoped to make you laugh, not scare you half to death." He wound his opposite arm around my back and pulled me against him in an apologetic embrace.

I pressed my cheek to his shirt, still grinning at my silliness. As if someone would try to hurt me, here, now, with a dozen witnesses at my side. "I'm clearly on edge. I didn't realize how much."

"Understandable," he whispered. "I really am sorry. I wasn't thinking about the week you've had."

I tilted my head back, peering up at his sincere, blue eyes.

The door across from us opened, and I flinched.

Matt rubbed my back with another soft laugh.

Two men looked out from inside the small office. One man I didn't recognize—and Grady.

"Oh," Matt said. "I was not expecting that. Do you think he heard you scream?"

Grady's eyes locked with mine, then swept up to Matt's face before sliding back to me. His expression flattened, and he closed the door.

The group shuffled forward, their fearless leader carrying determinedly on despite my outburst.

Matt released me. "I didn't realize he was here."

I shrugged, hoping for a casual look while my insides churned themselves into butter. "It's fine. He's probably working, and we're enjoying a lovely night." I forced my eyes to meet Matt's, refusing to look in the direction of the door.

Matt watched me, evaluating. "I probably should've asked before inviting you out tonight, but are you seeing Detective Hays?"

I opened my mouth. No sounds came out.

Matt shook his head. "Right. Sorry. You wouldn't have said yes to me if you were seeing someone. That was just a really intense death stare he gave me. We should probably talk about that."

I didn't know if Matt thought he and I should discuss Grady's angry face, or if he'd meant that he and Grady should discuss it, but either way, I felt certain it was a bad idea. "No need." I smiled. "Grady's like that. Intense. Focused. I'm sure the look on his face had nothing to do with us."

Matt gave the closed door another look. "All right." he smiled. "You know him better."

I wasn't sure what to say. Lately, I didn't feel as if I knew Grady at all. "So, what's next?" I asked, determined to salvage a perfectly lovely night. "I hope you know, because the group seems to be getting away from us."

Matt raised my hand and curved it over his elbow, then began to walk once more. "It's time for that dinner I promised you."

"Dinner?" I asked, genuinely surprised. "What was that colossal buffet outside?"

"Appetizers."

"This place is like heaven."

We strolled companionably to the Welcome Center's atrium, where the normally plain rotunda had been transformed into an intimate dining area. Collections of small, white pumpkins and pillar candles on mirrors centered every crimson tablecloth. A string quartet played at one side of the space, while waitstaff in traditional livery stood ready to serve at the other. Embossed, white place cards were tucked into glass bottles, filled partially with sand and a few colorful shells.

I gaped at the beauty and elegance of it all as Matt led me toward a small table at the window with a perfect view of the darkened sea.

"You like it?"

"It's amazing," I said, heart soaring as excitement filled me from toes to nose. "Everything about this is perfect." I inhaled deeply, attempting to name the main course by scent alone. "I can't believe you get to do this every year."

"I do," he said proudly as we arrived at our seats. "I think this year is my favorite so far." He checked the names inside the bottles, then smiled. "Yep. This is us. I requested this table, because I know how much you love to watch the waves." He gripped the stately mahogany chair, dragging it out for me to sit.

My heart stopped at the sight of a dagger jammed into the wood.

Two words carved menacingly below.

Final Warning.

CHAPTER

NINETEEN

Dinner was moved to another location in the building while Manteo law enforcement officers questioned event guests and staff. Matt and I stayed behind, lingering awkwardly in the atrium with Grady, while several officers processed the scene. He had his game face on as he gave us the third degree about why we were late to be seated, and why Matt had chosen a table so far away from the others.

Matt held his own, unfazed by Grady's cop face and no-nonsense disposition. Matt had seen him in action before, at other crime scenes, but this was the first time he'd been on the business end of Grady's determined detective routine. Bonus points to Matt because I hated when Grady got like this. I understood the reasoning, but squirmed every time, nonetheless.

Grady's jaw clenched, and a vein in his head bulged as my date continuously offered me comfort. A hand on mine, the gentle brush of his palm on my back. Matt kept me close and tended to my rattled nerves without regard or care for Grady's clear irritation. A fact that both endeared and panicked me. I didn't enjoy feeling like a victim, in need of security and comfort, but it was nice to know I wasn't alone.

I bit my lip against the building tears. It was only a matter of time before the emotions bubbling inside me reached my lids and spilled over onto my cheeks. I pressed the pads of my forefingers against the corners of my eyes to push back the tears. I hated to be seen crying, and this week was officially too much. After everything else I'd been through, my psychotic stalker had ruined my perfectly lovely date, along with several dozen others' night as well.

A camera flash startled me out of my head, and I blinked at the officer taking professional pictures of the crime scene.

"Excuse me," I said softly to Matt, needing to get away. "I'll only be a minute." I tipped my head toward the sign for the ladies' room.

"I'll come with you," he said, catching my hand in his, anchoring me in place. "Are we done here?" he asked Grady, politely, protectively.

Grady nodded.

"Then I'm going to take her home. I'm available anytime if you need anything else."

Grady's gaze slid to our joined hands before he turned away. "I'll be in touch."

Matt waited outside the ladies' room for me to pull myself together. Then, we rode back to Charm in silence. I sulked and cringed internally over the fact that my current drama had ruined our evening and an entire charity event. And I imagined Matt was plotting how quickly he could drop me off and escape my world of doom and gloom.

I breathed a little easier when the familiar streets of home came into view, ready to be done with this night.

"Care if I make a quick stop?" Matt asked, pulling into an empty space outside Sandy's Sweet Shack, Charm's most popular ice cream parlor.

"Okay," I said, unsure what was happening.

He jumped out and lifted a finger, indicating he'd be only a minute, then he ran inside. I barely had time to worry about being abducted before he returned, handing me a white, logoed bag across the space inside his Jeep. "Two pints of double chocolate brownie fudge chunk. One jar of hot fudge, already warmed, maraschino cherries, and a can of whipped cream. He was out of chocolate jimmies. I asked."

I stared at the bag as he reversed from the spot and headed for my home. "You bought ice cream?" I asked dumbly, attempting to catch up and connect the sweet treat to a night of upheaval.

"We missed dessert," he said smoothly. "Technically, we also missed dinner, but getting straight to the sugar seems like the right move here. I called Sandy and placed the order while you ran into the ladies' room."

I hugged the bag to my chest, warming impossibly further to Matt for the gesture. "I might be able to find some jimmies."

Matt carried the bag while I punched the keycode into my front door and turned on the lights in my café. Instead of choosing a table, he went to the gray wicker love seat and arranged the bag's contents on the coffee table before it while I snagged a shaker of chocolate jimmies from my cupboard. He passed me a pint of ice cream and plastic spoon when I arrived.

"Should I get bowls?" I asked. "Napkins? Drinks? Maybe bottled water?"

"Nope." Matt motioned for me to sit, then he headed to my refrigerator. "I'll get the water, and we can eat ice cream from the containers. It tastes better than way." He grabbed two bottles and headed back to me.

I smiled. "How are you single?" The words popped into my mind and out of my mouth before I could stop them.

He cracked the lid off his pint. "My mom and Nana keep asking me the same question."

I laughed. "Your sisters don't ask?"

"My sisters know too much," he teased. He opened the warm fudge and poured a layer over his ice cream, then offered the same to me. I accepted. "What about you? Why haven't you dated anyone since Wyatt?"

I pushed a spoonful of ice cream into my mouth to buy me some time, then accidentally moaned at the delicious intensity of flavor.

"Right?" Matt shook the can of whipped cream then filled the newly made hole in my ice cream with it. "I could do this every night."

"Then I wouldn't be the only one whose pants

don't fit," I said, spooning the whipped cream into my mouth.

Matt's eyebrows rose. "Not to overstep, but I think your pants fit just right."

I laughed again and felt the tension release down to my toes.

"Why aren't you dating anyone?" he asked again, circling back to the question I thought I'd avoided.

I spread a puddle of fudge across the top of my dessert with a pink plastic spoon. "At first, I was still hurting from Wyatt's rejection, I guess. After that…" I'd met Grady. "I don't know."

"Fair enough." Matt distributed the fudge and whipped cream, then added jimmies. He took a few more bites before speaking again. "You want to talk about why someone carved a warning into your chair?"

My heart sank at the reminder. "It's a mystery," I said. "I didn't even know I was going there until I was on my way, but somehow someone did."

"I called to list you as my plus-one yesterday," Matt said. "It could be my fault."

"No." I shook my head. "The only person responsible for what happened tonight is the person who did it." Or at least that was what Wyatt and Grady told me regularly when I assumed guilt I didn't deserve. "Grady was there when it happened. Maybe whoever did this had been following him to keep tabs on the investigation. Then got upset when they saw me there too."

Matt bobbed his head. "That makes sense.

Following the investigation would keep the criminal in the loop. Like listening to a police scanner for updates, only better. The killer would know if the police get too close." He turned on his cushion, facing me, and stretched an arm across the back of the love seat. "Detective Hays said you've had other threats since Ms. Wetherill's death. Why?"

I released a heavy breath, and the dessert turned to sawdust on my tongue. "Someone's looking for a map and thinks I have it. I don't."

"Any idea who?"

"Maybe." Burton and his wife, Aubrey, came immediately to mind, and I hadn't discounted any member of Dixie's unrecorded history society, including Tony and Finn. Though I wasn't sure what either of those men would want with one of Dixie's maps. Couldn't the bookstore just order whatever they needed? And hadn't Finn been working with Dixie, meaning he had access to whatever material she did? I blew out a breath. Too many questions. Not enough answers. "The weirdest part is that whoever it is wants me to believe the ghost of James Hudson is the one asking."

"The British sailor who beheaded Mourning Mable?" He looked simultaneously amused and horrified. Exactly the way I felt. "Dixie was dressed as Mable when she died."

"Yep." I set my dessert onto the table. "And the curator seemed to think the dagger in my chair tonight was part of the museum's collection."

Matt put his ice cream down too. "Creepy." He looked around us, through the windows, to the darkened sea. "Aren't you uncomfortable here? All alone in this big old house with someone threatening you?"

"Not really," I said. I knew from experience that someone wishing me harm could reach me anywhere, even on Main Street in broad daylight. There was no hiding from a killer with an agenda. "I have Maggie and Lou," I reminded him. "I think Lou's already saved my life once, so that helps."

I watched Matt's genuine and accepting expression. If I said a bird saved my life, then a bird saved my life. He was all in. No condescension. No argument.

"Caw!" Lou thumped against the patio door.

We jumped as the bird screamed from the deck. He hadn't been there a minute ago, and Matt looked as if he might've wet his pants.

"He probably wants shrimp," I said. "I usually give him something before I go to bed."

Matt laughed, his attention stuck to the silhouette of Lou on my deck.

Lou's wings were spread. His beak opened wide. "Caw! Caw!"

My heart sank a bit as I realized what had to happen next. "I had a great time tonight, despite the whole part where we had to call the police."

"Me too." He turned to smile at me, giving me his full attention once more.

"We probably shouldn't see each other again." I lifted then dropped a hand onto my lap. "My life is kind of bananas right now. No one else should have to deal with that. It's a bad time to try to get to know me. I'm not usually this big of a mess, and my attention is seriously divided. You deserve more than that."

Matt watched me, seeming to consider my words. "I understand, so this is going to sound strange. Do you have a date to the Harvest Ball?"

"No," I answered automatically, confused by the drastic change of subject. "Why?"

"How about this," he began. "Why not let me take you to the ball as a friend. Think of it as a safe way for you to not miss out on something you love, and if we have another great time together, that's just icing."

I smiled. "Like the buddy system?"

"Exactly," Matt said. "No expectations."

"I'd like that."

❧

Denise arrived early for work the next morning. She dropped her purse behind the counter and tied an apron around her middle while watching me as if I might explode. "Well?" she said. "What happened last night? Grady came home grumpier than usual, and your name was thrown around a lot in his office. It was the first time in a while Denver slept through the night, and Grady missed the opportunity for a few consecutive hours of rest. I assume you had a fight or were threatened again?"

I puffed air into my wildly overgrown bangs, then

tucked them into my hair. "I ran into Grady last night at a charity event in Manteo. Someone carved a threat into my dinner chair."

"Yikes." Her sharp gaze glided over me, likely in search of injury. "What did the threat say?"

I chewed the insides of my cheeks, working up the nerve to repeat it. "Final warning."

"Are you okay?" She moved closer, as if she might hug me, but stopped short. Creases gathered between her bright blue eyes. "When did that happen?"

"Around eight. The event was supposed to last until midnight and end with fireworks. Instead, it ended before dinner, with a heaping helping of my drama. The dining room became a crime scene. They had to move the entire meal. It was a mess."

Denise considered that a minute. "Grady was home kind of early. He usually stays with you a little while after these things. Making sure you're okay. Are you two fighting?"

"Matt drove me home," I said, feeling strangely uncomfortable. "He invited me to the event, and Grady was there when we arrived." That reminded me. "We saw Grady talking to someone in a suit. Any idea why he was at the museum?"

Denise started to shake her head, then stopped. "Wait. Actually, yes. I heard him on the phone when I went to get him for Denver's counseling session. He was going to talk to someone about the sword and flag piece left on your porch. It sounded as if the items were reported missing from somewhere. He wanted to see if his evidence was what the person on the other end of the line was looking for."

"That makes sense," I said. "Grady and I talked about reaching out to local museums a few days ago, and the curator from last night thought the dagger in my chair was from their collection. I wonder what he learned about the sword." I wished I could pick up the phone and call Grady, like I used to, but my pride had put her foot down on that.

Denise moved into her morning routine, prepping the shop to open. "I'm not sure. He never talks to me about his cases or anything personal, other than Denver."

"How is Denver?" I asked. "You said he had a good night?"

"Yeah. He's doing better all the time. He's a tough kid," she said, the glow of pride in her eyes.

"Well, he gets the strength honestly, and he has a powerhouse support system, so I'm not surprised."

She smiled, then cast me a curious look. "How'd your date handle the threat to your life?"

"He invited me to the Harvest Ball."

Her smile tightened. "Well, I suppose whatever is meant to be will be. No sense fighting it in this town."

I wasn't sure what that was supposed to mean, exactly, but I hated it.

CHAPTER
TWENTY

Senator Denver came for Denise at three sharp. She wanted to go with the family to her grandson's after-school counseling session. I was thankful anytime I saw the senator taking a personal interest in Denver. She was stern and standoffish, but she was also his mother's mother, and with Amy gone, Denver needed her more than she realized. It wasn't my place to say so, but I thought it frequently, and I sent them off with snacks for the waiting room. She handed me a clicker pen from her campaign swag in return.

I smiled politely and waved as they headed out. I was certain the senator didn't like me, but I was in no mood to try to convince her otherwise. And since Grady had pushed me away, I couldn't help feeling I no longer had a pony in that show.

Business slowed as usual around dinnertime, and I popped a pair of rum cakes in the oven then grabbed my laptop. I wanted to see what the gossip blog had to say about the upcoming election and commercial I'd made for Fran. Or if there had been any new updates on the Dixie Wetherill murder.

The mayoral election was the top story, and the ad wars were officially underway. After a thick paragraph about each candidate—Aunt Fran, Mary Grace, and Senator Denver—there were three videos waiting to be played.

I puzzled at the sight of a third. Had Mary Grace made a second commercial, or had the senator joined in on the fun? If she had made a video, I could only hope she'd been kinder to Aunt Fran than Mary Grace had been.

I clicked to play the video, and Senator Denver appeared outside the Capitol Building in DC. She spoke to a hoard of gathered press while the voiceover ran down a list of her stats, as if she were a professional ball player. Advanced degrees, retired military, having risen rapidly through the ranks, a career in local, then state politics, and finally, a seat at the big table as a U.S. Senator.

I shook my head at the screen. It was a powerful political ad, if she wanted to stay in DC, but it was all wrong for Charm, which said everything. And everyone who saw it would know. She didn't understand this place or the people. She could've shown us images of her home here, her relationship with her son-in-law, the local detective, or her precious grandson. Maybe some footage of her adjustment after big-city living. Watching dolphins and wild horses or just shopping local. Instead, she'd focused on her large-scale accomplishments that had nothing to do with Charm. Unfortunately for her, the voters lived here. And they needed a mayor who focused on them.

The comments for my ad were all lovely, though most were more words of nostalgia rather than commentary on the ad itself. I didn't mind. I'd made them feel good, and voters would associate those warm feelings with Aunt Fran at the polls.

Comments on Mary Grace's commercial were more about when her hair had gotten so big, and if her eyelashes were real. No one seemed to take the bait on Aunt Fran as the Grim Reaper, in the comments anyway. There was no way to know what folks were saying privately, and it worried me the ugly image might stay in some folks' minds, especially those who were too young or new to the island to have connected with my ad.

I scrolled on, searching new posts for information on the murder investigation. There wasn't any coverage of the incident in Manteo last night, or Dixie's death, but there was an article recapping Sandman sightings near my home, along with speculation that I had somehow provoked James Hudson and disturbed his eternal slumber. I resisted the urge to leave a comment on the complete idiocy of the premise, then scrolled farther, skimming a large article about the Harvest Ball I still needed to pick a dress for.

Procrastinating a wardrobe choice, I opened a new tab and went to the website where Burton claimed he and Dixie frequently shopped. BookYourBid.com looked a lot like eBay, with fewer bells and whistles. The color scheme was sepia, and the images were old timey. I selected the tab for Antique Books and Documents from my choices on the top banner, then scanned the current auction for signs of the book Burton was hunting. I didn't have any luck.

I moved on to checking the other tabs and various content before stumbling upon a list of previous auctions. I searched for the username Burton claimed Dixie had used: Island_Historian48. The results were bountiful. In fact, the only thing longer than her list of auction wins was her list of auction sales. Apparently, Dixie had sold a lot of books on this site, and she'd seemed to turn a lot of her buys around at a profit. A review of her star-rating and general activity showed she was notorious for side deals and swooping in at the last minute to bid over someone who'd never seen her coming. Exactly what she'd done to Burton.

Her behavior seemed like the sort that could tick off a serious collector. And I wondered again how mad Burton was about his particular loss.

Additional searches revealed that many of the books Dixie purchased contained maps of the islands. She'd also made a number of map purchases. Though it didn't seem as if she'd sold the maps. Only books.

I returned to her profile and skimmed her recent activity. She had a lot of positive reviews from buyers who'd gotten what they'd bought from her quickly and without damage. Others complained about her jumping in last-minute to outbid them on something they'd been sure was theirs.

Someone by the username The_Collector1800 had been more than a little upset. The account's profile picture was a ship inside a bottle, and The_Collector1800 had taken issue with Dixie over a map. The exchange was brief, but The_Collector1800 was clearly heated.

The_Collector1800: That map was mine.
Island_Historian48:
The_Collector1800: You should hand it over, but I'm willing to buy it from you.
Island_Historian48:
The_Collector1800: How much will it take?
Island_Historian48:
The_Collector1800: ????
Island_Historian48:
The_Collector1800: ANSWER ME
Island_Historian48: No.
The_Collector1800: Do the right thing. You don't need any more enemies on this site. That map is mine and you know it.
Island_Historian48:
The_Collector1800: Final. Warning.

My heart stopped on the last two words. The same words that had been carved into my chair. Common words, yes, but another heavy coincidence.

I took screen shots of the conversation in case it somehow disappeared, then sent the link to Grady in a text. He could make of it what he wanted, but I couldn't help wondering if that argument had been the catalyst for Dixie's demise.

I clicked on the profile for The_Collector1800 and read his bio. "A passionate historian and fervent collector." It didn't get much more generic than that on a site like this.

I searched for Burton next but didn't find him. He wasn't listed as himself, and I didn't know his username. I could only hope it wasn't The_Collector1800. Then again, maybe that would be better. *The devil you know*, I thought. But was it really better to know he was a murderer on the loose? Or to not have a clue who was after me?

Both options gave me goose bumps, so I closed the shop and went upstairs.

I flopped onto my couch, then reached for the manilla envelope of photos Grady had given me the night he'd dumped me. I rolled onto my side and dragged the coffee table closer, too exhausted to get up.

I lined the images up like a floor plan, placing the rooms in order on each floor. I wanted to restore as much of my home as possible to its original grandeur and charm, with a dash of personal flair, much like my approach to family recipes. But first, I needed to know what the original look had been. Unfortunately, my home seemed to be one of very few examples of Victorian architecture on the island, so I had nothing specific to go by. Until now.

Grady hadn't provided a photo of every room, and I

didn't recognize the spaces in a couple of pictures, but I was happy with what I had and did my best to make sense of it all. I used windows and doorways, arches and ceilings, to identify the various images by structural things that didn't change the way the décor had over time. He'd included a three pack of photocopied floor plans, showing the original blueprints as well.

I marveled at all of it, vowing to return the floors and woodwork to their former glory while promising to never install new wallpaper. I made mental notes to buy a stained-glass window for the first-floor bathroom and imagined the former ballroom filled with tables in a café expansion. I'd nearly finished the floors and baseboards in that room already. The wallpaper was a beast, but I was tenacious, and my steamer was slowly doing the trick. I'd finish that job eventually, but for now, I wanted to spend some time on my personal space.

My gaze dropped to the baseboard beside my built-in bookcase. It didn't look so bad today. I could barely see the minor misalignment in the baseboard. Maybe Grady was right. No one would notice such a small problem unless I pointed it out, which I wouldn't do. Funny how things looked so much better with a little time. I could've sworn the crack was a much bigger deal when it happened.

Maybe the bookcase had shifted back on its own, or all Grady's pulling had made a difference. Or maybe I just had a clearer head tonight.

As long as there wasn't any hidden structural damage caused by the shift, I was happy.

I went back to the photos, trying not to think about what I'd wear to the Harvest Ball, and also thinking it might be fun to dress up for work tomorrow. A sort of precursor to the ball, guaranteed to get customers pumped up for the big event.

I ran my finger over a black-and-white image of a woman on my front porch. The backside of the image had faded blue ink on a white label. Magnolia Bane. I inhaled sharply, realizing I'd never seen a photo of Magnolia before. I'd assumed she was statuesque and blond, but she wasn't. She was a brunette like me, with the lion's share of curves, and her gown clung to them from chest to navel before falling in long waves to her ankles. Her lips were cocked in a sneaky grin, and there was mischief in her eyes. I supposed that was right. She'd snagged the love of a wealthy married man, and he'd built her a mansion to keep her. I certainly didn't approve of the behavior, but I could understand the choice. Young women in that time had very little power, but Magnolia had found some and used it.

I squinted at her features, and another notion sank in. Despite the generations between us and her being only a cousin, not a Swan, our resemblance was uncanny. Looking at her so intently suddenly felt intimate. As did the fact that I lived in her home, with my inherited version of her face. I thought of her throwing herself from the widow's walk, and the image became violently real. Until then, it had seemed like only a story. Something Aunt Clara and her unrecorded history society would tell to warn girls away from older men.

I fell asleep thinking of her and the heartbreak it must've taken to do what she did. I couldn't imagine that kind of guilt, shame, or desperation, and I hoped I never would. I was infinitely sorry that she had.

CHAPTER

TWENTY-ONE

I woke nearly ten hours later, feeling like I could take on the world. I hadn't expected to conk out on the couch at eight o'clock, but apparently, exhaustion wins all battles. One minute I was considering texting Grady again to see if he got my message about the heated conversation on the book auction site, and the next minute, the sun was shining in my eyes through my sliding glass doors.

I thought of the perfect thing to wear to work while my coffee brewed, then darted up another flight of steps to the third floor to retrieve it. Aunt Clara had left an old steamer trunk of clothes at my place last year while I'd been filming a video for her. She'd needed multiple wardrobe changes, depicting various styles through the years, and had brought a mass of options.

My third floor was smaller than the other two floors and packed as tightly as the carriage house with things from previous owners. Thankfully, the trunk was right where I'd left it, at the front of the rest. I'd planned to return the trunk to Aunt Clara when I got around to sorting and organizing, but that day had yet to come.

I chose a cream-colored gown that reminded me of the one Magnolia had worn in the photograph of her on my porch. *Her porch*, I corrected internally, then puzzled. *Our porch?* The short sleeves had a bit of poof to them, and the empire waist was flattering on my middle. The square neckline was modest but comfortable. I pinned my wild curls into an updo befitting the dress's style and era.

I bounded downstairs several minutes later and opened the front door for Denise when she arrived. She whistled when she saw me.

Business was slow, as expected. Most Charmers were focused on the Harvest Ball happening later tonight and had stayed home to prepare. Denise handled the customers that made it in, then left early when people stopped coming all together.

I spent the day writing out everything I knew about Dixie and her death, as well as chronicling my multiple threats, by hand. I could type faster than I could write, but there was something therapeutic about seeing the information in my personal script.

I flipped back and forth between the numerous pages I'd filled, comparing and contrasting details, then creating a timeline.

It was highly possible that none of the people I'd listed as suspects had anything to do with Dixie's murder or my threats; but working through what I knew helped me feel like less of a sitting duck. It bothered me that Aubrey had muttered about wanting to knock Dixie's head off on the night she was murdered. She probably hadn't realized I'd heard her as she stormed past Aunt Clara's dressing room in search of Dixie, but I had. She was the first on the scene of Dixie's murder, after Aunt Clara and I, and she'd handed me a bloody candelabra while wearing gloves. She was at the Society's Kitty Hawk location the same night Dixie's office was ransacked, and she was looking for Dixie right before the ghost walk began. Could she have found her and lashed out? Perhaps doing something she could never take back? Maybe even tearing up Dixie's office in search of the book Burton wanted? I couldn't help wondering how she'd look in an old sailor's costume with a bloody sword on her shoulder.

Too short. I felt my train of thought come to a screeching halt. *The sailor couldn't have been her.*

What did that mean for my suspect list? Something? Nothing? Could I be sure the creepy sailor at the book launch had anything to do with my stalker situation?

The seashell wind chimes jingled, and I started. "Welcome to Sun, Sand, and Tea," I called, tense to my marrow.

Finn appeared, peeking cautiously around the corner from the foyer into the shop. "Hello." He was in a plaid shirt and tie, khaki pants, and boat shoes again. This time with a navy blazer folded neatly over his arm.

"Come in," I said, motioning him to the counter.

He cast his gaze around the café. Sunlight streamed through the windows, reflecting off the lenses of his round Waldo glasses. "Are you open?"

"Yeah." I sighed. "Everyone's getting ready for a party tonight. So, it's just me. Well, and you, now. What can I get you?"

"Tea?"

I laughed and pointed to the menu board. "I make twenty flavors. Pick your poison. Are you hungry?"

His expression opened into something like awe. "I didn't know there were that many flavors of iced tea."

"I get that a lot," I said. "There are more, actually, but these are what I've got on tap today. Do you like rum cake?"

He grinned. "I do. Did you know this area was a hotspot for rum running during prohibition? The number of speakeasies on the islands was believed to be incredible, and every home was said to keep a secret stash. Lawmen and priests included."

"That would explain the large number of rum-related recipes in my family's old cookbooks." I laughed, then sliced him some rum cake and served it with my grandma's traditional sweet tea. "Here you go. On the house."

His eyes widened. "Thanks. I appreciate it."

My phone buzzed with a message, and I ran the pad of one finger over the screen in three quick swipes. The little *Z*-shaped unlocking method I used to embrace my inner Zorro. Denise had sent a photo of Denver via text. I smiled at the little man in what could only be his daddy's boots and hat, a shiny badge on his little plaid shirt. I saved the image to admire later and marveled at the way my heart swelled every time I saw that kid.

Finn watched curiously as he worked his way through the cake.

I put the phone in my pocket and returned my attention to him. "So, what brings you to Charm? Was it my offer of tea?" I teased.

He forked another bite, then stilled. "No. Grandpa Tony." He seemed to note my smile, then laughed. "You were joking."

"I was."

Finn relaxed. "Grandpa Tony wanted to see Clara, so I drove. I need to return something to the Wharf Museum." He gave an impish grin. "And I thought I might see about that tea."

I smiled, acutely aware of the opportunity dropped into my lap. "The Wharf Museum?"

He pointed to the blazer now draped across the stool beside his. "I wore it as a volunteer during the ghost walk. Additional, unofficial museum security."

I remembered seeing him there with a group of men in matching jackets.

I waited while he took a few more bites of cake before I pressed on, hoping the sugar would loosen his lips, if he had something to tell. "Did you decide to look for Dixie's family treasure?" I asked. "I thought about it after I left your store. I was too quick to dismiss the idea. I think it was a nice suggestion, to honor her that way. I'm sure Dixie's daughter would love to have whatever you find. It would be a unique and special tribute to her mother." And it seemed fair as long as the treasure was kept in the family.

He shook his head. "It was a fun thought, but I don't have the time. Chasing buried treasure might be better suited for retired people. How about you? Any luck figuring out what she wanted with you, writing your name like she did?"

"Not a clue, but I'm working on it," I admitted.

Finn scanned the room, nodding in approval. "This house is remarkable," he said. "The architecture is outstanding. It must've been a real showstopper when it was built. There's nothing like it now, but back then it must've blown locals' minds."

I had no doubt. "I grew up thinking it was haunted," I admitted. "My friends used to run past on the beach because it seemed so ominous up here, giant and empty. There were all sorts of stories designed to keep us from venturing inside and getting hurt. But all I could see was its beauty. I dreamed of getting a peek in here one day."

"You got more than a peek," Finn said, swigging his tea, then pausing to savor it.

I smiled. "I did. Funny how things work out."

Finn finished his tea and cake, then checked the time and gathered the navy blazer once more. "I hate to eat and run, but I want to return this before I pick Grandpa Tony up."

"No problem." I tried to smile, but my gaze locked on the jacket. "Are you a Friend of the Museum? Is that how you got the volunteering gig?"

"Yeah." He adjusted his glasses. "It's a good deal. When I'm there, I'm surrounded by history and people who love it, which is fun. And sometimes those people become my customers, which is great for business."

"Do you have access to the entire place?" I asked.

"Sure." He shrugged. "Except the offices."

"What about the archives?"

Creases gathered on his forehead. "Those are usually locked up. Why?"

"I'm thinking of joining," I lied.

Finn tucked a generous tip beneath his empty plate and smiled. "You should. We have a lot of fun."

I walked him out, contemplating whether or not I should become a Friend of the Museum just to see how much access the volunteers really had.

I closed Sun, Sand, and Tea an hour early, then headed over to Molly's Market for another roll of painter's tape. I wanted to finish working on my bookcase, but I'd run low on tape and couldn't go on without buying more.

The evening temperature was delightful. At least fifteen degrees warmer than it had been all week. I lifted my face to the breeze as I made my way along the boardwalk toward town. I felt inexplicably safe in my historical gown and truly content despite the recent threats and my emotional upheaval.

I smiled at the Little Library as I passed, dressed for

fall in a garland of colored leaves and lovingly stocked with themed reads by its owner and creator, Amelia. I picked up my pace as I crossed the fallen log over the marsh, connecting the boardwalk to Ocean Drive. Many of the shops had their CLOSED signs up, and I hoped Mr. Waters hadn't gone home as well. Molly's Market was the town's only general store. It was run by Mr. and Mrs. Waters and named after their daughter, my old babysitter, Molly. The market had nearly everything anyone could need, and I'd been a regular all my life.

"Hi, Mr. Waters," I called, hurrying in to retrieve the painter's tape.

He raised bushy gray brows at me as I rushed past. "Good evening, Everly. You look lovely. Is that your costume for the Harvest Ball?"

"No." I grabbed the tape and headed to the counter. "I'm going home to change. I'm glad I caught you before you closed." I set the tape on the counter. "Hoping to do some more painting as soon as possible."

"How's it coming?" he asked.

"Slowly. But I'm having fun."

"That's what counts." He barked a laugh. "We've got to have fun, you know? No one's promised tomorrow, so we make the most of today." He scanned the tape, then pushed it back to me. "I liked the campaign ad you made for Fran. You really did her justice. My wife and I have watched it twice."

"Thanks," I said. "I'm glad you liked it, but I can't take all the credit. I had a lot of help."

"We would've helped," he said. "My wife and I love Fran. She's got our vote. You can count on that. And if you ever need anything…" He pointed to his chest.

I slid the roll of tape over my hand and onto my wrist like a bracelet. "Will do."

He winked. "Four dollars."

I fished a five from my purse. "Will I see you and Mrs. Waters at the ball?"

"You know it. Are you going with that nice detective?"

I worked to keep my smile in place. "No. Matt Darning invited me."

"Ah!" Mr. Waters gave me change and crossed his arms. "Matt's a nice boy. You'll have fun."

I noted the time on the clock over the door and started. "I have to run. Gotta get home and change before he comes to pick me up. I'll see you soon," I called, already pushing open the door.

"See you at the ball," he answered.

I moved along the sidewalk, feeling impossibly lighter. Aunt Fran had a real chance at the election. Senator Denver had played her cards all wrong, and Mary Grace was Mary Grace. If the town wanted her, I'd have to consider moving, or holding a Charm-wide intervention to see how many voters were drinking at the polls.

I stared at the mass of election signs collected on the square and in every yard I passed, hoping I was right about Aunt Fran's upcoming win. She had far fewer signs than the competition, but maybe that had nothing to do with her number of supporters.

"Hey, E!" a familiar voice called. "Where are you running off to?"

I turned to see Wyatt jogging in my direction.

"Why are you dressed like a ghost?" he asked.

"I'm not," I said. "Shouldn't you be on your way to pick up Denise for the Harvest Ball?"

"I'm headed there now." He gave my dress another look, then shook his head. "I saw you and thought I'd better walk you home. The sun's already set, and it's not safe to walk alone after dark, especially with someone threatening you."

I considered telling him I was fine and he should go see Denise, but he was right. The sun had set, and twilight was upon me. The boardwalk would be dark and covered in shadows before I made it home. I wasn't a fan of that imagery or what my mind would surely conjure in the places I couldn't see. "Where's your truck?"

"Outside the grill," he said. "I grabbed a burger."

I turned and began to walk. "How's Cowboy Club? Are you still having as much fun as you'd hoped?"

"I am," he said, easily keeping pace at my side. "Turns out I like kids. I had no idea until the boot camp this summer. They're all a hoot. So determined and honest. And they help each other up when they fall. It's refreshing."

I smiled. "I'm glad you're happy."

He smiled back, though I sensed some hesitancy in his eyes. "Are you?" he asked. "Happy?"

"Sure." I nodded. "I'm okay."

"Okay and happy aren't the same thing," he said, pulling up short and catching my elbow gently in his giant hand. "Someone's threatening you again."

I bristled. "I know that. And I'm fine."

He heard the lie in my voice. I saw the recognition in his eyes. "All right," he relented, clearly seeing everything I tried to hide. "Just checking." He pushed his hands into this jeans pockets and began to walk again.

I huffed and followed suit.

"Are you going to the ball with your aunts?" he asked.

"No." I crossed my arms, irritated at the discussion. I liked Wyatt, had even loved him once, and the transition from lovers to friends was complicated and a little bizarre. Suddenly the man I'd pined over for years was more like an annoying older brother, always trying to parent and protect me. I appreciated and loathed him for it. Which only confirmed my sibling analogy was probably on target.

"Denise and I can pick you up," he said. "No sense in going alone."

"I'm going with Matt." I glanced at Wyatt in search of feedback.

He did a long, slow whistle. "Twice in one week. Y'all must've really hit it off. What does Grady say about that?"

"Nothing," I snapped, rubbing the chill from my arms. "Why on earth would he care who I'm dating?"

Wyatt raised his brows. "If you say so."

I deflated a bit, then dared a look in his direction. "I don't know what I say," I admitted. "What do you think?"

Wyatt raised his shoulders, hands still tucked into his pockets. "I think he's going to be sorry. I speak from experience."

My heart softened, and my tummy rolled. "Yeah, well, I don't want a dummy," I said, letting a slow grin slide over my face. "I want someone who knows exactly what he wants and that it's unquestionably me."

Wyatt offered me a small smile as we stepped off Ocean Drive and onto the fallen tree across the marsh to the boardwalk. "And that's how it should be," he said.

We walked in companionable silence for a few minutes, until Amelia's Little Library came into view, and Grady picked up his pace. "Give me just a sec," he said, rushing forward to select a small paperback. He tucked it into his back pocket while he waited for me to catch up. "Amelia's got me hooked on reading. Louis L'Amour."

"She has a way of doing that," I said, "connecting people with the books and authors that speak to them. It's her special brand of matchmaking."

We walked on. Wyatt whistled, and I pondered my most recent threat. My "final warning" that felt like a guillotine hanging over my head.

"You okay?" Wyatt nudged me with his elbow.

"I'm fine."

He chuckled. "You keep saying that, but the lady doth protest too much, me thinks."

"Shut up." I rolled my eyes at the reformed cowboy quoting Shakespeare. Amelia was far too good at her job.

Wyatt walked me to the door, and I invited him in for a jar of tea. Surprisingly, he agreed.

We made it as far as the foyer before he swung an arm wide, stretching it across my center like the mechanical gate in a parking garage.

I stopped short, nearly running into the makeshift barrier. "What?"

He caught my eye, then pointed into the café. "Someone's been in here." He pulled his phone from his pocket and tapped the screen as I pushed my way forward.

I flipped on the café lights and marched determinedly through the space. He was right, and I fought the urge to scream. Someone had overturned my café's bookcase. What kind of monster threw books on the floor?

I spun around in search of additional damage, but saw none, then made a circuit through the first floor with Wyatt on my heels.

A window in the former ballroom was broken. "Dang it!" I growled.

We returned to the foyer, and I grasped the doorknob to my private staircase. Unlocked. I said a small cuss, then hollered up the stairs. "I'm home," I called, "and I'm not alone. We know you're in here, and we've alerted the authorities, so you have about two minutes before Charm PD arrives to arrest you."

Wyatt pressed me back and angled his way up the steps ahead of me.

"We're coming up!" I called. "I have a cowboy! And pepper spray!"

Wyatt shot a crazy look over his shoulder at me, then mouthed the words, "What are you doing?"

I shook my head and shrugged.

We stepped into my living space and found the floor covered in cowboy romance novels. All my neatly filled boxes had been dumped, the contents clearly ransacked.

I gaped at the mess, the reality of it finally breaking over my head like a tidal wave. Someone had been inside my home. Inside my private living space, and I felt the tears of anger and frustration begin to fall.

Wyatt curled an arm around my shoulder, wiggling his phone in his opposite palm and tugging me closer to his side. "Grady's on his way. Let's meet him outside."

CHAPTER

TWENTY-TWO

Wyatt left when Grady arrived, bowing out to pick up Denver and Denise for the ball. He'd called a local handyman about replacing the broken glass in my window before he left, and the guy had graciously agreed to come right over.

Matt texted to say he was caught up at work and running late. I encouraged him to take his time. I wasn't even sure I still wanted to go out after some lunatic had broken in, but I didn't tell him any of that. He was working, and given the nature of his job, I figured he had his own crises to tend to.

I hovered as Grady took photos, asked questions, and examined the messes made on each floor. Nothing appeared to be missing, so he didn't call for backup. He took fingerprints and said he'd talk to the lab when it opened tomorrow. Then he helped me pick up all my books and followed me upstairs to wait while the handyman fixed my window.

"Whoever did this was probably waiting for you to

leave," he said. "When you left in costume, he or she likely assumed you were heading to the ball and would be gone for hours. I think you surprised the intruder by returning so quickly, and I also think you're lucky Wyatt was with you. People caught in the middle of a crime will usually do whatever it takes to get away with it. If your burglar was still here when you arrived, that person would have been more likely to attack and less likely to run if you were alone."

I looked down at my dress, having temporarily forgotten what I was wearing. "I'm not dressed for the ball," I said, feeling numb to the reality of my situation. "I wore this to work for fun today."

He huffed. "That was your takeaway?"

I went to the kitchen in my living quarters while Grady returned the last few paperbacks to a box. "Can I get you something?" I asked, then poured two glasses of sweet tea while I waited.

He looked up and saw me working but didn't protest, so I cut us each a thick slice of lemon cake to go with the tea.

"Are you going to the ball?" he asked.

"Maybe," I said. "I'd planned to before this happened. Now, I don't know."

Grady collected a plate and cup, then followed me to the couch.

We each chose a cushion, then set our drinks on the coffee table.

Grady dug into his cake. "I guess your date was ruined the other night. That was too bad."

I frowned. He didn't look as if he thought it was too bad at all.

"The death threat wasn't super romantic," I said casually, "but we made the most of the night anyway. It was lucky you were there, I guess. Why were you there exactly?"

He paused, mid chew, then finished before speaking. "I got a hit on the sword stuck in your porch. The curator responded to my inquiry from earlier this week. When he checked the archives to see if the item belonged to them, he found the sword and a number of other things from that era had gone missing."

"Like the dagger used to carve the chair," I said.

Grady nodded.

"So, someone with access to that museum's archives is the one who's threatening me," I surmised. "Have you compiled a list of people affiliated with both the Festival Park Museum and Dixie Wetherill? Society members? Volunteers? Friends of the Museum? A volunteer at the Wharf Museum says the archives are kept locked, but I think someone with enough motivation and access to the general area could bypass a lock if need be."

"Who did you talk to from the Wharf Museum?" Grady grouched.

"Finn. He owns Historical Pages in Hatteras and is the grandson of Tony from the Society in Kitty Hawk," I said. "Tony is chasing Aunt Clara, so I've run into Finn once or twice this week."

Grady fixed me with a hard look, then went back to his cake. "Leave this alone, Swan. I've got it covered.

If you need something to look into, how about pricing a proper alarm system for your home? Maybe a few cameras too?"

I put the suggestion in the back of my mind for later. Something about dressing my house up like Fort Knox felt like saying I would definitely have another intruder, and I needed to prepare. I didn't like that. "Well, did you get my text about The_Collector1800?" I asked. "He seemed pretty miffed with Dixie, and he was trying to get a map from her. Just like the stalker is trying to get a map from me. Could be the same person in search of the same map, especially if he or she saw me in Dixie's office before the maps went missing. Is there a way to find out who uses the The_Collector1800 account?"

Grady pressed the tines of his fork into the cake, then locked me in his blank stare. "Leave this alone," he repeated.

"No." My spine stiffened, and my limbs went rigid. I absolutely would not stop trying to figure out who was threatening me. No one should have to live like this. Just waiting for the next scare to come. Or worse.

Grady's face flushed red. "I mean it. This kind of unnecessary interference on your part always ends poorly for you, and frankly, I can't take another moment of thinking you're dead."

I pointed my fork at him, exasperated and shocked he couldn't understand my reasoning on this. As usual. "If my stalker isn't caught soon, I might be dead," I snapped. "I dig into these things because I want to stop the wackadoodles before they get tired of making threats and actually hurt me." I jolted to my feet, a wellspring of emotion taking over.

Grady stood too, looking down at me from his dumb, lofty height. "I know you think you're helping, and I'm not doing things right, but poking around in my investigations is precisely what keeps putting you in the path of these criminals, and they all eventually try to kill you. When are you going to figure that out?"

I crossed my arms and fought the urge to stomp my foot.

He glared. "One of these days, Everly, I won't be there in time. I won't reach you fast enough. Won't figure it out before it's too late, and I cannot live with that."

The heat in Grady's eyes seemed to shoot straight through me and pool in my core. The familiar electricity crackled and snapped, softening my resolve and raising gooseflesh over my arms. Heat rushed across my stupid cheeks, and I hated the way he made me feel. Hated that he could be so oblivious to absolutely everything between us. I wanted to grab him by his ridiculously broad shoulders and shake him. Or shove him. Or kiss him.

My phone buzzed on the coffee table beside my tea, and a photo of Matt's face appeared on the screen.

Grady stepped back and scrubbed a hand through his hair.

I took the call, feeling an invisible rubber band stretch between Grady and me. "Hello?"

My limbs shook with misplaced adrenaline as Matt apologized again for being hung up at the hospital. He offered me a rain check and promised to go straight to the ball as soon as possible, but he couldn't say when that might be. He disconnected before I could respond, and I returned my gaze to Grady. "Matt can't make it to the ball."

Grady's jaw locked. "You were going out with him again tonight?"

"Yes."

"Why?" he asked.

I stared, momentarily stunned by the change of tone and topic. "What do you mean *why*?" I asked. "Because he invited me, and he's a genuinely nice guy."

Grady's expression wavered, emotion flashing quickly over his features before settling into something like disinterest. "You really hit it off with him the other night? Or is it something else?"

I felt a bolt of anger rip through me, but it immediately fizzled. My shoulders drooped. "Yes, Matt and I hit it off, then I told him I didn't think we should see each other again. My life's kind of crazy. It seemed like the right thing for me to do."

"What about the ball?"

"He offered to take me as friends," I said.

Grady's frown eased.

I squared my shoulders and regrouped. "Now, he's stuck at work, but I can get to the ball without him. After I pay the window guy and change my clothes."

I checked the time. "Do you need anything else from me about the break-in, or are we done?"

"I can take you," Grady said, his voice low and cautious. "To the ball. If you want."

I wanted to scream. "No, thank you," I managed politely, despite my rising blood pressure. "I can take Blue."

"You're still mad at me." He managed a sheepish look. "I thought you might've forgiven me when you brought me the lemon cake."

"There was nothing to forgive," I said, my mood shifting fast to aggravation. I mentally tallied all the things I was still upset about. Like the fact that he'd shoved me out of his life without any warning earlier this week. I understood Denver needed him, but lots of people had kids and friends. Heck, some had kids and a spouse or significant other. Grady had used Denver as an excuse to push me away, and that wasn't okay. I'd thought he and I were friends, but what did we really have between us if he was willing and able to shut the door in my face anytime things got complicated? "I'm not mad. I'm fine."

"Great. So let me drive you to the ball."

"No."

He glared. "Then admit you're mad."

"I will not."

"Then I'm driving you to the ball."

I pressed my lips tight, and my blood pressure skyrocketed. "Fine," I snapped.

"Fine."

Someone knocked on my door, and I jumped.

Grady went to answer it.

The handyman offered him a clipboard and pen, looking as if he'd overheard more of our conversation than he should have, and he knew it. "I just need a signature for the window."

Grady scribbled across the paper, then returned the clipboard to him.

The man flicked his attention to me, then back to Grady before hurrying away.

Grady followed him downstairs, then returned to me with a smirk.

"What?" I grouched.

He retook his seat on the couch and reached for my unfinished slice of lemon cake. "I'll wait here while you change."

I spun on my heels and stalked away.

I returned thirty minutes later, having swapped the Magnolia tribute gown for a long black dress I'd also found in Aunt Clara's trunk. The bodice was fitted, the neckline low and heavily embroidered, and the skirt nearly reached my ankles. I'd added a thick, purple crinoline under the dress for dimension and a pop of color. The purple peeked out as I walked. I fastened a large ruby amulet on a gold chain around my neck for luck. The jewel had been in my family for generations. I slipped a pair of black ankle boots onto my feet, then went heavy on the eye makeup and lipstick.

Grady stood when he saw me, eyes going wide

before narrowing as they traveled over my ensemble. A small curse ejected from his lips.

I pulled the pins from my hair, unleashing the kraken. For once in my life, the unruly, dark curls worked with the outfit. I squared my shoulders and ran both palms over my bodice, feeling confident, independent, and powerful.

No ghost sailor, paramedic, or detective was going to ruin that for me tonight.

CHAPTER

TWENTY-THREE

The Harvest Ball took place on a large historic property on the sound side of town. The land had once been farmed, but for as long as I could remember, it was merely a site for field trips, weddings, and the annual Harvest Ball. The property perimeter was aglow, outlined by roughly ten million candles, each secured inside a small glass jar, and more twinkle lights than the entire town used at Christmas. The house was less than half the size of the barn and used mostly as a staging area or food prep. A pier out back stretched twenty feet into the sound, with ropes of leafy garland strung post to post. It was a beautiful sight, but the main event took place inside the massive, two-story horse barn.

The barn was red, trimmed in black, with a wide loft on one side and a genuinely cavernous interior. The doors were propped open and held fast by piles of hay bales. An abundance of pumpkins and gourds lined every flat surface, and more white twinkle lights wrapped exposed beams and railings. A trio of teenagers sat in the loft, feet dangling above me as I entered. The lucky high schoolers were in charge of playing songs from before they were born and paid well to do it. I'd had the job twice in my youth, hauling a complicated speaker system and pile of CDs into the loft with me, then feeding an orange extension cord through the planks to power my equipment. These days, teens had pocket-sized wireless speakers and phones with endless playlists. All they needed was a full battery, and they were good for hours.

I waved to a couple dressed in red plaid shirts and overalls, their new baby planted in a pouch on the dad's chest. The baby's pouch was designed to resemble an ear of corn, as was the knit cap on the child's head. I sidestepped a pack of pint-sized pirates, each demanding another walk a plank made of hay, and curtsied to a series of princesses holding court near the refreshments, then I went in search of my aunts.

Grady stuck close but said little. I did my best to ignore him.

Aunt Clara spotted me first, then wrapped me in a hug. "Where's Matt?" she asked as Grady stepped around to my side. "Oh, dear." She blinked at him, then looked back to me for an explanation.

"Matt had to work," I explained. "He'll meet me here if he can. Grady drove me so I didn't have to make the trip alone."

"Nice to see you, Clara," he said, offering her a handshake.

"Oh, dear," she whispered again as she shook his hand.

"There you are!" Aunt Fran's voice reached me before she did. She stopped short to eyeball Grady. "You."

I bit the insides of my cheeks. I'd unloaded the whole of my frustrations about Grady to my aunts by phone after Amelia's book launch party. I'd inadvertently stressed out Aunt Clara and put the good detective on Aunt Fran's hit list in the process.

Grady shifted his weight. "Good to see you. The campaign seems to be coming along nicely." He offered her his hand as well.

She narrowed her eyes but accepted his shake. "Thank you. Will your mother-in-law be joining us tonight?"

Grady stretched his neck, looking uncomfortable. "I'm sure she'll make an appearance eventually. All these voters in one place. How could she miss it?"

"Well," Aunt Fran said. "Vote for Swan." She pulled a campaign button with the same saying from her bag and pressed it into his hand.

He tipped two fingers to his forehead in a weird salute but didn't comment or put on the button. His gaze drifted then, moving from Aunt Fran to Aunt Clara, then to me. "You're all dressed as witches?"

"Every year," Aunt Clara said.

A slow grin spread across his mouth, and he chuckled. "That must get folks wound up."

"It does," Aunt Fran said, squinting at him, appraising. "What do you think of it?"

"The costumes?"

"Us portrayed as witches," she asked.

I sighed, then reminded myself that if Grady was uncomfortable, it was his fault for hurting my feelings and getting on Aunt Fran's bad side.

"Go with it, I guess," he said.

I made a crazy face. "Why would we do that? What does that even mean?"

"It means that maybe we should spend less time denying things and more time embracing the truth in them," he said.

Aunt Fran's lips twitched, fighting a smile. She crossed her arms. "Explain."

Grady turned to me. "You're unusually gifted in the kitchen, right? Everyone knows it."

I liked the sound of that but inched my chin up on principle. "And?"

"And?" he parroted. "People notice. They can't explain it, but they want to. They know your family came here from Salem, so they whisper *witches*. Who cares?"

"And that makes me what?" I asked. "A kitchen witch?"

He shrugged. "When was the last time you burned something you made? Anything. Or undercooked a dish? Overcooked one? Got a recipe wrong? Were unhappy in any way with the results of what you created?"

When I didn't answer, because I literally couldn't think of a single time, he turned to Aunt Clara. "Your dedication to the life and preservation of American honeybees isn't exactly a common practice." He jerked his gaze from one aunt to the other. "Your store is like some bizarre hometown apothecary. People line up for the products you make, from the bees you raise and gardens you cultivate. It's...I don't know. Witchy."

"Witchy?" I repeated.

"Yeah," he said. "Witchy."

I gawked.

Aunt Fran smiled.

Grady rubbed a palm over his face, then met my eyes with an intensity I couldn't begin to understand.

"All right," Aunt Fran said. "I accept your answer, Detective Hays. Now, here." She pulled a camera from her bag of campaign buttons and passed it to me. "Let's get a few good photos of me at this party and show folks I know how to have fun."

I dragged my attention away from Grady and followed my aunt around the property, snapping shots of her until we spotted Denise, Wyatt, and Denver.

Grady squatted and opened his arms to catch his son as Denver ran full speed in his direction.

"Having fun?" I asked Denise.

"Always." She'd worn jeans and a denim jacket over a thermal shirt, apparently leaving the costumes to Denver, who was in yet another fantastic cowboy getup. Wyatt wore the same T-shirt and jeans he'd had on earlier, though he'd added a tan barn coat.

Wyatt extended a hand to Grady. "I see Everly found a ride. She refused mine."

Grady gave me a look. "She only rode with me because her date had to work."

My temper flared, and I caught Denise's stunned expression, then Wyatt's confusion. "Excuse me," I said, intentionally ignoring Grady. I patted Denver's shoulder on my way back to the barn.

Aunt Clara caught me at the open doors, worry etched on her brow.

"Is everything okay?" I asked, looking instinctively past her for Aunt Fran. I found her surrounded by people, all looking delighted for a moment of her time.

"I think Fran is going to win this election," Aunt Clara said. "And I know I said I'd be okay if she did, but what if I'm not? I'm worried. And selfish. Mostly the last one." She pressed a fist to her lips, completely forlorn. "I don't know who I am without her."

I slipped an arm around her narrow back and leaned against her side. "You are Clara Swan—historian, gardener, soap maker, beauty product creator, sister, aunt, and friend. You are all that and so much more. You're anything and everything you want to be."

She smiled appreciatively. "A bee witch?"

I laughed, seeking Grady with my gaze. "And a bee witch," I agreed. "You know, Aunt Fran will need you more than ever once she's mayor. It's going to be a big adjustment for you both. You'll have more to do at the shop, and she'll need a trusted confidant she can lean on after tough days at work. Someone who will never spill her secrets and will always let her be herself, not just the mayor." I squeezed and released Aunt Clara, then pulled back to look into her eyes. "And with her so busy, you and I will get to spend more time together."

She smiled. "I'd like that very much."

"Me too."

A strange chugging sound drew my attention to the long gravel driveway, and a pair of headlights appeared. It took only a moment to recognize the vehicle as a farm tractor and the big-haired silhouette beside the driver as Mary Grace Chatsworth-Vanders.

"What the devil is she doing on a tractor?" Aunt Clara asked.

The vehicle stopped before us, and the trailer behind it became visible. Dozens of hay bales lined the bed.

Guests spilled from the barn to see what was going on.

Mary Grace struck a pose and raised a megaphone to her big mouth, more prop than necessity, I was sure. "Who wants a hayride?" she called, waving people closer. "A vote for me, Mary Grace Chatsworth-Vanders, is a vote for the ride of your life," she yelled, pumping her free fist into the air.

Children ran for the tractor, and their parents followed.

"Yuck," I said, heading into the barn.

Aunt Clara joined me. "I guess we'll see what impresses voters next week at the polls."

I shook my head at the possibility folks really would have the ride of their lives tonight and get confused about how to make the right choice while voting next week.

The music stopped suddenly, cutting a popular country music dance number down to silence. A moment later, that piña colada song by Rupert Holmes came on. I looked into the loft, wondering what had happened, and witnessed a landslide of colorful balloons and beach balls being dropped from above. For a moment, everyone stilled, then the music got louder, and Senator Denver strutted inside, wearing sunglasses, despite the hour, and toting an armload of beach bags printed with her face and the words FOR MAYOR underneath.

So, this was her grand entrance.

She shook hands, posed for pictures, and handed out her swag bags to eager recipients.

I waited, annoyed and a little impressed that the senator had gotten slightly more on track with her campaign. We were a beach town after all. Who didn't need another big burlap shoulder bag?

Aunt Clara ran over to get one.

I could've lived without the senator's face on mine, but I supposed every bag was reversable with enough effort.

I waited while Aunt Clara worked her way through the crowd.

A man in a werewolf costume slid into position at my side, and it took a minute for me to realize it was Burton. He had a beach bag hooked on one shoulder and a look of determination on his face.

"What are you doing here?" I asked. I looked around for signs of Wyatt or Grady in case Burton had come to hurt or abduct me.

"I'm getting something to eat and looking for my book," he said. "There's going to be food later, right?"

"No one here has your book," I grouched. "I looked for it at Historical Pages too, by the way, but it wasn't there either. And it's definitely not at the Harvest Ball."

He stared at me a moment. "You looked for my book?"

"Yes. Because I don't have it," I said. "I figure it has to be somewhere." I crossed my arms and sighed. "There's a buffet over there." I pointed to a crowd of people still talking to Senator Denver. "Behind them."

Burton nodded. "I think Dixie might've hidden my book," he said. "I talked to her daughter this morning, and she let me go through the office. I looked at every cover, and it's not there. I spent hours."

"Did you ask to look inside her home?" I suggested. "Or check inside her car? Maybe it's already been sold and is in transit somewhere. I don't know, but you've got to stop following me."

"I'm not following you," he said.

I performed a dramatic eyeroll. "I see you every day now."

"It's a small town."

"Not that small," I said. "And you're from Kitty Hawk, not Charm. So, if you're the one leaving me ridiculous threats and pretending to be an old sailor ghost to scare me, you can stop. I don't believe in ghosts. I don't have any maps, and you're wasting your time."

Burton managed to look offended. "I'm not stalking you or pretending to be anything. I'm just looking for my book," he said. "Book. Not map." Burton looked away, swaying with the music. "I'm here more often because I like it. Charm is more fun than Kitty Hawk."

"You have a life and a wife in Kitty Hawk," I said. Finn's theory of Aubrey as a barnacle came back to mind. And it was wrong. I'd seen Burton several times this week without her anywhere around. So, what had she been up to while he was away? "How long have you been in Charm today?"

"A while. Why?"

I tried to imagine Burton skulking near my home, waiting for me to leave, then breaking in and rifling through all my books, looking for his. "You say you want a book, not a map, but your book has maps."

"So?" He shrugged. "I don't care about the maps. I want the book for my collection."

I couldn't tell if he was lying. "What about Dixie? Did she want the book or the map? Did she want it for herself or to resell?"

Burton watched me carefully. "I don't know."

I sighed. That was the problem. The only person who could answer my questions was Dixie, and she was gone. "Do you believe in buried treasure?" I asked, trying to sound more casual than I felt and nearly holding my breath as I awaited his answer.

If he and Dixie both believed there was treasure buried on the island, and both thought a map in his book could lead them to it, how far would Dixie go to stop Burton from reaching it first? Would she swipe the book from him? And how far would he go to stop her?

Burton turned to face me, clearly irritated and no longer content to stand at my side. "If you don't have my book, then why are you so concerned about what makes it valuable?" he asked, a new and menacing edge to his voice.

"Because I'm starting to think someone killed Dixie for it," I said.

And that person was likely standing right in front of me.

CHAPTER

TWENTY-FOUR

I told Grady about my run-in with Burton, then asked to go home. I said my goodbyes, then climbed back into Grady's truck and unloaded everything on him, including the details of my trip to Historical Pages and all my theories he didn't want. Surprisingly, he only listened and didn't complain.

At home, I changed out of my costume and into pajamas, then pulled knee-high fuzzy socks over my pant legs and went to make a cup of hot tea. I checked all my window locks on both floors, stuck brooms in the bases of my sliding doors to prevent unwanted intruders, and dragged the baker's rack in front of the door at the top of the interior staircase on the second floor. The rack didn't weigh much, but anyone attempting to open the door would knock it over, and at least that would wake me.

I settled on the couch with the tea and my laptop, then looked again for the book causing Burton to lose his mind. Maybe I was beating a dead horse, but it was the only lead I had, and the one that kept coming back around. I hoped that someone trying to sell a copy might have taken pictures of the maps inside. I paused on an ad featuring the corner of one colorful map and words like limited-edition, hand-drawn, and gilded. Apparently, there were very few books made with those maps inside. The limited-edition volumes were worth nearly ten times more than the others, which were still going for several hundred dollars a pop, depending on their overall condition.

I scanned other references to the book, looking for new information until my tea grew tepid, and I'd nearly given up.

Then I saw something I hadn't read before. A woman in the UK described her thrill after winning a copy of the limited-edition volumes in a blog post. She claimed her excitement came from the rarely covered story of the "Sad Man's Treasure."

I scrolled the article, looking for the typo again. Surely, she'd meant the "Sandman's Treasure." But there was no mention of James Hudson, only someone she called the Sad Man, and extensive exposition on how much she could relate to his heartbreak.

Personally, I couldn't sympathize with a man who'd murdered a woman's husband, then cut off her head when she didn't fall for him, but maybe things were different in the UK. Obviously, the names associated with our legends were.

I opened a new window and searched for legends of the Sad Man in North Carolina, just to be sure I wasn't confused. And I was shocked at the number of links that came back. I nearly fell onto the floor as I read the details.

The legend of the Sad Man had nothing to do with James Hudson or Mourning Mable. The Sad Man was a wealthy businessman in love with two women. When he lost both his lovers to suicide, he was forced to live out his days alone, slowly going insane. With no heir to inherit the wealth, he hid his greatest treasure and died.

I read multiple articles on the subject twice, then once more for good measure.

A wealthy man in love with two women, who lost them both to suicide, and was left without an heir. Maybe I was overthinking, a definite habit of mine, but that story sounded incredibly familiar.

I'd never given any thought to what happened to Lou's fortune after his death. I'd assumed his money had simply been lost, used up or squandered while he wasted away, no longer working or trying to maintain his fancy lifestyle.

I closed the laptop, pondering the possibility that Lou had hidden his wealth in my house. Then started on the first floor and tested every original shelf, light fixture, and loose floorboard for a false passage or hidey hole big enough to hide a treasure.

I fell asleep hours later, feeling silly and exhausted, thinking I was a moron for seeking hidden treasure in my home, and simultaneously wishing I could find it.

I dreamed of blue-moon lunacy, murder, and British ghosts, then woke to the infuriating vibration and beeping of my bossy fitness bracelet.

Within an hour, I was dressed in workout gear and headed into the day. An unexpected dose of adrenaline set me out the door at just after dawn. Part of the reason, I suspected, was the date.

October thirty-first.

I power walked through the brisk morning air, breathing deeply and feeling the burn build in my legs. It'd been days since I'd gotten my heart rate up and my muscles singing. And I'd missed it.

I also suspected the nut pretending to be a sailor ghost had something grand planned for me tonight. Halloween. The night when the official blue moon would be high in the sky.

And it was those sorts of thoughts that were sure to give me an ulcer.

I shook my hands out hard at the wrists and blew away deep chest fulls of air. I let my mind go, let it ferret out my various points of stress so I could analyze and dismiss them. Seek and annihilate.

Surprisingly, the election was first to take the mental stage. I wanted Aunt Fran to win, but I had no idea what else I could do to push voters in her favor. And it left me feeling helpless.

I hated that.

From there, I tallied my issues stemming from the ghost walk. My house was broken into, for starters, and it scared me. Someone had left a threat on my porch, on Blue, and carved into my chair at a fancy dinner. Also scary. And again, I'd felt helpless every time.

I was noticing a pattern.

Grady had pushed me away this week, and I suspected Matt might literally be the world's perfect partner, but I couldn't date him because my stupid, moronic, idiotic heart wanted someone else completely.

I picked up my pace. I needed this walk like I needed air.

My arms pumped. I thrust my legs with each new stride, putting my whole body into it as I barreled along the boardwalk.

Fog hung thick across the marsh and old weathered boards beneath my feet, creating a creepy Halloween aesthetic. I didn't mind; nothing short of a gator would stop me now. Though it would be an arguably fitting end to my crazy week. *Sorry lunatic stalker, your plaything was eaten by an alligator. Move along.*

I thought of Burton's obsession with the missing book, and his wife's general angst. The online anger of The_Collector1800 and the oddly flirtatious Tony Grayson. Stranger still was his friendly cartographer grandson, Finn. Finn had claimed to like Dixie when no one else did. Was it because they had common ground? Was it because she'd dated his grandpa? Somewhere during my late-night list-making, he'd begun to bug me most of all. Why had Dixie been nice to him and no one else? Maybe she'd needed him for answers to her map questions. Maybe that wasn't it at all.

I rolled my shoulders and stretched my neck as I walked, feeling the heat spread through my limbs. I passed Amelia's Little Free Library with a smile, startled by the unexpected motion of a heron in the marsh, a wiggly fish speared in its beak, then hightailed it across the fallen tree to Ocean Drive, where the air smelled of pancakes and fancy coffee. Both seemed like a nice reward for such a high-intensity walk.

Amelia was on the sidewalk outside her shop when I arrived, tying balloons to a sign advertising signed copies of her new book. "Hey," she said, brightening at the sight of me. "I feel as if I've barely seen you this week, and I know you could use a friend right now." She looked so sad I nearly hugged her. She also looked fantastic in her knee-high socks and orange, cowl-necked sweater, clearly dressed as Velma from Scooby Doo for Halloween. I doubted she'd want to smell like my sweat.

"I'm okay," I said. "Your book launch was a hit."

"It was," she said, finding her smile. "Macy loved the party, and I'm down to my last dozen copies here. Which means I've sold about seventy on my own. That's really good for my little store."

I lifted a hand, and Amelia slapped her palm against mine. "Nice."

"I missed you at the Harvest Ball the other night," she said. "I was going to call, but your aunts said you left early with Grady. Did you two make up?"

I rolled my eyes. "No. I was just tired and being annoyed by a werewolf."

She chuckled. "Well then, watch out tonight. There's a full moon."

I felt the familiar chills of being watched slide over me, and I looked in every direction for signs of someone else on the street. There was only Amelia and I, plus folks going in and out of local cafés.

"I'm still planning to be at your place for the election party," she said. "Dad and I have been collecting and making decorations on the side for weeks. It's going to look amazing, and with your refreshments being served, I'm not sure who'd bother attending any other party."

I smiled, hoping she was right. "I'm sure the senator has something grand planned at the estate." A place my humble old Victorian could never measure up to, and everyone had clamored to get a look inside at Christmas.

"Yeah," Amelia said with a grin, "but she already played the fancy-house card by putting her place on the lineup for the progressive dinner in December. Now everyone's been there, and even if they wouldn't mind taking another look, the novelty is gone. They'll show up to encourage whoever they voted for, and I'm betting that's Fran."

My smile grew, and I suddenly missed my best friend desperately, though she was right in front of me. "I needed to hear that. You want to come over and have cake together tonight? We can catch up on everything we've missed this week."

She dropped her chin and raised a brow. "Name the time."

"Nine?" I asked. "Just come on over after you close. I'm not attending any of the Halloween events after work. I've been in survival mode all week, and I need the night off."

She nodded. "I'm kind of partied-out myself. I'd rather share dessert with my bestie."

"Perfect. We can keep the *Town Charmer* up for coverage of the parties, so we won't miss anything."

"It's a date," she said.

"Text me when you're on your way, and I'll come down to watch for you."

Clusters of women and children began to head our way, emerging from local restaurants and climbing from golf carts in nearby slots.

"Story time," she said, lowering circle-framed glasses from the top of her head to the bridge of her nose. "And they would've gotten away with it too, if it wasn't for that meddling tea maker." She curtsied.

"Bravo." I shook my head and took a few steps backward, in the direction of Blessed Bee. "Have fun. I'm off to check on the aunts. Don't tell Grady you think I meddle."

"Oh, he knows," she said.

I ducked into Blessed Bee and headed for the counter. "Good morning," I called.

"Everly!" Aunt Clara's voice lifted cheerfully from the back of the store. "Come on in. We've got our hands full, but you can help."

I laughed and jogged toward her voice.

Aunt Clara and Aunt Fran were pouring something

that smelled like heaven into a series of shallow tins. They'd pinned their long hair back and donned aprons, safety goggles, and gloves.

"What are you doing?" I asked, inhaling the delicious scent. "Is that lip balm?"

Aunt Fran's attention flickered to me briefly, then back to the work at hand. "It is. Honey and almond for moisture and healing." She filled the containers as Aunt Clara lined them up, pushing finished tins out of the way to make room for more.

I jumped in, dragging the full containers into orderly rows on the far side of their workspace. "I just saw Amelia. She's getting ready for story time," I said. "She got me thinking about the Harvest Ball. I never asked you if I missed anything by leaving early."

Aunt Fran shot me another look, this one sour. "After the hayride, Mary Grace started up a projector and played her commercial against the side of the house. I was a twelve-foot-tall Grim Reaper for the whole town to see at once."

Aunt Clara wrinkled her nose. "Mary Grace sat on that dumb tractor, waving like Miss America, so proud of herself for slandering Fran. It was awful."

I cringed. "I'm sorry I wasn't there for you." I'd really dropped the ball this week on my duties as a niece and best friend. "Maybe I can make another ad or find a way to get more exposure for your commercial."

Aunt Fran finished her job and set the empty pot aside. "You've already done more than anyone could ask," she said. "All while running a successful business, navigating a complicated personal life, and dealing with a murder that had nothing to do with you. Until it did." She shook her head with a sigh. "We're proud of you, Everly. Right down to our toes. You're probably the strongest woman we've ever known. Isn't she, Clara?"

Aunt Clara nodded. "We say that all the time."

I hurried around the table to gather them in a group hug. "I'm all sweaty," I said, fighting a sniffle.

Aunt Clara squeezed me tighter. "You are lovely."

Aunt Fran released me to tug off her gloves and goggles. "I took a look at the menu you emailed for the election party. I know you want me to make selections, but it all sounds delicious. Why don't you choose whichever recipes you're in the mood to make that day and surprise me? Detective Hays was right. You can't go wrong in the kitchen."

I smiled. "Okay. I have to get back home and shower before I open the café, but I wanted to stop and say hello." I waited a moment, a thought rattling in my mind, then turned to Aunt Clara. "Do Burton and Aubrey always fight?" I asked. "I couldn't help noticing they've been at each other's throat since the night of the ghost walk, every time I've seen them anyway."

"Kind of," she said. "I think Aubrey's a little insecure. It's why she spends so much time worrying about her appearance, and Burton's sort of aloof."

I'd have pegged him as more of *a goof*, but I nodded. "She's embarrassed by him?"

"Heavens, no," Aunt Clara said. "She thinks that man hung the moon. She suspects everyone else does too."

I recalled her line about Dixie having her hands on something of everyone's, and suddenly things began to click. What if Aubrey hadn't been talking about a book or map? What if she'd been talking about her husband? "Any chance he was having an affair with Dixie?" I asked, rolling the possibility over in my mind. There was a significant age difference between them. Burton was probably in his forties, and Dixie had easily been sixty. Still, stranger things had happened.

"I don't think so," Aunt Clara said. "I never picked up on anything like that from those two. They mostly argued about books they both wanted. Who'd get them first, where, and at what price."

At what price, indeed.

I made a mental note to ask Aubrey what she'd meant about Dixie, then said my goodbyes to Aunt Clara and Aunt Fran. Aubrey was too short to have been the mysterious sailor from Amelia's book launch party, but she might still be helpful in figuring out what I was missing.

CHAPTER

❧❧

TWENTY-FIVE

I hurried upstairs to get ready for my day, taking a little extra care with my hair and makeup. I felt good after the exhilarating walk and proud I'd skipped the pancakes and fancy coffee. I'd saved twelve bucks and helped my waistline.

I headed downstairs to Sun, Sand, and Tea, then propped my phone on the counter and taped myself prepping a few sample menu items. I planned to post a poll and let viewers choose their favorites, though ultimately, it would be Aunt Fran's decision. And hopefully, a celebration party, not a consolation event.

"Red, white, and blue is the preferred color pallet, and fall is the general food theme," I told the camera. "I have a few quick recipes you can make for your own election party next week, and an idea or two I might be serving here. Let's start with a quart of juicy, homegrown organic strawberries." I displayed a pair on one palm. "I have a small dish of white chocolate wafers, already melted, and a bowl with blue-colored sugar, ready for dipping." I tipped each bowl toward the camera before getting started. "Make an assembly line with washed berries at one end and a tray with wax paper on the other. Move your clean, dried berries from bowl to bowl, dipping them two-thirds deep into the white chocolate, leaving the top third of your berry bright red. Then dunk the bottom third into the blue sugar and rest the finished strawberry on wax paper for the chocolate to set. You'll get three bands of perfect color top to bottom. Red. White. Blue." I set my sample berry onto the tray, then moved on to a freshly peeled sweet potato.

"Sweet potatoes aren't red, white, or blue, but they fit the fall theme very well, and who doesn't love a sweet potato?" I asked. "Today we're making simple, delicious sweet potato chips. Start by soaking your potatoes in cold water for about ten minutes to make them easier to peel. Then pat them dry, peel, and slice them as thinly as possible for the crunchiest chip. Next, you want to heat your oil to about 375 degrees, and line a plate with paper towels to absorb extra oil from the finished chips." I sliced my sweet potato, then added the pieces to the oil, making a show of setting a timer and removing them after a few minutes. "You'll want to season your chips while they're still hot. I use a mix of sea salt, ground black pepper, paprika, and a pinch of sugar, but you should use whatever works for you." I seasoned the chips as I spoke, then dusted my palms. "There you have it. Two recipes that will be perfect for your election day party or any fall festivity. Easy. Simple. Delicious. And remember, when you're at the polls, vote Swan for Mayor." I raised one of Aunt Fran's buttons in front of the camera and wiggled it a moment before cutting off my live stream.

I cleaned my workspace, then took down the flyer for Widow's Brew and drew a countdown on my chalkboard menu beside the Voter's Delight special. Just five more days and that deal would be gone.

Denise arrived at ten, and before she managed to tie on her apron, the chimes rang again. The café didn't open for an hour, and folks rarely ignored the OPEN/CLOSED sign, so Denise and I moved together toward the foyer.

"Hello, darling," Aunt Clara called. "It's only me. And a few guests. I hope you don't mind."

I hurried to the archway and spotted a few faces I recognized him from the Society for the Preservation and Retelling of Unrecorded History. Kitty Hawk chapter. Burton and Aubrey were there, along with several others. "Welcome to Sun, Sand, and Tea."

Aunt Clara led them into the café and directed them to a set of tables near the windows. "Impromptu meeting," she said. "These guys dropped by Blessed Bee to deal with some chapter business, but I simply didn't have the room for a proper sit down. I suggested we take the show across town. I hope you don't mind."

"Of course not," I said. "Is everything okay?"

Aunt Clara wrinkled her nose. "We had to organize the details of Dixie's memorial over email and through texts, thanks to the Kitty Hawk police, so that ought to flop like a fish. I suppose if we have chapter business to tend to, anywhere we can get together in person is better than that."

The group nodded their agreement.

"Is something wrong with the headquarters in Kitty Hawk?" I asked.

Tony frowned. He traded glances with the other members of the group before answering my question. "Dixie's daughter is going through her mom's office. She's having a tough time, and we felt it would be rude to carry on with our regularly scheduled meetings while she's grieving and hurting in the next room."

"Understandable," I said. "Well, welcome."

Denise smiled from her place at the counter. She'd counted heads and lined ice-filled jars before her. "What kind of tea can I get you started with?"

I visited with the guests while Denise filled and delivered their tea orders. Iced chai. Strawberry mint. Black tea with vanilla, and of course, good old-fashioned sweet tea. "What's on the agenda today?" I asked.

Tony smiled at Aunt Clara. "The whole Society isn't here, because this is a board meeting, and we are the board, minus Dixie, of course."

Aunt Clara's thin brows drew together. "I'm not a board member."

Tony chuckled. "We know," he said, "but we want to talk to you about an expansion of our society. To Charm."

Aunt Clara's eyes went wide. "What?"

The others smiled warmly and traded knowing looks. Everyone was clearly in on this, except for my aunt.

"Expansion through the islands was a long-time goal on Dixie's agenda, and we thought it would be nice to honor her by finally opening a sister group in your town. Who better to head that up than you?" Tony asked. "If you'll accept."

Aunt Clara set her fingers against her cheeks. She turned wide blue eyes on me, a smile blooming between her hands.

And I knew. This was what she needed. This was her mayoral election. She wouldn't become an afterthought to her sister, she would simply be one of two busy siblings who supported each other and the things they loved. I nodded at her. *Go for it*, I said silently, willing her to get the message.

She dropped her hands to her lap and smiled at the group. "I'd be honored."

"Wonderful," Tony said. He turned in Aubrey and Burton's direction.

Aubrey pulled a thick stack of papers from her bag and passed them to Aunt Clara. Two narrow lengths of twine hugged the stack around its center. "These are our bylaws, articles, and governing protocols. You can use them to establish the same for your chapter. As secretary, I have access to all our documentation, and you're welcome to anything you need. Just ask. I'll add you to the board's email loop tonight."

"A Charm chapter," Aunt Clara said softly. "Thank you."

I rubbed her back, feeling the appreciation and enthusiasm roll off her in waves. "I know it's early, but this feels like a reason for cake. Any objections?"

Several of the members patted the table. Everyone beamed in acceptance.

"I'm on it," Denise said, already rattling around behind the counter.

Burton stood and arched his back in a stretch. "I missed the last trip our group made here," he said. "Someone said they've got a tour?"

A few others nodded.

I barely remembered that, but he was right. I'd been new to town, and I'd left Aunt Clara in charge of the shop while I'd dragged tea samples around town in Wagon, trying to drum up business.

"Any chance I can get that tour?" he asked.

"Absolutely," I said, "but not today."

His smile rose, then fell as he heard the whole of my answer.

"Sorry. I'm renovating and wasn't expecting company. You're welcome to explore this floor if you'd like." I didn't mean it but felt obligated to offer a consolation prize, so as not to ruin Aunt Clara's moment.

Burton stood and walked away, heading into the former ballroom and future café expansion. The rest of the group stared after him.

Denise delivered a generous slice of blueberry

Bundt cake for everyone, then met me behind the counter while the group discussed new business.

"Want me to follow that weird guy?" Denise asked, leaning in close and keeping her voice low.

"Yes, please." I smiled. "Thank you."

Denise vanished.

Aubrey stood next. She made her way back to the foyer, presumably to find her husband or the restroom.

I rushed after her, suddenly desperate to ask the question I'd been chewing on for days. "Aubrey?"

She spun on me with her usual frown.

"The other day, in Kitty Hawk, you said Dixie had her hands on something of everyone's. What did you mean?"

Aubrey's gaze flickered to the table where she and Burton had been sitting, then jumped quickly back to me. "Nothing. I was in a foul mood and spouting off. It didn't mean anything. Excuse me," she said, moving smoothly in the direction of my first-floor restroom. A room nearly everyone asked for directions to the first time around.

Had she seen it on her way in? Or had she been here before?

And if the answer was the latter, had she come for the tea or something else entirely?

❧

Grady arrived at noon, hat in hands and taking me in slowly while I returned the gesture. The fitted blue jeans and gray V-neck T-shirt were casual but flattering and paired with a black windbreaker. His hair was damp and rumpled from a recent shower, the scents of his soap and shampoo filled the space around him. "Can we talk?" he asked.

"Sure." I poured him a jar of sweet tea, then glanced around the nearly empty café. Aunt Clara's meeting had wrapped up quickly and returned her to Blessed Bee within the hour, though I was sure she'd be beaming for days.

Denise had the handful of customers under control, which meant I had time to chat with Grady.

"What's up?"

He set his hat and hands on the counter, then checked over his shoulder for eavesdroppers before turning sincere gray eyes on me. He tapped the tea jar with long, steady fingers. "Thank you."

"No problem." I narrowed my eyes at him. He had a strange, tentative expression that I wasn't used to or sure what to do with.

"I want you to know I wasn't trying to hurt you before," he said quietly.

I leaned against the counter, unsure how to respond.

The overhead lighting cast long shadows of his lashes across his cheeks. "I was wrong to push you away. I know that now, but at the time, I thought I had to. I didn't think there was a choice."

My heart rate sped. "We don't have to talk about this right now," I said, tossing my gaze pointedly around the room.

"I know." He stood and moved behind the counter with me, placing his back to the room. "I'll be quick," he said, "but I felt it was important to say this sooner rather than later."

I nodded. And waited.

"Between the demands of my job and what Denver's going through, there wasn't enough of me to go around. And I thought I had to sacrifice something to make things right."

I crossed my arms, unsure I liked whatever he was doing. Was it an apology? A list of excuses? And if it was the latter, how could I trust him not to do something like this again? The next time his life got too complicated?

Also, why was he behind my counter?

"I thought keeping my priorities in line meant cutting out something that I loved," he whispered. "I can see now that my premise was faulty."

I lifted a finger, mentally replaying his confession. Did he say he thought he had to cut out something he loved? *And he'd cut me.* I couldn't force the question from my dumbfounded lips, so I lowered my finger and let him continue.

"It's been a long time since I was happy," he said, checking over his shoulders again. "I think somewhere along the line I started to believe I'd had my chance at happiness, and that time had passed."

"With Amy," I said.

Grady worked his jaw. "I was wrong. I realize now that I don't have to pick and choose what's important to me. And picking one thing doesn't mean not picking another. I never should've tried to push you out of my life, because you're one of the most important things in it."

I peeked around him to see if the entire café was hearing this, because I wasn't sure I was awake anymore. "You want me in your life," I said, heart hammering. "As your friend."

His chin moved slowly left, then right, heated eyes blazing.

I sucked in a ragged breath and tried again. "You want me…"

He dipped his chin once, nearly infinitesimally, before I said another word.

And I imagined my heart exploding in my chest. My lifeless body falling to the floor and no one ever understanding how a slightly chubby but otherwise healthy woman in her twenties had dropped dead behind an iced tea counter.

"Everly?" Grady whispered, his hand coming to rest on my elbow. "I'm truly sorry."

The seashell wind chimes over my door jostled, and Denise called out, "Welcome to Sun, Sand, and Tea!"

I gasped, then laughed.

Grady smiled. "Can we talk more later?"

"Yes, please," I said, cheeks flaming.

Grady returned to his tea at the counter; his wary expression became a broad smile as Denise hustled past.

"Okay," she said, dragging the word into syllables. She filled a jar with ice, presumably for the newest customer, then gave us each a mischievous look. "So, what's up?"

I pressed my lips together and shook my head.

"Something," she said, turning with a full jar of tea. "What was all that whispering about? Inquiring minds want to know."

"I came across a legend that had me wandering my house like a lunatic, looking for hidden treasure last night," I blurted. "I think this case is getting to me."

Denise frowned. "Sounds like it." She left with the tea, and I mentally bounced a hand off my forehead.

Grady squinted at me. "The Sad Man's treasure?"

"You know about him?" I asked, mystified and thankful I wasn't the only one who'd heard of him in my town.

Grady shifted, pulling his phone from his pocket and navigating to a photo. "I found him yesterday too. Clara was wrong about Lou being an ancestor of Dixie's, but his name did turn up on the family tree." He turned the phone to me, and I leaned in close for a look. Grady had zoomed in on the words Louis Franco. The name was attached to another by marriage.

"Betsy Wetherill," I read. My stomach rolled. Lou's wife had been Dixie's ancestor. "So, Dixie hated the Swans because she blamed Magnolia for her affair with Lou. Not because their relationship had sullied Lou's name. She blamed my family because Lou's affair led to Betsy's suicide."

It was absolutely irrational to hold a grudge against an entire family over something that happened nearly 170 years ago, but I could almost understand why it might affect a dedicated historian the way it did. "Send that photo to me?" I asked.

Grady tapped his phone screen. A moment later, my phone dinged with a message.

"Thanks."

He polished off the tea, then reached for his hat. "I've got something to follow up on this afternoon. Can I stop by tonight? So we can talk more."

I ignored the little hum Denise made as she flitted past me with the broom.

"Yeah." I nodded quickly, my heart swelling painfully once more.

"Good." Grady's lips twitched, and the skin at the corners of his eyes crinkled. "If it gets too late, I'll call."

"Still come," I said.

"I will."

With that, he was gone.

❧

The hours until closing numbered seventy-thousand and ninety-two, I was sure of it. I'd dodged Denise's questions and thwarted Matt's invitation for a walk on the beach after closing with as much calm and composure as I could muster. All while watching the hands on the clock move backward.

I locked up at seven sharp, then pounded up the stairs to get ready for my night. Amelia was coming at nine. I hoped Grady was coming any minute. I couldn't be sure, and I didn't want to call or bug him. So, I looked for ways to stay busy.

I put the dresses I'd borrowed back into the steamer trunk on the third floor, then took a stroll around the crowded space, wondering if one of the boxes or floorboards hid a treasure.

My widow's walk was accessible by a short ladder and trapdoor tucked behind a tower of boxes and a seamstress form. I shivered at the thought of it. The long, flat stretch of roof was lined with a small iron fence that would never pass a modern safety code. In days past, lonely wives of sailors would watch the horizon for signs of their husband's returning ship. In reality, it was the place where Magnolia had taken her last earthly steps.

A whisper of wind tickled the back of my neck, and my shoulders climbed toward my ears. Something clattered against the floorboards, and I jumped. A tarnished silver candlestick rolled past my foot, then paper letters settled beside a trunk nearly identical to Aunt Clara's. Two golden script letters were visible beneath the dust. M.B. "Magnolia Bane," I whispered, running my fingertips reverently over the latch.

Unable to resist, I cleared everything from the trunk's lid and opened it. Stacks of old clothing were smashed inside, along with shoes, hair pins, and horribly yellowed sheets of paper. I flipped through the papers, most too faded to read, then moved on to admiring the clothes.

An elaborately detailed white gown stole my breath when I touched it. I pulled it from the trunk and held it against my body, desperate to try it on. I checked the time then tossed the dress over my shoulder and carried the faded pages downstairs.

Clearing out my third floor was going to take weeks, but I had a feeling I wouldn't mind the work.

By eight o'clock, I'd dressed in the fabulous gown. It had likely been commissioned as an elegant party dress but would make a gorgeous wedding gown. I flopped onto the couch with my favorite cowboy romance novel and three leftover brownies in the shape of bats.

I read all my favorite passages from the book, then set it aside to process the possibility of soul mates united. I rolled onto my side, arranging the long, satin folds of my dress over the edge of the couch. The unfinished bookcase ruined my reverie. I had everything I needed to work on it right now, but my heart was still soft from imagining my hero and heroine riding into the sunset on horseback. I just knew they'd be married forever, and their offspring would grow up with two parents and endless love. It was all I'd ever wanted. I could smell the air of the Montana plains and feel the warmth of my cowboy's arms around me.

I reached for the stack of faded letters and tried again to make out the words on the brittle paper. Impossible.

I sat up and went to turn on another light, tripping over the length of a gown that needed a bustle or a hoop to manage its length.

The winds of a brewing island storm rattled my windows, fitting for a Halloween night like tonight. Full moon? Blue moon? Super moon? Killer on the loose? *Check*.

I caught my toe again and dropped several sheets of paper. They floated gracefully to the floor, landing near my bookcase.

"Caw!" Lou called, drawing my attention back to the sliding doors. "Caw! Caw!" The winds blustered around him, bending distant trees and rushing clouds across the sky.

I shook my head as I collected the papers. The corner of the last remaining sheet curled as I reached for it.

I pulled my hand back.

The paper drifted toward me, and I nearly swallowed my tongue.

Then the faint sound of wind whistling through cracks caught my ear.

I collected the paper and placed my hand where it had been. A cold breath of air rushed across my skin, and a thrill curled in my stomach. I set the papers aside and accessed my phone's flashlight app, then directed the beam at the narrow break between the bookcase and baseboard.

Dusty, but finished wooden floorboards appeared in the space behind the wall.

I sat up, mind racing, then crawled the few feet to

the coffee table to get the envelope of photos Grady had given me the night he told me we were through. I'd already reviewed the photos several times. I hadn't recognized all the rooms in the pictures, but I'd assumed that was because so much had changed over time. What if the real reason was that I'd never seen one or more of those rooms?

I gave the photo of rough, hand-drawn floor plans another look. The area beyond my bookcase was shaded with diagonal lines. I'd assumed the lines represented a revision. The reimagining of the space as a whole and elimination of a small section.

It took a minute for my brain to catch up. I'd thought I broke my house earlier this week, when in fact, I'd identified a doorway to a hidden room.

I scrambled to my feet, hauling yards of fabric off the ground so I wouldn't trip again. I stared at the freshly stripped built-in bookcase and tried to imagine how to move it. The shelves were bare, no secret lever to swing it wide or spin it around. I slid my hands over the wood, feeling every inch. I traced curious fingertips along the decorative edges, where the unit reached the wall, seeking a hidden hinge or someplace to curl my fingertips inside.

"Think," I said. *What had I been doing when the case had shifted before?*

My hip ached with the ghost of a memory.

I'd been on all fours, scraping loosened paint, and my hand had slipped. I'd jammed my hip against the baseboard and earned an unsightly bruise.

I moved away from the bookcase and dragged my gaze along the baseboard instead. A narrow strip of ornately carved wood stood vertically at the seam of two long, horizontal pieces, protruding a bit above the rest and jutting slightly forward. I scanned the baseboard for another seam connector like it and found none.

Was this where I'd hit my hip?

I pressed my toe against the strip in question and heard the familiar click.

My breath caught, and I moved back to the bookcase, then pressed my palms against it, pushing in the direction it had gone before instead of trying like I had to pull it back in line with the baseboard.

And the bookcase glided away.

A bolt of laughter erupted from my chest. I had a secret room. No. *A secret library*, I thought, already imagining it filled with books. I peered into the dim and dusty space, then stepped cautiously inside.

A desk and chair were positioned in the corner. An old banker's light stood on the desk, and a large wooden crate in the corner had three letters stenciled across the top. RUM.

I felt exactly like an island Indiana Jones as I took a spin around the small room. At least eight feet by ten. No windows. Bootleg rum.

I pulled the chair away from the desk, contemplating whether or not it would hold me, and froze when a cigar box on the cushioned seat came into view. A stack of letters inside had been tied with a red ribbon.

Delicate script identified the intended recipient as: My Dearest Lou.

My heart hammered as I carried the box back to my couch, carefully setting the bookcase into place on my way out. Much as I wanted to stay and explore, the heebie-jeebies crawling over my skin demanded I wait for Amelia or Grady.

I sent a text to them both, saying they were going to flip out when I showed them what I'd found.

Until then, I'd take a closer look at the letters.

I sat on the couch, then opened the first envelope, a love letter from Magnolia. My cheeks heated as I began to read her private words, and I refolded the letter, no longer willing to be so intrusive. Instead, I flipped through the stack, examining the paper and handwriting. Each was addressed the same way and in the same beautiful script. Beneath the stack of letters, a folded paper lined the cigar box with a message written in a heavier, less tidy hand.

Oh, how I miss you, my dearest Magnolia. I shall treasure our times to the end of my days. Your sweet words are diamonds and gold. Nothing in this world will ever be worth more.

All my love,
Your Darling Lou, the saddest man alive.

"The Sad Man," I whispered to myself, my heart squeezing with pain for his loss. "And these letters are his hidden treasure."

My bottom lip jutted out. I retied the ribbon, then set everything back into the box the way I'd found it. I returned the cigar box to the hidden room, then saw my way out again. I'd show Amelia the room later, but I'd need to find a special place for the letters if I decided to use the room for myself.

I gathered the faded pages from the trunk and headed back upstairs with them. Whoever they were written for, it wasn't me, and I needed to put them back where I found them as well.

The bulky material of my beautiful but ridiculous gown dragged on the dusty floor and steps as I climbed. I couldn't help feeling a little heartbroken for Magnolia, who'd given her heart naively to a man who could never marry her, and I was utterly gutted for Lou's wife, who'd found him with someone else. My poor heart had been crushed by Grady this week, and all he'd wanted was to say we were just friends.

But tonight, we were going to talk about something more. And I felt lighter at the very thought.

I stepped over and around a million ancient things as I made my way to the back of the room, superstitiously avoiding all shafts of moonlight through the windows. I didn't need any astrological interference in my sure-to-be-fantastic night.

My mind flashed back to the ghost walk, and I shivered. I'd marveled at the moon and its light moments before discovering Dixie, dying beside my name in the dirt. So much had happened since then. So much had changed. I'd found the Sad Man's treasure, something she'd believed was hers. Dixie would've been disappointed with the letters, but I wasn't. I understood Lou's sentiment. Love was all that mattered. Not gold and jewels, big houses or expensive things. Then again, if the curse was correct, it might've been Magnolia's love that had killed them all.

And for a moment, I rethought my excitement over seeing Grady tonight. Was I sure the Swan love curse was a lie? Sure enough to risk Grady's life? To leave Denver an orphan? Was I *that* sure?

I thought of Denise wondering if finding dead bodies was part of the curse.

Then thought of something I hadn't before. Finn had volunteered at the Wharf Museum.

He was a historian who would've known all about James Hudson and possibly been able to gain access to things associated with the sailor. His captain's sword. The flag from his ship. The uniform. Finn was certainly tall enough to pull that off. He'd been in town before my house was broken into. He knew Dixie was looking for a family treasure.

A shaky new theory took form in my mind as I reached the old steamer trunk. I set the papers on top, then dropped my skirt to reach for my phone. Which I'd left on the couch.

What if it had been Finn who'd been following me, assuming I had a map he and Dixie had talked about together? I thought of the missing basket of rolled maps from her office and the piles of rolled blueprints at Finn's bookstore. What if he'd worked with Dixie to deduce the Sad Man was her ancestor's cheating husband, and the location of the treasure was in my home? And they'd used old blueprints to try to find it?

I froze as a long creak stretched from the staircase to my heart.

A feral hiss came from the shadows, and Maggie prowled into view. Her luminous green eyes fixed on the shadow crawling up my stairs. Her hair stood on end. Her tail bushed out like a lightning rod.

Then Finn's face came into view.

CHAPTER

❦

TWENTY-SIX

I ducked behind a stack of boxes, gathering the insane length of my dress in one hand and preparing to run. I considered, briefly, that stripping out of the gown would be to my benefit, but pride kept me tightly corseted. That and the fact that I doubted I could shed the thing quietly enough to avoid being found. I scanned the area, hoping for a path back to the stairs that I might navigate unseen. There was none, short of crawling on the ground, which would make far too much noise in my massive dress.

Finn had reprised his role as the creepy sailor from Amelia's party, easily blending with all the other costumed people while on his way to kill me. Half of Charm had some sort of house party planned tonight. The larger community events had passed, but it was still Halloween. And my town didn't let that go uncelebrated. I wondered idly how he'd gotten inside this time. Another broken window? Was he the one who'd broken in before?

He dragged the sword beside him, pressing it into the floor as he went, carving a narrow and jagged path into the old, wooden floorboards. Creating a maniacal scrape as he moved.

I counted my blessings for the hiding place, however temporary, and the time to think. Finn miraculously hadn't seen me when I'd seen him, his attention drawn to Maggie as she'd growled low in her throat. Warning him. Even now, as he prowled the sprawling, overpacked space, she followed.

Panic grew in my chest as reality fully set in. I was trapped. And Finn was armed.

Killing me here, dressed in this gown, on Halloween, under the blue moon, would be the final, fitting chapter in a story he'd been spinning all week.

The air around me became thin and difficult to pull in. Each of my breaths grew louder. Like wheezy screams, audible from outer space and certain to register with Finn at any minute.

I peeked between boxes, peering into the dimly lit space cluttered with everything under the sun and listening to the gut-wrenching sounds of his footsteps. And his sword.

"You can come out, Everly," he said gently. "There's no need to hide. I'm not going to hurt you."

No. Of course not. How stupid did he think I looked?

I craned my neck in every direction, certain there was a way out. I just had to think of it. And for a moment, I visualized myself running full speed and launching at him, preferably while he stood in front of the staircase, where we would plummet onto the floor of my living quarters. He would be hurt much worse than me, and I would be able to escape. Run to the couch. Grab my phone. Call for help as I ran down to my foyer, then outside.

If only he'd move back in front of the stairs.

If only I could run carrying twenty-five yards of heavy fabric.

And if I wasn't a total chicken. I was incapable of doing anything so drenched in bravado. If I tried, he would undoubtedly see me coming, lift his sword easily, and impale me.

I needed a real plan.

The moon loomed large and eerie outside the window, watching me cower. Watching him hunt. The glow illuminated much of the space, despite the fact that no lights were on. None were necessary.

Wind whipped and whistled through cracks and crevices around us, under rafters and window frames, rattling the glass and every last one of my nerves.

An icy whisper danced across my cheek, tousling my hair and drawing my attention to the rickety ladder behind me. The ladder to my widow's walk. Partially obstructed by my barricade of boxes.

I inched toward it, considering. Finn hadn't seen me. He didn't know I was there. Not for sure. And once he'd checked every inch of my cluttered third-floor storage, he would leave.

All I had to do was stay hidden and wait him out.

But I couldn't stay where I was much longer. He'd nearly reached the end of my floor, moving in the opposite direction. Soon, he'd come my way.

"E-ver-ly," he sang. "Come out. Come out. Wherever you are."

I stared at the ladder, unsure it would hold me. Afraid to go and unable to stay.

"I saw you going through Dixie's office the night she died. I turned the whole place over, looking for the map after you left, but it was gone. And you were the only one in there."

I scoffed at his casual wording. *The night she died.* As if he'd had nothing to do with it.

"I have your phone," he said casually. "You left it on your couch. No way to call for help, I guess," he taunted. "I've already texted your sweet friend and that pain-in-the-backside detective that you have a headache and need to cancel plans. They were both on their way over. It's cute that your password to this phone is a big *Z* across the number pad. Convenient too. I noticed when I dropped by for tea the other day. I always tell people how important it is to pay attention, because we never know what will come in handy. And that philosophy just keeps working for me."

I mentally kicked myself for choosing ease over security. And loving Zorro.

My phone beeped. Another incoming text.

"Good news," Finn called. "Detective Do-Good says he got a match on prints from your broken window. It seems Aubrey Chase broke in here looking for that book her husband's been whining about. Police picked her up. She confessed. What an amateur."

I digested the bead of information. *I'd been right.* Aubrey was the one following me from the start. Looking for Burton's book. *But she wasn't Dixie's killer.* That guy was with me now.

My stomach dropped and roiled.

"Should I write him back?" Finn called, baiting me. "Okay. Okay. I will. Let's see." He cleared his throat. "Oh, thank you," he said in a terrible falsetto. "My hero." He tapped my phone screen and chortled. Then scrolled. "Uh oh. What's this?" he asked, his usual tenor returning. "You texted him less than an hour ago to say you found something pretty exciting. That wouldn't happen to be my treasure, would it? Tell me, Ev-er-ly," he sang, breaking my name into syllables. "What. Did. You. Find?"

I rubbed sweat-slicked palms against the dress. My teeth chattered with sudden excess adrenaline. My mind scrambled, and my throat burned with the need for breath. No one was coming for me. No one would know what had happened to me. And I would be an unsolved tale on the ghost walks of the future. Just like Dixie.

I pressed clammy palms against the sides of my burning face, trying to regulate my erratic thoughts and find a place of peace as heat scorched over my body and sweat began to drip. I needed to think. But the storm of unbidden images flashing in my mind were painful and blinding.

I was dragged into the woods, shot at, chased. I saw

my friend bleeding. Unconscious. I'd been poisoned. I'd been drowned. I was hit with a car. Forced to the edge of a cliff. I'd felt the life leaving my body. More than once.

And it was happening again.

I flared my nostrils, desperate for air. I opened my mouth, and a whimper emerged.

Finn's footfalls stopped.

He clucked his tongue and turned on his heels. "I knew you were up here. You almost had me, but I knew. And now we're going to play a game. You're going to tell me what you found and where you hid it, then I'm going to kill you." His footfalls began again, accented with the ghastly scrape of his sword against my floor.

My eyes blurred as I thrust myself forward, grasping almost blindly at the narrow, splintered wood of the ladder, forcing my feet against the gown and between the rungs. I jerked the material, ripping the fabric and exposing my shoes. Breathing loudly as I thrashed and pulled my feet free. Up the ladder's narrow steps. Up. Up. Up.

The wind howled, long and hard above the trapdoor overhead, and the latch fell free.

I raised one trembling arm to push it open, praying silently to make it outside before Finn caught me.

An angry hand curled around my ankle like a vise, and I screamed as my body was jerked back down the ladder. The arm I'd been holding on with felt ripped from my body. I was certain it was dislocated.

I gripped the ladder tight with my other hand. The trapdoor remained closed above me.

"Ah, ah, ah," Finn said, still holding tight to my ankle. "I think you have the Sad Man's treasure, and that is mine."

I kicked at him with my free foot and held on to the ladder for my life. My good arm wrapped around the side, the fingers of that hand clutching one rung.

"Help!" I screamed, desperate and knowing no one could hear. Not inside my home. On the third floor. With the howling ocean winds outside. "Help!" The word presented itself again and again on instinct, leaping from my throat and tongue, an outlet of desperation. "Please!" I sobbed, still kicking wildly.

My foot collided with something soft, and Finn swore. A horrendous crash echoed behind me.

I threw myself forward, up the ladder once more, and slapped the trapdoor wide. I scrambled outside, into the relentless wind, then slammed the wooden barrier closed behind me.

I collapsed onto the trapdoor, holding it shut with my weight and immeasurably thankful for the extra dress sizes. My shoulder and hip screamed with searing pain.

A deluge of unstoppable tears, combined with mind-numbing fear and a frigid, biting wind to render me nearly blind.

The sounds of children's laughter pricked my ears and drew my attention to the world beyond my madness. I wiped frantically at my eyes with my good hand and peered at the distant beach.

There were people along the shore, wearing costumes and building a bonfire from driftwood. The eerie blue and green flames licked into the air.

I could see the people. Could they see me too?

Not from where I was seated, I realized. I was little more than a dot of shadow on the massive roof of a home atop a hill.

And there was only one way down.

Something bumped against the trapdoor beneath me.

"Open up," Finn called. "We're not finished."

"We are," I said. "Go away. Please!"

He pounded harder against the wooden square between us. Fast, jabbing thuds at first, then a teeth-jarring shove that lifted me and the trapdoor an inch off the roof.

Finn began to laugh. "You're sitting on it," he said brightly. "I thought it was locked somehow, but it's just you. And I know how to move you." The familiar scrape of his sword on wood sounded beneath me.

I scanned the narrow widow's walk, seeking an escape. The flat strip of roof was no more than ten or twelve feet long and five or six feet wide. The wrought iron fence along the edge was no higher than my knee and broken in places from age and rust.

Beyond the widow's walk, my roof was made of treacherous slants and angles, impossible to navigate on foot in this wind.

The tip of Finn's sword emerged through the wood at my side, twisting and grinding at the ancient, weathered boards until more and more of the blade became visible.

"Stop!" I cried. "I don't have what you want. Just leave!"

The blade disappeared, and the board I sat on went still. I held my breath in anticipation, with nowhere to go but overboard and to my death.

The blade returned in a rush with an earsplitting crack.

I dove away as the wood splintered beneath me, narrowly avoiding a fall down the ladder into Finn's arms.

Instead, I landed on the widow's walk, facedown and with a thump. The air rushed from my lungs. My head ached, and my vision blurred. I'd hit my head on the rusty iron fence. A warm trickle of blood spilled over my lids and across my cheeks and nose. My stomach heaved.

Finn climbed out of the hole, off the ladder and onto the porch, his sailor uniform beating against him in the wind. He stood over me, grimacing, sword in hand. "You've stained your dress and torn it all up. That was a piece of history."

I blinked, unable to clear my vision. I swiped at my face. Crimson stains appeared on my hands, reminding me of the night I'd found Dixie. My gown was tattered and torn from my trip up the ladder, filthy from my dive onto the roof. "Please don't," I begged, blurry gaze locked on his sword. "You don't have to do this."

"I do," he assured me calmly. "Because I want

that treasure. I'm the one who made the connection between the Sad Man and Dixie's distant relative. I'm the one who figured out the money was hidden here, and I'm the one who unearthed nearly two-hundred-year-old blueprints for this place. No one else did a darn thing, so whatever you found, it's mine."

My head fell back against the roof as sickness coiled over me. Pale-gray clouds rushed across the starry night sky, and a moon so large it seemed I could touch it, stared poignantly down.

"Meow!" Maggie darted onto the widow's walk with a wail and a cry. She circled my head and hissed at Finn, her hair and tail bushed out once more.

"You hit Dixie with the candelabra," I croaked, willing the world to stop tilting. "You took it from her dressing room at the museum, then used it to knock her out so you could kill her without any fight."

"Correct. Now, get up," Finn said. "Tell me where the treasure is, or I'll stab you like I stabbed Dixie."

"There isn't any treasure," I said, blinking wildly and willing my vision to clear despite the pain.

"Liar!" he screamed. His eyes went wide and crazed without warning. His cool exterior completely gone. He raised his sword overhead, gripping the hilt with both hands, then plunged it into the train of my dress with a horrendous thunk.

I screamed until my lungs ached and I was sure there was no more oxygen left in the world.

Finn yanked the sword free and raised it again. "Next time, I aim for flesh."

Maggie arched her back and hissed, ready to attack.

"Don't," I whispered. "Don't do it." He would surely toss Maggie over the edge if she came within reach, and I couldn't live with that. "Please don't," I told her softly, begging with my blurry eyes. "Go away. It's okay. Just go."

"Talk," Finn said, his impatient gaze jumping around us.

I wondered if my scream had gained some attention from those on the beach. Maybe they would call the police for me. Maybe I could scream again. My churning stomach and thundering head didn't think so.

"There's no treasure," I croaked. "Only old love letters." My tongue was thick and fast becoming glued to the roof of my mouth.

Finn bent forward, grabbing hold of me in one fell swoop. His sword clattered to his feet as he hauled me to mine. "Maybe this will get you talking." He tipped me forward, leaning my head and shoulders over the little fence and giving me a blood-curdling view of the world below.

Wind whipped my hair across my face and pulled at the torn material of my gown.

And the only thing I could think of was my ancestor, Magnolia, standing here, in my place, and wanting to jump. "I don't want to die," I whimpered. "Please don't let me die."

The wind picked up in an angry blast, rattling the heavy sword behind us and blinding me again with searing pain and nausea. I added probable-concussion to my growing list of injuries, and I struggled not to vomit.

Finn groaned and released me so suddenly, I collapsed, not realizing how much of my weight and balance had been on him. I rolled onto my back, the stout iron railing of my widow's walk pressed against my side. I praised the stars, moon, and sky that I hadn't landed on the other side of my little fence or worse…fifty or sixty feet below.

Finn screamed nearby. His voice ratcheting into an earsplitting pitch. "No!" he called into the raging wind. "No, no, no, please! No!"

I strained to lift my head, pulling back the curls covering my face and eyes, dragging the locks through the blood still flowing slowly down my face.

Finn was on the outside of my fence. He clutched the small iron posts with ghost-white hands, his body hanging helplessly over an impossibly steep roof pitch, feet dangling above a great precipice.

Maggie was gone, and for a moment, I feared Finn had taken her over with him.

"Maggie," I called, the word reverberating through my skull, a shuddering sob close on its heels.

"Please," Finn begged. "I'm sorry!"

I blinked, unable to lift my head or limbs again, my stomach pitching, body weak, and vision dimming. And then I saw her.

A woman dressed in white. Standing just before him. Looking disdainful and a lot like me.

"Magnolia?" I whispered, knowing, even as I said it, the thought was insane. Impossible. The result of my head injury. A trick of the light. *Light from the blue moon.*

Except Finn saw her too.

His eyes were wide with terror and glued to the woman, who slowly turned her porcelain face to mine.

She lifted a finger to her lips, the delicate material of her gauzy gown blowing wildly in the wind.

"Everly!" Grady's voice boomed in the night, ripping through my head and chest.

"Here!" I croaked, cringing with pain and effort.

He burst into view, gun drawn and determination on his brow.

In that moment, Magnolia was gone.

"Everly!" Grady darted toward me, only missing a beat when Finn cried out once more. Grady slowed to stare, his head swiveling from my attacker to me.

I waved him back, forcing my heavy but working arm to move. "Help him," I said. The words arrived in deep, choppy grunts. "Killer." I choked. "The killer."

Grady turned reluctantly for Finn, taking more time than I thought necessary to offer a hand across the little railing. He hauled him up, then flattened him onto the roof and wrenched his hands behind his back. His soulful gray eyes met mine with intense regret and apology.

I nodded. He'd done the right thing. It was going to be okay as soon as the roof stopped spinning.

My eyes began to shut as Maggie came into view, perfectly safe and grooming her paw. She exchanged a low, guttural sound and slow blink with Lou, who cawed from his perch on my weathervane.

CHAPTER

✦

TWENTY-SEVEN

I drifted in and out of consciousness as my fuzzy world filled then overflowed with people. Emergency lights cast garish streaks across the luminescent moon. I strained to make sense of the warbled voices, acronyms, and sounds lifting into the night around me. The white noise of walkie-talkies. Hurried voices of first responders. The soothing cadence of a woman's soft hum.

"How are you doing?" Matt asked, his blurry face poised above mine. "You and I have to stop meeting like this." He pressed warm fingers against my wrist, my neck, my head.

His partner, Jane, smiled warmly from her space beside him, working diligently to clean blood from my face. "I think a bandage will hold it," she told Matt. "I can get the wound closed with some glue and avoid stitches, but it's going to scar."

He nodded. "Everly? Can you tell me if you're injured anywhere else?" he asked. His hands coursed gently, strategically, over my body. "This blood is probably from the head wound," he told Jane.

"My arm," I said, the gurgle of sound unrecognizable to my ears.

"What happened to your arm?" Matt lifted my good hand and pushed the dress sleeve up to my elbow, turning it slowly before moving on to the other.

I screamed.

"Okay." He stilled. "No visible injury or bruising."

"Dislocation?" Jane asked.

Someone sighed.

The teammates shifted, rising from the roof and changing positions.

I whimpered when Matt knelt on my opposite side and manipulated the injured shoulder. Then cried out when I could no longer keep it in.

"Dislocation," he agreed.

Jane pressed her hands against my collarbone.

"One," Matt said.

Before I could fathom what they were doing, a rocket of pain nearly shot me off the roof. I screamed, and the stars danced. The pain ended.

"You'll need a sling," Matt said. "It'll be tender for a while, but it will heal."

"Hey!" Grady called, his voice hard and sharp. His heavy footfalls pounding in my direction. "What are you doing to her!"

My eyes closed, and I let the sweet relief of my freshly set shoulder pull me under.

❧

"Everly," Aunt Clara said sweetly. "My poor, sweet girl."

Careful fingers stroked my hair and cheek as my aunts whispered endless words of love.

"I'm so sorry this happened to you," Aunt Fran said. "To think we could have lost you."

I fought to peel scratchy eyelids back, immediately struck by a blinding overhead spotlight. I choked on the too-strong scent of bleach.

"No, no," Aunt Clara said. "Sleep now."

❧

"How is she?" Amelia's voice tickled my mind. "Dad and I got here as soon as we could."

"They didn't want to let us back," Mr. Butters said. "I had to say we're family."

"You are, dear," Aunt Fran replied.

❧

I dreamed of falling. Of flying. Of entering the proverbial light and being greeted by a hundred of my ancestors. They passed me around in their embraces, then set me back into the light.

❧

"What's on her forehead?" a small voice asked.

"A bruise."

"Why's it so big? My bruises don't look like that," the little boy stated flatly. "I don't think it's a bruise."

"It's a bruise." Grady's voice was low but strong. Amused but steady.

Something hard and cool touched my arm. It glided over my skin, raising gooseflesh in its wake. "How long has she been sleeping?" the boy asked. "Is that green Jell-O?"

"Denver. Let her rest."

My heart rate picked up at the sound of his name. *Denver.* I rolled my face in the direction of his small voice and peeked at him.

He bounced a small plastic pony down my arm. "Is she going to eat that Jell-O?"

"No," I whispered.

His gray eyes opened wide.

I recognized the space around me as a hospital room. Sunlight crept through the closed blinds, and an assortment of machinery beeped at my head. An IV tube was taped to my hand and attached to a nearby bag and stand.

Denver yanked the pony away from me and stared. A moment later, his arms went wide, and he threw them as far across me as he could reach, kneeling in the bedside chair and laying his little body across mine.

Tears stung my eyes as I stroked his back. "I'm glad you're here."

Grady came into view on my opposite side, emotions warring in his expression as he watched his son holding onto me.

"I'm glad you're here too," I told Grady, my voice hoarse and froggy.

He stepped closer, dragging his gaze to my face. "Denver was worried."

"But not you," I said.

Denver's head popped up. "Daddy says you're infuriating."

I laughed, and pain tunneled through my shoulder.

Grady swiped the Jell-O off my bedside table and passed it to Denver. "Here. A little gift to keep your mouth busy."

Denver giggled and accepted the bribe. "Thanks!"

"You want to tell me what happened?" Grady asked, angling for a seat on my bedside.

"Finn from Historical Pages stopped by," I said dryly. "What happened after you arrived?"

Grady blew out a long breath, looking away for a beat before pulling his eyes back to mine. "I was running late last night because I got a confession from Aubrey Chase. She admitted to following you around and breaking into your place. I texted you to tell you about Aubrey and to say I'd be there soon. You responded by calling me your hero." He wrinkled his nose, and I laughed.

"I'd expected you to respond with a million questions or tell me you'd known it all along. When you didn't, I knew something was wrong."

"Finn had my phone," I said.

Grady nodded. "We found it on him."

"You *are* my hero."

I let my heavy eyelids shut again.

"Is she going back to sleep?" Denver asked. "Already?"

My lips curled into a smile, but I left my eyes closed.

A familiar zip of electricity crackled in the air a moment before Grady pressed a kiss to my cheek and whispered, "Sweet dreams."

❧

Aunt Fran and Aunt Clara collected me at dinnertime. After nearly twenty-four hours of observation, I was deemed seaworthy and launched. A mild concussion. Varying splinters, cuts, and bruising. Plus, a healing but previously dislocated shoulder. When compared to the injuries I could've sustained by falling from my roof, it was a lucky day.

We picked up a bottle of prescription pain medication in the hospital pharmacy, then headed home in Aunt Clara's new Prius. She'd sold the Bel Air to Aunt Fran at a massive discount when her sister couldn't bear to see it go. That seemed about right to me.

Thankfully, my aunts had brought me a change of clothes, so I didn't have to leave in borrowed scrubs or the massive, wholly ruined antique dress I'd been wearing. Aunt Clara vowed to do her best to salvage the gorgeous gown, but I wasn't in a real hurry to put that one on again.

I stayed at the homestead, in my childhood bedroom, until Election Day. Resting, healing, and being catered to like an infant or a princess. I'd shamelessly adored every moment.

Then, it was time for the party.

☙

Amelia and Mr. Butters turned Sun, Sand, and Tea into a perfectly patriotic campaign party center while I worked some one-armed magic in the kitchen. They'd swapped out half my beach-themed décor for American flags, bald eagles, and loads of "Vote for Swan" propaganda. I'd removed my seashell centerpieces, and Amelia had draped the tables in white linens, then sprinkled them with red and blue confetti. Mr. Butters had added framed photos of Aunt Fran through the years.

He'd also hauled the flat-screen television down from my living quarters and tuned it to the local news, for continuous election updates.

Despite the sling, I'd managed to make six apple pies, twelve dozen wings, a myriad of assorted side dishes, from baked macaroni and cheese to homemade curly fries, and a burger bar worthy of magazine coverage. After ten hours of prep and setup, I was sure my title as Kitchen Witch remained firmly in place.

People began to arrive after five, and they kept

coming. Each with a little I VOTED sticker proudly on display. Aunt Fran was elated, and I was exhausted.

I took a seat at the counter, thrilled to be alive to participate in Aunt Fran's big night, whatever the outcome.

By the time the polls closed two hours later, my first floor had exceeded capacity. Guests spilled onto the rear deck and wrap-around porch. They mingled on my lawn and in my gardens, where Amelia and her dad had erected additional tables and strung twinkle lights around my gazebo and through the trees.

I was on the verge of sleep despite the noise and chaos when I felt the air electrify.

Grady threaded his way through the crowd, eyes fixed on me and looking stunning in a nice black suit. "You certainly know how to throw a party."

"I had a lot of help," I said, "but thanks."

He looked me over, gaze lingering on my forehead, eyes searching mine. His suntanned skin and ethereal eyes were impossibly more pronounced by the presence of his stark white dress shirt. "How are you feeling?"

"Good." I did my best to perk up my smile, but fatigue had moved in the moment I'd sat down.

"You look beautiful."

"Thanks. You clean up well yourself," I said. "Is the Senator's party a jacket and tie affair?"

He shook his head, loosening the tie. "I'm on my way home from court on the mainland."

I stilled, then straightened, a shot of adrenaline

coursing through me. With everything on my plate today, I'd forgotten where he'd been.

Aubrey had confessed to taking the photo of me with the candelabra then leaking it to the Town Charmer, apparently thrilled to have something someone wanted. She blamed emotional despair over a troubled marriage for her crimes and received a slap-on the-wrist by local courts for stalking me and breaking into my home. She was ordered to pay restitution, see a counselor, and assigned one hundred hours of community service to be completed by the end of the year.

Finn, on the other hand, had been transferred to a higher security facility than was available on the islands. And his attorney was entering his plea today.

"How'd it go?"

"He's going with insanity." Grady laughed humorlessly. "What he did was definitely insane, but he isn't. He's calculating and cold. I just hope the judge and jury will see past that doe-eyed, goofball appearance. I'll do everything I can, but it could still be tough."

I rested a hand on his arm in understanding. "Don't beat yourself up if they go easy on him. Pretending to be the ghost of a two-hundred-year-old murderous British sailor isn't exactly the definition of sanity."

Grady's lips tipped in a lazy half smile. "And it didn't help that he claimed a ghost tried to toss him off your roof."

An image of Magnolia flashed into mind. The thought came and went like a blip. A forgotten memory, trying to return without quite succeeding.

"Crazy or not," Grady continued, "I can put him at the Wharf Museum on the night of Dixie's murder and at the Festival Park Museum in Manteo. He volunteered to help with the annual inventory. A role like that would've given him access to the relics he needed for his role as James Hudson's ghost. Thankfully for me, he was thorough in his documentation and planning. He kept a detailed log of preparations for Dixie's murder in an old, leather-bound journal at his shop. He knew what he'd need to get the job done, and he chose the ghost walk as his time to strike. The goal was to attack while she was in costume, then blame the ghost who'd killed Mourning Mable. He thought people would be willing to believe it, and he'd lurked around your house in the old sailor costume, hoping to sell the same ghost act twice."

"And it was all for a treasure that doesn't exist," I said sadly.

Grady bobbed his head in agreement. "As soon as Dixie convinced Finn there was treasure here, he started making arrangements to keep it. Then, being the woman she was, Dixie stole the blueprint he found for her and hid it so she could come for the treasure on her own."

"She doubled-crossed her double-crosser," I mused.

"Yeah," Grady said, "and it cost her." He scanned the crowd briefly before turning back to me. "How's Clara doing? I hear Tony's moving to Florida."

"Clara's fine," I said. "She and Tony were just getting to know each other better when this all started."

Whatever attraction they had died when his grandson tried to kill me. Now, Tony was selling the bookstore and moving to the Keys for a fresh start and room to process. I didn't blame him. It would've been awkward to stick around the island with everyone knowing his grandson was a killer. "He was horrified when he found out what Finn had done. I'm sure a little distance will help his heart begin to heal."

"Everly Swan?" a woman called, cutting through the room in my direction.

"Yes?"

"I'm Harriett Wetherill." The small blond offered her hand and a sad smile. "I believe you knew my mother, Dixie."

I blinked. The Harriet Wetherill I'd met was taller, thinner, and several years older. Yet, this woman looked so strikingly similar, I was momentarily dazed at the sight of her. "You were named after your grandmother?"

"Yes." She furrowed her brow, then shook it off. "I wanted to bring some things to you." She lifted a canvas tote in my direction. "My mother's friend Burton helped me go through her office and make sense of all her books and keepsakes. All of these had to do with your family, or you," she said. "I thought you'd like to have them. And there's a folded set of floor plans in there that look like they might be for this place. I found them tucked into the back of a photograph of my grandmother on New Year's Eve."

I nodded. Dixie had hidden the plans to my house,

i.e., the map noting my secret room, with her mother. "You look just like her," I said, unable to stop myself.

Harriet's frown returned. "I never knew her. She died in childbirth having Mom."

Grady turned curious eyes on me while I floundered.

"I—saw the photo," I said, "in your mom's office. I know the one you're talking about."

"Right," she said, "Well, anyway, these are for you." She gave me the bag and a small smile. "I think she wrote your name on the ground because she wanted to tell you something," she said, nodding as I felt my breath catch. "The police told me about that. Then, I saw all of this stuff about your family and knew she wasn't accusing you. She was trying to tell you something."

"What?" I asked, nearly holding my breath for the answer.

Harriet shrugged. "I don't know. I'd like to think she was sorry for the grudge she held. She was a bit eccentric at the end, crankier than when I was young. Obsessed with maps and treasures. I hear the man accused of her death came for you too. Maybe she wanted to warn you."

"I think you're right," I said. "She tried to save my life."

Harriet's eyes glossed with unshed tears, and she nodded. "Thanks for saying that. Mom was always my hero. It's nice hearing someone else thinks of her that way too."

Someone cranked up the volume on the television. "Numbers are coming in!"

Harriet swiped her fingertips under her eyes. "I'll let you get back to your party. I found that book Burton was hunting, and I promised I'd drop that off tonight too. I hope your candidate wins."

Me too, I thought. "You can stay if you want," I offered. "Everyone's welcome. There's plenty of food and tea."

"Thanks." She nodded kindly but drifted toward the door.

"Bye," I whispered.

I peered into the canvas bag of books and journals, feeling confused and appreciative. I thought of how I might've met her grandmother's ghost, and how I'd possibly seen Magnolia's spirit on my roof. I was sure the latter was a result of racing clouds, a supermoon, and my head injury. But what about the former?

Maybe I should be the one pleading insanity.

"Here." Grady set a bottle of water in front of me.

I hadn't noticed him leave. "Thanks." I uncapped the bottle and sucked in deep gulps of the liquid.

Grady took the bag from my hand and set it on the counter in front of me. "You want me to run this upstairs for you?"

"No. I'll get it," I said. "In a minute."

I caught sight of Lou in my peripheral vision and turned to smile at him on the deck. "Lou came." A memory rattled loose in my head, and I looked to Grady for confirmation. "I think he was on the roof with me that night. On the weathervane." The image was fuzzy and faint in my mind, but there, nonetheless.

Grady slid his eyes from me to the gull. "Yeah," he said. "He was. Did I tell you how I knew to check the roof for you?"

I glanced briefly in Lou's direction before returning my attention to Grady.

"I drove over here on a hunch," he said. "I thought it was odd that you didn't have any follow-up questions about Aubrey, and I had more I wanted to tell you."

"I had questions," I said. "But I was a little busy when you texted. Plus, Finn had my phone."

Grady's jaw tightened, and his gaze darkened, the way it always did when I spoke Finn's name.

"You know, in a strange way, it's kind of nice to know Finn and Aubrey were both stalking me. I'd started to think I was losing my mind there for a while."

"Paranoia was the better option," Grady said. "That's a lot less likely to kill you than an actual murderer."

I rolled my eyes, then scrambled mentally backward over our conversation. "So, how did you know to come all the way up to the roof to save me?"

He frowned. "When I got here, your cat was pacing on the porch. She headed straight for the truck when I pulled in, then back to your door."

I remembered Maggie's disappearance on the roof. The way I thought she'd been tossed over the edge with Finn when he fell.

"When I got to the porch, the wind blew, and the door swept open," Grady continued. "The door to your living space was unlocked, and Maggie led me upstairs. Then she started meowing. Loud, and on repeat, until I followed her to the staircase leading to your third floor. I could feel the wind blasting and hear someone screaming."

"Finn," I said.

Grady rubbed his clean-shaven cheeks, then locked a palm against the back of his neck. "I didn't know what to think when I saw you laying there. In that crazy dress. Blood speared all over it. On your face and hands. Then there was this man, hanging off your roof." His gaze turned dark. "And you said 'killer.'"

"I'm sorry," I told him, meaning it to my core. "I didn't realize it was him until it was too late, and he had my phone."

Grady groaned. "It wasn't your job to know, Swan. This one's on me. I was at his shop with a warrant while he was here. With you."

"A warrant?"

He nodded. "Finn was the only name on my list of Dixie's known acquaintances who also had a relationship with both the Wharf and Festival Park museums. It didn't take long to confirm his role in taking inventory at the latter, and we knew he was present at the former when Dixie died. Aubrey filled me in on the nature of his personal relationship with Dixie, and it was enough for a warrant."

"They were reviewing maps and looking for

treasures," I said. "Then they thought they'd found one here."

Grady stepped in close and opened his arms.

I gripped him around his waist, not caring who saw me or what they thought. A dull ache pounded in my head. "Thank you for saving me again."

"Always," he whispered against my hair.

The room around us erupted in cheers, and Aunt Fran squealed.

I jumped, heart seizing and breaths short, but Grady held me close.

"She won," he said.

I wiggled free, noting the bright and genuine smile on his lips, then the elation on Aunt Fran's face. There were tears in her eyes and on her cheeks as she became part of the town's largest group hug.

"By a landslide!" someone called. "The others never had a chance!"

"My mother-in-law is going to be intensely unhappy," Grady said. "I should probably go over and see her. Make sure she contains her anger until Denver and Denise are headed home. The senator is not accustomed to losing. Especially not in a tiny island election. Or to a beekeeper."

"A bee witch," I corrected with a laugh, then I stood and reached for his hand. "Do you have a minute before you go? I want to show you what I found."

He towed me into the foyer and waited while I unlocked the door to my private staircase. "What did you find?"

I swung the door opened and climbed a step before looking back. "Right before Finn showed up, I found the Sad Man's treasure." I watched closely for his response.

Humor left him at the mention of Finn, but curiosity quickly pinched his brow. "Show me."

I led him to my bookcase, then pointed to the little decorative strip of vertical wood on my baseboard. "Press that with your toe. Try to make it flush with the baseboard."

Grady frowned, but obeyed.

And the bookcase swung backward a few inches, revealing the room.

"No." He moved cautiously to the opening and pushed the bookcase like a door, then stepped inside.

"Can you believe it?" I asked, joining him in the cozy space. "Amelia helped me clean it while the apple pies baked." We'd dragged accents from the third floor to warm it up. A rug for under the desk. Generous stacks of old books. A clock. And an oil painting of a woman dressed in a cream gown and floppy hat, standing in my gardens, overlooking the sea. The material of her dress billowed in the wind. She held the hat down with one reaching arm, her dark curls alive on the breeze.

Grady's attention fixed to the image, and he approached with caution. "Is that…" He turned to me, unsure.

"Magnolia?" It was my guess too. "I don't know," I said. "There's no name anywhere, and I can't make out the artist's scribble at the bottom. But I think so."

He raised a finger to the woman's bent arm, with a hand unseen. A long white tail fell from it, almost invisibly mixed with the fabric of her cream gown. "She's holding a white cat?"

"Maybe," I said. There were so many things about the past that I would never know, and as much as my aunts liked to explore, understand, and preserve historical details, I wasn't sure I agreed. Not where individual lives were concerned. That felt a lot like prying. Some things simply weren't ours to know. Like the words of Magnolia's love letters.

Grady smiled as he took in the details of the room, chuckling at the ancient case of rum, then staring at the cigar box on the desk.

"The treasure is in there," I said. "Love letters from Magnolia to Lou. Take a look. Read the paper underneath the letters."

Grady lifted the box's lid carefully, then examined the contents. He didn't untie the ribbon on the letters. He knew, like I did, that the contents weren't meant for us. "This is pretty great."

"I thought so."

He set the box aside, then reached for me.

I went willingly into his arms, careful not to jostle my sling and set off my aching shoulder.

He tucked a mass of wild curls behind my ear, then rested his chin on top of my head. "We still need to have that talk, Swan."

"I know," I told him, feeling my heart break as I pulled back an inch. "I want you to know I understand why you tried to push me away. I've had lots of time to think about it while my head healed. And I get it. Waking up to Denver with his little pony on my arm in the hospital, I realized what a terrible person I am to have in his life. He's already lost so much. And his dad is a lawman who's never guaranteed to come home at night, and I am absolutely cursed. Denver deserves more than another person to worry about. Regardless of what I want, I get that now."

Grady's gaze narrowed. His hands rose to cup my cheeks. "I know what he deserves, but the problem is that Denver adores you. Exactly as you are. Wholly, unquestionably, and without reserve. And he's not alone."

My heart fluttered, and a tiny gasp escaped me. I searched his eyes, trying to decipher what was being said between the lines. "He isn't?"

"No. In fact, we're both a lot better with you in our lives," he said. "Denver is happier, and I'm..." He paused, considering. "At peace. Entertained." He smiled. "I'm more myself when I'm with you than I have been in years. Maybe ever. I've slowed down. Found a pace I like. I'm making memories with my son and protecting a community I feel like a real part of."

I chewed my bottom lip, letting his perfect words settle in my heart. "You're sure it wasn't me giving Denver nightmares?"

"Yeah. Matter of fact, he's been missing you. He thinks we should visit more often."

I smiled. "What about you?"

Grady drifted closer, stopping only when our bodies aligned and the toes of his boots nudged the tips of my shoes. "I'd like to see you more often too."

My smile widened. "You should know I'm just getting out of a complicated relationship," I said. "A really amazing guy recently broke up with me."

"That guy sounds stupid."

I laughed, and one of Grady's arms wound around my back. "I get myself into a lot of trouble," I warned. "I'd make you crazy, and I need rescuing a lot more often than I can stand."

Grady's gaze flickered to my lips. "I will always rescue you, Everly Swan. And there's something else you should know about me."

"What?" I rose onto my tiptoes, rapt with anticipation and praying the next words out of his mouth were, *I want to kiss you.*

He caressed my cheek with a gentle stroke of his thumb and said something epically better. "I don't believe in your curse."

Swan's Savory Sweet Potatoes

Nothing says fall like a baked sweet potato! Except maybe pure maple syrup. Try the two together and you'll say, "Delicious!"

Yield: 8 Servings | Total time: 40 minutes

8 small or 4 large sweet potatoes
2 ½ tablespoons olive oil
3 tablespoons pure maple syrup
1 tablespoon fresh thyme leaves
Salt and pepper to taste

Preheat the oven to 425°F.
Prepare a baking sheet with olive oil or cooking spray.
Cut the sweet potatoes in half lengthwise.
Flip the sweet potato halves, rounded side up, and cut multiple shallow slits across each sweet potato.
Line the potatoes, flat-side down, on the prepared baking sheet.
Combine the oil, maple syrup, and thyme in a bowl.

Brush the potatoes with the maple mixture. Sprinkle with salt and pepper.
Bake 25 to 30 minutes or until potatoes become tender.

Bite-Sized Apple Pies

Bring everyone's favorite fall treat to any gathering, and leave the messy pie pan and server at home!

Yield: 16 servings | Total time: 30 minutes

2 (8-ounce) tubes crescent roll dough
1 (21-ounce) can apple pie filling
3 teaspoons sugar
1 ½ teaspoons ground cinnamon
3 tablespoons butter, melted

Preheat the oven to 375°F.
Prepare a muffin tin with baking spray.
Separate the crescent rolls.
Place the center of one dough-triangle into each muffin tin, allowing the ends to stick out.
Top each triangle of dough with apple pie filling.
Blend the sugar and cinnamon, then sprinkle over each generous dollop of pie filling, reserving half for later.
Wrap the ends of the crescent rolls over the top of the pie filling.
Drizzle the melted butter over each little pie.

Sprinkle with the remaining cinnamon-sugar mixture.

Bake for about 15 minutes, until golden brown.

Serve warm, with vanilla ice cream or caramel syrup as desired.

Easy Peasy Lemon Basil Iced Tea

Refreshing and simple, you don't need to visit a seaside café to enjoy this light citrus tea, but it sure would be nice!

Yield: 7 servings | Total time: 3-4 hours

1 lemon
10 fresh basil leaves
4 green tea bags
Optional: 3-4 teaspoons honey
7 cups hot water

Slice the lemon thinly, and add to 1 quart jar or pitcher.
Top with basil leaves and green tea bags.
*Add 3–4 teaspoons of honey to pitcher if desired.
Pour the hot water over the ingredients.
Steep for 15 minutes.
Remove the tea bags.
Place into the fridge for 3–4 hours, or until chilled.
Serve over ice.